Praise

"Soukup conducts a chorus of seductively unreliable first-person voices to relate a heartbreaking coming of age ... parable that delves into the depths of human despair and celebrates the redeeming power of compassion. *Ashes, Ashes* is unflinching acknowledgement of society's unseen. You may be uncomfortable watching, but you won't look away."
DAVID R. ROTH, AUTHOR, *THE FEMME FATALE HYPOTHESIS*

"Soukup perfectly captures how growing up with trauma leads to harsh choices and, ultimately, a kind of grace."
DAN KOPCOW, AUTHOR, *PRIOR FUTURES*

"Fredrick Soukup returns to familiar territory—rural Minnesota and its disenfranchised—capturing the abject despair of foster care youth while at the same time offering up a heartbreaking murder mystery."
JANET GOLDBERG, AUTHOR, *THE PROPRIETOR'S SONG*

"Soukup offers up a heartfelt and genuine slice of life. His characters jump from the page with crackling dialog that transports the reader into an intoxicating, though often terrifying, world. Truly gripping."
STEVE ZETTLER, AUTHOR OF *TWO FOR THE MONEY*

"Edgy. Smart. Exhilarating. This breathtaking thriller of small town intrigue demonstrates the heartbreak and redemption that can rise from the ashes of a pillaged youth."
MARTHA ENGBER, AUTHOR, *WINTER LIGHT*

About the Author

Fredrick Soukup's works include *Bliss* (2020) and *Blood Up North* (2022). He's been named an IPPY Bronze Medalist, a semifinalist for the American Short Fiction Prize, and a finalist for both the Erik Hoffer Book Award and the Minnesota Book Award. *Blood Up North* won the NYC Big Book Award for Literary Fiction and *Ashes, Ashes* was long-listed for the Petrichor Prize.

He lives in Saint Paul with his brilliant wife, Ashley, and daughters/muses, Clare and Nora.

fredrick-soukup.com

ASHES, ASHES

FREDRICK SOUKUP

www.vineleavespress.com

Ashes, Ashes
Copyright © 2024 Fredrick Soukup

All rights reserved.
Print Edition
ISBN: 978-3-98832-055-1
Published by Vine Leaves Press 2024

Cover design by Jessica Bell
Interior design by Amie McCracken

To Becky, Jenny, and Brandon

Ring around the Rosie

Heath

Far as Moms go, she isn't the worst. She tells me and Baby Milo a goodnight prayer. Tells us to sleep good for the first day of school tomorrow. Tells us she knows we'll act right in class. She closes the bedroom door and the dark swoops in real fast like a ninja. I'm antsy and I'm buzzing. Antsy and buzzing since I'm getting the hell out of here right quick to find my brother, Bunkie.

Baby Milo is a wuss who gets the runs from creamed corn. I can't take him with me. Not because of the runs but since he'll slow me down by being a wuss and all. Today he's got sniffles and hack-ups. I've got them coming soon, I can tell. The house is creaky and ornery that way. Rumbles come from the basement pipes. "The basement is the house's tummy and sometimes it makes silly noises" is what Mom tells Baby Milo so he don't shit himself about ghosts. She really isn't the worst. Probably there's no one better. But she don't have ice cream. Not in the freezer upstairs or the freezer downstairs. No trampoline either. Except the main thing she don't have is Bunkie. That's my brother. He'll be so proud of me.

I change out of my jammies and put on jeans and sneakers, a sweatshirt and a hoodie. The window slides open real easy. It's cool out, just a little rainy. So what? I'm about to leave and Baby Milo sits up in bed.

"Tell her you didn't see nothing."

"Whatcha doing, Heath?"

"Going for a gallon of vanilla."

"Can I have some?"

"I'm not coming back."

"Without you I'm scared of the dark."

"The dark is the same even if I'm gone."

"But the basement—"

"Be tough, Milo."

He's crying hard now. Sucking in air like he could just die from crying. He turns the green nightlight on, and his tears are green pus like his eyes are all wrong and might need scooping out. "I'm sorry," he says. "I'll be better. I promise I won't ask so many questions. I promise I won't talk so much—"

"It's not your fault at all but if you wake up the house and she comes in right now, I'm gonna be a ghost. I'm gonna be a ghost and I'm gonna haunt you in the dark every night."

He keeps crying and nodding. Sometimes he's like that, a robot built just to cry and nod.

"Wait a second," he says. "I wanna give you something."

He hands me a playing card from his baby games. The wizard on the card wears a big dopey wizard hat and looks like a true dipshit. "He's worth five hundred quibbles."

"Holy shit, five hundred?"

"He's the best one."

"You better keep it, then."

"No, take it. Really, where you going?"

"To find Bunkie. I gotta tell him a story."

"What story?"

"Best story anybody's ever heard."

"Tell me."

"No."

"How come?"

"Shut up and don't wake nobody."

"But what about all the monsters?"

"Oh, Milo. I'm no wuss."

He won't take his card back and it's time to leave, so I tuck it in my pocket and slug him on the shoulder and throw my hoodie's hood up over my head and I'm gone out the window.

Too bad Baby Milo didn't have a hat to give me instead. Rain streams down harder than it looked to be streaming back in the bedroom. My clothes weigh ten thousand pounds. My fingers are all rubbery and slick and cold inside the pouch of my hoodie. It's slow-going even when I run. I don't like leaving places with something I don't really need, except I keep checking to make sure the dipshit wizard hasn't slipped out of my pocket.

At the far edge of town is the church where Mom would take us, and we'd have to be quiet until afterward so we could go to the diner. Baby Milo would pretend he couldn't decide between milk and orange juice so Mom would get him a glass of each. He isn't the dumbest. Past the church is the long forest road out to Bunkie's grandma's house ten miles away. Kids have been saying that since she did her time over the meth and whatnot, he lives with her again. Hanging with him will be good fun because he's the king. I've seen it all. I've seen him steal from an antique store. Seen him chase chickens and throw rocks at traffic lights and give the finger to that woman in a floppy hat who looked down her fat nose at us. Bunkie is the king. That's my brother.

Tomorrow, bright and early. I'll see my brother tomorrow. The front steps of the church aren't covered. Except there's a little scoop of an awning over the belltower door and since there's rain it's better to sleep here by the church than out in the woods. So long as I'm up and gone before Mom sees that I ran off on her. Because she might get to shining flashlights down alleyways. She might get to calling around the neighborhood and calling the police and calling Liz from the big brick building in Brainerd. Liz has got a neat little nose and brown eyes that are the color of dead grass. She chews peppermint gum and I wish she'd breathe on me more, only she don't even come around her desk. I wish she'd be Mom. Even if it's just for a bit. Liz loves ice cream.

I'm asleep before I even get a chance to pray Mom don't find me.

It's morning when I wake up sucking screws down my throat. All everything is wet and cold. Some ancient lady in a polka dot dress pokes me in the chest with the knob of her cane. Parents must've been lizards. Her wrinkles have wrinkles. Plus, her tongue's doing too much like she might lick her own eyeballs at any moment. One of those kimono dragons.

Kimono says, "You coming in for rehearsal?"

"Huh?"

"Must be you're joining the choir. Wait, you're one of Jessica's fosters, aren't you?!"

"Nope."

"You are! I've seen you at service before. Come on in with me, warm up. I'll give her a call in a bit. I used to babysit her, believe it or not. Hector?"

"What?"

"Heath. That's it. Heath."

She holds out her scaly hand. A limp fish. She weighs less than I do. Not a chance she could help me up and anyway I'd rather not turn limp-fish too.

"I don't wanna get sick."

"That's sweet of you, honey," she says.

She slinks away toward the front door. Her purse is as big as she is. Start running and she won't catch me even if she had another hundred years to live. But Bunkie though, he might see if she's got something I can eat.

"Say, you got any food?"

Kimono has a little scaly trigger finger that welcomes me to follow.

There's a kitchen in the basement. She makes coffee and sets out some stale chocolate chip cookies and a glass of milk. Then she slinks up the staircase. A slinker, this Kimono. The heater ticks. The fridge hums. Upstairs pastor moans a song. One time I caught him chewing tobacco in his office and he gave me some to keep me quiet about it. The kitchen air is cool and dead-still and ready to strike. This is how murders begin.

Her and pastor could come downstairs at any moment. I scarf all the cookies and drink all the milk and empty out her purse on the countertop. Coins jangle and roll along the floor. In the cupboards are the goodies. Screw-top glass bottles of juice and plastic bags full of church crackers. I fold her purse inside out. It's hard to do because the purse is made of some type of leather like maybe the skin of Kimono's sister or something. I have to put my foot inside and pull on the straps with both hands. I fill it with goodies and sling it over my shoulder. I'm about to sprint out of there but then I get to thinking.

In one of the drawers is all the knives a boy could ever want. I take the biggest one. Something you'd use for slicing watermelon. I put it in the purse. Just in case. Because when it's all done and I'm a man someday, I'll bring old Kimono her purse back and she won't even recognize me because I'll be a monster-killer. A monster-killer is what I'll be. Like Uncle Bob. A monster-killer.

Soon there are the woods and I slip in deep to where there's cover. Fuck the wood ticks and ivy and shit and squirrels. Fuck all the scratchy branches and fuck the itches. I'm on fire. Then there's a four-wheeler trail that creeps along the ditch of the road to Bunkie's Grandma's. I'm safe from town now. A few cars pass by here and there. Mostly it's just me and the sun hating on me. My neck is hate-burning and the church juice is warm and goofy and I eat half the bag of Pastor Mudtooth's crispies. Real warm and real goofy, that church juice, so it must be that God isn't just a story but more of a buzzing in your brain and in your heart and in your stomach. That's the whole *duh* of it. God is the good buzz. The best juice there ever was.

Then suddenly there they are. Monsters, three of them. They circle around me at the edge of the woods. They're tall as road signs and strong as wolves. No more good buzz. No more God. I know what type of air dead boys breathe, see, since it's what I'm breathing now.

Two girls and one boy. Siblings, probably. They sit on mountain bikes and drink energy drinks out of cans. Their bones sweat through their shirts, three skeletons the color of damp. The taller girl stands between her brother and sister. She has a scar on her cheek that is the shape of a fishhook and she's the prettiest thing the woods have ever had.

"Who are you?" she asks.

"Marvin," I lie.

"How come you're not in school?"

"I don't go to school around here."

"We're ditching out," the other girl says.

Scar-girl glares at her and looks at me and says, "How come you got a purse? Tampons?" They laugh at me. "Marvin, you got any cigarettes?"

I shake my head no. "There's juice, though. Maybe if you like it—"

"Maybe if we like it *what?*"

"You guys won't try nothing, will you? To hurt me?"

"Why would we?" the boy asks. His bangs are glued to his pink forehead. His eyes are real blue and almost closed. Maybe they don't get more open than that. They look at me like there's a good answer if only I could find it.

"Okay," I say.

Then everyone is forever passing the juice and eating cookies and riding bikes around and around this mountain-bike track in the woods and jumping off ramps made of packed dirt and flying high, almost to the branches of ginormous pines. It's muggy out here. I put my sweatshirt and hoodie by the purse. Two bikes have baseball cards in the spokes but the boy's bike don't. I give him the wizard card and he ties it to his spoke with one of his shoelaces and then his bike revs when he rides too. The good buzz comes back and everyone laughs and everyone jumps higher and higher and everyone wants ice cream.

Scar-girl sends her little sister back to their house for a gallon tub of Neapolitan. The girl is gone for a thousand loops around the track. Then the boy starts puking all over a patch of moss. He's crying as he runs off where his sister went with her bike. It's just me and Scar-girl now. After many more loops she stops and rests her arms on her handlebars, then her head on her arms, where there are purple welts.

"Dad must not have gone to work. I better go back. See you later."

"But what about the Neapolitan?" I had my hopes up.

"Won't be any today."

"And Baby Milo's card?"

"What the hell's a Baby Milo?"

She walks away with both bikes.

"I don't care about the scar," I yell after her. "I think you're real pretty."

She acts like she didn't hear me. Maybe I didn't yell loud enough. Sometimes I do that. Maybe I didn't yell at all. Only whispered to myself kind of. Sometimes I do that too.

I leave Kimono's purse by a dirt ramp and start after her. I need that card. If Baby Milo was here I might wanna smack him once good because I don't wanna go on without it. It's all I have until I get to Bunkie.

She's out of sight by the time I make it through the woods. But there's only one trailer there, with lilac bushes on the side. In the lawn there's enough toys and tools and dirt bikes and four-wheelers for a garage sale. Them friends of mine aren't around nowhere. Must be inside. But nothing happens when I go up onto the front steps and knock on the door. Dead-quiet inside and out.

Then a man behind me says, "You the one got my kids sauced?"

I turn. I'm on the steps and he's on the ground but he's still taller. He's a strong beast. Hunched over. Twisted up. Snarled. Two maul heads for fists. A monster in tight black jeans and cowboy boots. His yellow hair goes down to his shoulders and there's an unlit cigarette hanging from his lips. His eyes got no whites to them. Only dirty pinks. He pulls the cigarette from his mouth like it's a toothpick and spits on the ground. He's got a toolbelt on. Hammer in the holster. If he wanted to he'd bash my brains right through the door.

"Fuck you want?"

"My card."

"Speak up!"

"My card!"

"How about you get your scrawny ass off my property, or I'll thump you?"

"You use the hammer?"

"Huh?"

"And the wrench?"

"What do you mean? I use everything."

"But it's your own daughter."

He don't understand the question. He's not real sharp, this turd.

"You got about three seconds, kid."

"Getting my card first."

"What card?"

"In the spokes."

The bikes were right by me the whole time. They're leaning up against the lilacs on the side of the trailer. When I follow him over there his snakey back muscles wriggle. I could save them friends of mine. Save Scar-girl and take her with me and we'd be together for always. If only I wasn't a dumbass who left my knife in the woods. He goes right to the bike with the card and unties the shoelace and pulls the card out right quick like he put it there himself.

His pink eyes got more dirt in them now. He rips the card up once, twice, three times and holds it out to me.

I take the paper shreds and leave. A man like this, see, you don't gotta listen, but you do gotta hear. Someday. Someday I'll be a killer of monsters.

I go back for the purse. A few miles down the highway there's an ash tree with chubby roots. My stomach sloshes around in my head and my eyes water until I blow chunks all over them roots. I stumble to the next tree and sprawl out and think of what Bunkie would do if he was me. Because he wouldn't just die here, I know that.

So I keep walking along the ditch with the purse. All the cookies are gone. Another drop of juice would kill me. When I don't cry from it all I sing Alanis because she's the greatest. Clouds cover up the sun. Then the sun hacks back through the clouds. There's a breeze for a while. Then it's quiet. My shoes crunch along the dead leaves in the ditch. Here and there a driver going down the highway waves. Then the sun sets behind me and my shadow stretches out long. It's like an alien has taken over my body.

A row of buildings comes up out of the distance and I just know it's special before I even get close enough to see it all. Bunkie's gotta be nearby.

There's a restaurant and a gas station and a liquor store and whatnot else. I go into the bathroom to rinse my mouth out and drink as much water out of the sink as I can. There's a dumpster behind the restaurant. A buffet. I eat half a hamburger and half a fish sandwich and some fries. Then I'm real tired. There's also a big plastic bucket full of heater butts. A couple on top of the rest are still smoking out. I bring a dying one back to life with a few drags and smoke as many butts as I can one after another, down to the filter. Then I take out all the pieces of Baby Milo's card and set them out on one of the stone walkway blocks and make sure they're all there. That turd ripped both the wizard's ears off.

He's no different than Murphy. Murphy. His room was up in the attic where he did his pills and whatnot else. A trick he'd pull sometimes, his eyes rolling back in his head like they just might stay white forever. Got a demon taking over his body. Murphy. Always walking around with his shirt off and his chest out. Naked and skinny-strong and scarred up from evil he'd done and a tattoo of a Jesus cross. Black stencil on his grown-man boob. He'd get so mad there were purple veins in his forehead and neck, bulging out like fat worms. Didn't matter that I did nothing to him either. Every chance he got he spat in my food. In my cereal. In my macaroni and cheese. Even my ice cream.

Then I'd wake up to him yelling at me and slugging me in the nuts and pulling me out of bed and pushing my head against the bedroom window like the glass could shatter and I'd fly out onto the roof and roll down into the lawn. And he'd chew cinnamon gum and stink from sweat and cigarettes and his girlfriend. He'd make me smell his fingers covered in sour swamp. Fuck him and those smelly fingers. He'd laugh and want me to cry but I wouldn't since that meant I'd lose. I couldn't lose. Not to Murphy. Because that meant I was a baby. A real wussy baby.

That's the whole thing of why I need to see Bunkie. Last time I saw him at our old Mom's place, he was the one running off and I was crying, and he said, "Don't be scared."

"But I am."

"No, you're not. You're tough."

So, he'll be proud of me when I tell him how I beat Murphy. Pounded him to nothing with Uncle Bob's help.

Bunkie's my brother. He loves me and I love him.

***

I wake up on the scratchy doormat behind the liquor store. Not sure if it's late in the day or early in the morning. I swallow a bunch of times trying to pop my ears because it feels like I'm underwater. Except every time I swallow, a hundred bees sting my throat. The door behind me is open. A man inside laughs. He didn't wake me up on the way in so he can't be the worst. Boys have been kicked hard for less than that.

When I go in, the man is still laughing. He's heard the funniest joke ever told. The radio's playing that whiny Savage Garden again. "Truly Madly Deeply." He's sitting on a stool behind the register and watching *The Price is Right* on a little TV. His belly hangs over his belt like one of those garbage bags full of maple leaves. He was born on that stool and hasn't moved since. His hairline starts on top of his head and his hair is slicked back greasy. Behind him is the office door. Above the door is a clock with hands.

"He's awake!" Greasy cries. He turns on his stool to face me.

"What time is it?"

He looks at me. Then at the clock. Then back at me. "Almost ten."

"But is it tomorrow yet?"

He seems all weirded out, like I'm licking my own snot. "It's ten in the morning if that helps you any."

"Can I use the bathroom?"

"It's for employees."

"I gotta go to the bathroom."

"Figured as much. What's your name, son?"

"Kirby."

"Kirby *what*?"

"Scurvy."

"Kirby Scurvy?"

"That's right. How about tape? You got any of that?"

"What for?"

I show him the card and he smiles and clears the counter next to the register. Brushes aside a pop can and a magazine and a take-a-penny cup and a stack of wallet-size Vikings' schedules. He lets me sit on his stool while I tape the card back together.

After, he says, "Bathroom. Go back through that office, open the far door, go down into the basement, take a right, third door on the left. Careful, it's a mess down there."

He goes to organize the first row of liquor. The bottles clank behind me as I walk through the office and open the door. It's so dark down there I can't see the bottom, and the stairs are the type you don't ever come back up. I don't have my knife. Better to just piss myself. I turn back.

On the way out, I ask Greasy if he knows Bunkie.

"He's my brother. I'm trying to find him."

"Bunkie, huh? Bunkie Scurvy?"

"No, we got different last names."

"What's his?"

"Don't know. I could guess."

"I don't suppose that'd help. Say, I haven't seen you around here before. You got parents to call and come get you?"

"Yeah, my mom's out in the car. We're looking for my brother together."

"I hope you find him, Kirby."

I leave through the front and use the restaurant bathroom instead.

There's a park across from the liquor store. A swing set and a merry-go-round and a sandbox. All day I sit on the grass at the edge of the sandbox, asking people do they know Bunkie. Have they seen him. Do they know where he lives.

Don't nobody know shit.

The wind burns my eyes out. My headache is a heartbeat in my skull. I forgot Kimono's purse behind the restaurant but I'm feeling too shitty to go back for it. Then I'm hungry as ever too and think about what Bunkie does when he's hungry as ever. So I sneak into the back of the restaurant and steal a busboy apron and walk around to the front and wait until all the waitresses are in the kitchen. I go inside and tell a man sitting right by the window with his brand-new plump steak that there's something wrong with his food and so I better get him a new one.

For a long time, I'm a king like Bunkie, eating my steak with no silverware. Sucking my fingers until they taste like fingers again. A king because for a while it don't matter how fucked I've gone and fucked myself. The sun is bright all over the park for many hours and I tie my hoodie and sweatshirt to the merry-go-round and spin it real fast so that they fly out. Invisible boys hanging on for dear life. Then later I get bored and sit on the merry-go-round that burns my butt through my jeans and it matters now how fucked I've gone and fucked myself.

Except maybe Mom is missing me. She really isn't the worst one. Even though she don't let me watch *Scream* or *I Know What You Did Last Summer* and even though she don't let me jump off the roof and even though she don't got a trampoline. Still, she never forgot me at the grocery store or let my brothers steal my shoes. Maybe she's up in her bedroom thinking about loving on me like she loves on Baby Milo even when he's snuck himself some creamed corn but couldn't make it to the bathroom in time. Maybe she bought a trampoline just hoping I'd come back.

Then a woman comes along pushing a stroller. She's got on black running shorts and a windbreaker that's bright and pink and new-looking. Her red-brown ponytail sticks out the back of a baseball cap. In the stroller a baby is fussing about something.

I walk up behind her. I speak quietly since the baby might be trying to sleep.

"Ma'am," I say.

She don't hear me. My voice is never loud enough.

"Ma'am," I say again.

She don't hear me this time either. Only she feels me staring at her. She snaps her head around and looks down at me. It's almost a glare. Mostly it's a grossed-out frown. I know why. There are holes in the knees of my jeans. My hair is a clump of sweaty brown shag.

"Sorry to bother you, ma'am. You know a boy named Bunkie? That's my brother."

"No, I'm sorry."

"How far is it to Crosslake?"

"About fifteen miles."

Fifteen miles! How many years of walking is that? And I've already walked for years already! That stretchy little baby snarls at me and fusses quiet now because he knows I'll never find Bunkie and I was dumb to even try.

"Maybe could I use your cellphone? I wanna call my dad to come get me. I'm sure he's worried since I ran away. I tried to get back home and got lost. I'm a dumdum."

"Of course!" she yelps. She starts digging in a bag under the stroller. "If he doesn't answer I'll give you a ride home. You live close by?"

"He'll answer. He don't do nothing but watch TV and wait for someone to call him about a job."

"What does he do?"

"That's all he does, ma'am."

"Here you go, sweetie," she says, handing me the cellphone. "You know the number?"

"Uh-huh." The baby's crying now. "Is it a boy or a girl?"

"A boy. Charles. What's your name?"

"Wendell," I tell her. "Is he too warm in the sun, maybe?"

"No, I forgot his binkie."

"What's a binkie?"

"A pacifier."

"I wish I had one for him."

She smiles.

I step away and call Liz at her big brick building.

"It's Professor Bunghole."

"Where you at, kiddo?"

"Out and about."

"You sound sick. What happened with Jessica?"

"I'm ready to go back now."

"Why'd you run away?"

"I didn't."

"You did, though."

"Sort of."

"What happened?"

"I ran away."

"You got shoes this time?"

"Kinda." One of the soles isn't connected to the top no more.

"When's the last time you ate?"

"I just had steak."

"I won't ask."

"I thought Bunkie could get me a new pair of shoes. That's why I ran."

"You two are always getting each other into trouble."

"I'm not gonna make it where I thought I could. I'm fifteen miles away. Liz, can I get some socks? My big toe's poking through."

"Of course, kiddo."

"And can you call Jessica to please come get me?"

"Honey ... It's stressful for her to deal with runners."

"I didn't run, though."

"What, you fell out the window and rolled out of town?"

"Liz."

"I'm not mad, kiddo. I'm just being straight with you."

"But it was just to see my brother."

"You also stole an old woman's purse, a bunch of communion wine and wafers. I'm not mad. Anyway, I think I got a place for you. But you gotta stay put. You gotta do school. It's dangerous for you out on your own."

Sometimes she talks this way, like I don't know things. "Okay, Liz," I say. "But ..."

"What?"

"You ever kill a monster?"

"Huh?"

"You ever kill one?"

"What?"

"A monster."

"Like, in a video game?"

"No."

"Kiddo, did somebody hurt you?"

"I didn't let them, Liz."

"Whose phone is this?"

"Some lady's."

"You don't know her?"

"No."

"Nice of her to let you use it."

"Real nice. Nicest lady there ever was, probably."

"Where are you, I'll come get you?"

I hand the lady her phone and she sees it's all sticky.

"Can you tell Liz where we're at?" I ask.

"Your dad's name is Liz?"

She rummages through her diaper bag for a wet wipe to clean her phone's screen with. Then she introduces herself to Liz.

Turns out, she really is nice. She stays with me at the park while I wait for Liz. She even asks me what's wrong when I get to crying. I don't tell her. The thing is, I can't tell Bunkie the story now.

How it was Murphy, see. Murphy. It happened on that spring day after school when he pushed me down in the gravel driveway at our Mom's house. His eyes were just slits of black on his face. Behind them there was no boy. Because he had the brain of a monster then, I could tell from his eyes, just slits of black. My backpack was full of books and so I was stuck on the ground like a turtle on its shell. He cocked back so fast I didn't even see his fist coming. The side of my head exploded, and I was staring at him with no tears because he couldn't win unless I lost. And I wouldn't lose. Not to him. Then he looked up and his eyes grew big and there was a rush of air above us and suddenly I was free.

A man took Murphy by the ear and pulled him across the driveway and knelt on his spine. Murphy's face was in the gravel and his limbs were flailing like he was an insect stuck in something gooey. Murphy jiggled loose and ran down the driveway toward the house and I knew right then he'd never bother me again.

The man helped me up. A sandy blond ponytail went about to his butt. He was wearing jeans and work boots and a plaid t-shirt. "Hi, I'm Robbie."

"Robbie."

"Call me Uncle Bob."

Uncle Bob was Mom's brother, turns out. That summer he was working on his truck engine in the garage that was cool and sticky and grey all over. He must not have known what to do about the engine since it never started up for him. But I'd sit on the riding lawnmower next to him and he'd say how he'd protect me just the same way he protected all the other good ones who came through Mom's house before me. Said he looks out for the good ones who wanna be good. Said he could tell right away just how good I wanted to be. His eyes were droopy and sad but when he laughed his belly shook and his face looked like he was hurt somewhere inside. His room was upstairs in the loft above the garage. One time he left for a whole week to fish in Canada and I cried. Because he'd saved me. Because he showed me how to fight back. The best story anyone's ever heard. Someday. Someday I'll be good like him. Even better. So good at killing monsters I don't even have to.

Liz comes and talks to the woman. I jump into the back of her car.

"You wanna sit in front?"

"I've never sat in front before."

"Today could be the day."

Up front it's nice and cool. She gives me a plastic bag full of socks and shirts and jeans and underwear and a pair of new sneakers. She buys me a hamburger and milkshake at the drive-through. I'm still hungry afterward so she takes me through for more. Liz. Neat little nose. Eyes dead-grass brown. And today there's a scar on her neck. A mouth sown shut. Red like chewed up gummy bears.

"What happened to your neck?"

"A tumor. I had surgery to get rid of it."

"What if you died?"

29

"It wasn't that serious."

"I bet there's no cancer in Heaven."

"I suppose there isn't."

"Where am I going?"

"Most the homes are full right now. There's one woman who said she can take you in. Her name is Gwen Bonnie."

Name sounds made up. Gwen Bonnie. "Is she nice?"

"Oh, yes." She nods and smiles, so happy to tell me this Bobbie woman is nice.

"I'm glad you're not dead."

"Me too."

"I'd give you my neck if I could."

She smiles again. This one's the type that makes your heart tingle.

Then I remember ... "There's more than you even know."

"More *what?*"

"Monsters. More of them than ever."

I look away, except feeling her looking at me hurts and I get to worrying.

"I wanna go to Bunkie's," I tell her.

"You can't."

"But I still wanna."

"I'm sorry."

"Then can I please, please, please go back to Jessica's? I swear I won't run off nowhere."

"Jessica's house is full right now."

"I'll sleep in the garage. I'll make a fire in the back yard and camp out. Tell her I'm sorry and I'll be better. I'll help with the laundry and the meals, and I'll go to school and won't cause problems at all!"

I'm sobbing hard now, howling like an ass-whooped doggie. A major baby. Sobbing so hard she pulls over to put her arm around me. When I'm done being a wussy, I think about giving her Baby Milo's card so she can bring it to him. But it's all smudgy and ripped up and taped together. Anyway, I'm starting to like that wizard even if he's a dipshit.

Then she takes me to my new house and shows me my new Mom. Mom is just like the old Moms. Maybe friendly but probably not. She's got a big van that seats a dozen kids at least and is supposed to be white but is grimy. All that, same as ever.

Liz drives off and it's just me and Bernie or whatever standing out on her lawn. I try not to look at the house because the windows are all full of kids staring at me. One of them has ears that are two ginormous seashells sticking out of his head. A girl has tucked some hair into her nose like she's trying to make herself sneeze. A third is a boy making faces. Maybe at me or maybe at his reflection in the window.

I look her over good. She's a giant. Her mouth is a scowl with lipstick and beneath her makeup is all these rash-looking scars and her grey eyes are smooth and glassy and dim and stupid. The worst thing is her crooked nose. A lightning bolt zagging down her face.

"What's wrong with your nose?"

"A snowmobile accident. Older brother was driving through a playground, pulling me on a sled. He went under a seesaw. Guess which one of us ducked."

"Did you tag him back?"

"I happened to, yes. I woke him from a catnap by hitting him with the telephone set. I used to be wicked."

"Does your brother live here with you?"

"He's dead."

She scrunches her face up like she's trying to sniff her upper lip.

"Any other questions before we go inside?" she asks.

"No."

"Do you know where you are?"

"No."

"You're in Sibley, Minnesota. My name is Miss Bonnie. This is my house."

"Okay."

She don't start for the door yet. She waits for me. Then I up and ask her. "I wanna be good. What are you? You a good one? I'd rather just run now than wait. I'm not even hungry or need a bath."

"You see all those kids in the windows there? They're like you. They came here real scared."

"I'm not scared."

"Fine.

"I'm not."

A shit-eating smirk on her. "Okay, you're just as not-scared as they were at first. This is their last foster home. It'll be yours, too. The one you didn't run away from."

"Okay."

"Because you won't have a reason to run away from this house. If you ever think you do, tell me."

"Okay."

"Okay?" she says.

"So, you can help me?"

"As best I can."

Miss Bonnie has two little dogs. Scruffles and Deadfishbreath. Scuffles is scruffy and Deadfishbreath has breath that smells like dead fish. If you don't watch them, they pee all over.

Sometimes, when you're watching them, they pee all over. On the kitchen rug. On the carpet in the living room. On our homework. In our shoes. I wake up sometimes wondering if they peed on me.

Living there are Shrump and Jessup and Susanna B and Susanna C and Slim Pickles and all the other kids. After meals we put our dishes in the sink. When we get home from school one of us has gotta put them in the dishwasher. Then one of us puts them away. These are the rules of life. Break them if you wanna, but who'd wanna since Miss Bonnie can be a crusty scab? Stinking like an ashtray. Sometimes you can't really see her through the smoke. And she's scowling at me, and she's mean and she's monstering at me. And it don't matter any how much makeup goes on her face since there's still that red rash on her brow and nose. Those cheeks are just peach taffy and there's saggy bags under her eyes and her jowls go drooping like an old dog's. So, I have nightmares where she grabs ahold of her throat-skin and pulls her face down over her cheekbones and stretches it out. Then she lets it loose again. Some of them kids living here are ten-times bigger than me and they're scared of her just the same!

One day I got a cold. A real one but it's not as bad as I play it up. Except I wanna ask her the thing so I stay home.

It's just me and Miss Bonnie in the van going from school to school to courthouse to shelter to dollar store back to school to secondhand store and over and over. The cup holders are stuffed with coins and gum wrappers and receipts. Outside, trees jump by the window a thousand at a time. The radio crackles old rock songs. I know them all and if she don't like me singing, she don't say so. Sometimes she hums along with me. Sometimes she hums the last song that was on, like we're listening to different stations. When she hums, I sing quieter so I can hear. Never heard no woman sing like her before. Raspy and low and real pretty.

"Miss Bonnie, what are you singing for?"

"I don't know. Why are *you* singing?"

"I'm not singing no more."

"You're not singing *any*more."

"I didn't know you could sing, Miss Bonnie."

"Everyone can sing. You have a beautiful voice, too."

"Really?"

"Very beautiful."

I don't sing for her. Because now I gotta ask her the thing. I'm scared to but I may not get another chance to ask.

"Miss Bonnie?"

"Yes?"

"How'd you make everyone afraid of you?"

"Who's afraid of me?"

"Everyone."

"Why do you say that?"

"Because you don't ever gotta be mad."

She frowns since I stumped her. "I choose not to get myself worked up over small things. There's enough big things in life to get worked up over."

"Okay."

"What I'm saying is that there's no problem being mad will fix."

I haven't found the answer yet and so I drum on my thighs and get to huffing. She's crawling under my skin now. Monsters can do that. Soon as I find the stones to ask, I blurt it out.

"No wonder you're not afraid, you're a monster!"

"I'm afraid all the time."

"No, you're not."

"I am."

"Of what?!"

"I'm afraid I'll lose one of you kids."

Her scowl is real scowly now, like she hasn't been lying. She sniffs her upper lip. Sit there and think on it all I want, I can't figure out what she's up to.

"And I'm not a monster," she says. Like it must be true just because she says it is. And maybe it is true. Except that's just the thing a monster would say, that she isn't one.

I tell her, "Then you're a monster-killer."

"I'm not that, either."

"You have to be one or the other."

"In that case I suppose I'm a monster-killer."

"Like I said."

"What are you, Heath?"

"I'm no wuss, tell you that. That's the only way to become a monster-killer someday."

"Of course."

"I don't feel sick no more."

"*Anymore.* Yes, you look much better."

She buys me a cone with two scoops and says don't tell nobody else when they get home from school. Alanis comes on the radio. We sing.

For a while after that there's mostly just school. In gym class I'm good. In recess I'm good. In math I'm not the shittiest one. In science and English and spelling and all that I'm the shittiest one. When Jonesy calls on me to read, I'd rather eat the page instead. And I go crazy every day waiting to get out of the classroom because there's at least a billion little wild things happening all over. Birds and squirrels and rabbits. Throwing snowballs at cars in the school lot. Otis's show-and-tell python with a mole bulging in its belly. One day Richie Gibbenshitz says Jonesy keeps his urine in jars in his bedroom and drinks it up when the moon is just right, and I laugh and laugh and then there's that day in gym when we're playing track-and-field and Chandra Sanders throws a discus and it bounces off Mr. Delmar's forehead and he falls to the gym floor. All Jell-O. Crumpling down like she knocked the bones out of him.

Mr. Delmar is mean after that. Real mean. Telling Monica Spencer she's chunky. She isn't anyway. She's just perfect. Just the perfect type of eyes and lips and ears and she's got clean elbows and knees, and she eats food with her mouth closed and her smile is crooked and real pretty, and she don't pick her nose any, far as I can tell. Once, she tells me to quit staring at her and I say I'm not and she says I'm still doing it and so I run off to the bus where I sit forever thinking about saying will you please, will you please, Monica, please will you. Because when she's there I think about her. And I can't think about her and them monsters at the same time.

But then something else happens. The worst thing ever. Just I didn't know it was the worst thing at first.

Bunkie comes to Miss Bonnie's. Bunkie. Bunkie! My brother and all his stuff in a garbage bag. Except Bunkie is a different Bunkie now. He looks smaller. He's scrawny and shy and don't hardly look at me and won't say what happened to his grandma. And there's more! He's not alone. Murphy's with him. Goddamn Murphy!

It's weird because Murphy ignores me. He and Miss Bonnie are good friends somehow. They're right away playing Monopoly together and the games last for days and days. Maybe Murphy's changed or maybe he's picking on someone else that I don't know about or maybe he's just too sleepy to thrash me no more. Probably he's still afraid of Uncle Bob.

I wanna tell Bunkie the story real bad. Except he ignores me too.

One day me and Murphy are raking leaves out front, and I ask him what's wrong with Bunkie.

"Who the fuck is Bunkie?"

"The boy you came with."

"That's Dorian. He's my brother."

"Mine, too."

"No, he's my actual half-brother."

"Bullshit!" My arms are limp now and so I can't rake no more and I know he's making shit up to hurt me, but it still hurts. I spill all the words at him. "His name is Bunkie since we all shared bunks with him because he snored bad up on the top bunk, so we took turns sleeping on the bottom one, well, we didn't take turns, because we made the newest brother deal with him. It was me for a while, then it was Greg Meatloaf—"

"Shut up, Heath."

"You don't even know Bunkie."

"His name is Dorian and he's my honest-to-god blood-brother. Different dads, is all."

"Bunkie—"

"Shut up! I swear to God ...!"

"Swear all up and down! Uncle Bob will pound you again!"

"Robbie?"

"Right."

"You must be the dumbest motherfucker alive. Don't know shit about shit."

He looks at me like he might whack my head off with his rake. He just shakes his head and keeps raking.

I run inside, right up to Bunkie. "Murphy's telling lies that you and him are brothers for real even though I did all what you said, Bunkie, I really did because I don't wanna be like him and I don't wanna be a wussy baby and I'm not and he was spitting in my mac and cheese and in my ice cream too but I didn't cry once since I'm tough like you said, tough like you said, just like you because you and I are brothers for real and not him!"

Even now he won't talk. Except he nods sort of like I'm a true dumbfuck and should've known all along that he and the monster were closer than me and Bunkie could ever be and so I run upstairs to my room and sit on the bed for a long time staring at a book that I can't read because my head is all mushy thinking of him and Murphy chasing chickens together and throwing rocks at traffic lights and giving fingers to everyone. I'm so pissed I could climb out the window and jump onto the awning above the front door and run at Murphy and tackle him so he beats on me. Instead, I decide to not call Bunkie Bunkie anymore. Dorian the Mute is his name now. Fuck them both, I decide.

And I decide another thing, too. Because I have an idea. The best idea anyone's ever had, probably.

It's not even that cold out yet.

***

Everything I could ever wish for comes on Halloween.

Only it don't seem to start out that way. Me and my older brother Ricky get in trouble with Miss Bonnie for jumping over the seats on the school bus while Don is taking us home. She told me don't keep sitting by Ricky on the bus. Except I've never laughed so hard, him flying upside down over the bus seats. Don stops the bus and yells at us while we're laughing and laughing. So, Miss Bonnie won't let me or Ricky go nowhere since we're grounded. Even though tonight everyone will be at the movies in Brainerd. Monica too! And Miss Bonnie can't ground me if I'm not around and so that means tonight is the night.

Ricky helps with the plan. He just don't know it. He gets us a ride to Brainerd with his friends since they'll be at the mall next to the theater. Up front his friends share a cigarette that's shaped funny and smells like Murphy. I take one puff and I'm so woozy and nervous after that I have to keep checking that I still got what I need for my escape. They're there. Extra socks and fruit snacks in my hoodie pocket.

When I get out of the car I panic because I can't find the theater. But it's right where it's always been. Still, I have a hard time making it to the entrance. I wobble in. Inside is a trick-or-treat party. Everyone's dressed for it but me. If Ricky and his friends are too grown up for that stuff, so am I. Werewolves and cowgirls and baseball players and ghosts. Ace Ventura and Michael Myers and Beetlejuice. All everything you could think of. They look stupid. Except then there's Monica Spencer who's a cat. Long black tail and kittycat ears and whiskers on her cheeks done with black marker. Her hair is in a perfect ponytail. Her tennis shoes are perfect and white. Her smile is crooked-perfect like always and I feel stupid dressed in normal clothes.

There's a *Chucky* movie playing. Chucky's a killer doll and I honestly don't much like the way he looks on the poster. I get in line behind Monica and hope she and her friends buy a ticket to something that isn't *Chucky* so I won't see no more of that doll. But she buys a ticket to *Chucky* and that means I have to go. My stomach gurgles.

I'm lucky. It's crowded in the theater but there's an open seat behind her. It's worn slick-smooth and crusted in spots from soda spills. I watch the previews and she nibbles popcorn one kernel at a time since she isn't scared at all of what's coming.

Who knows what the movie's about. Shit, I'm not watching. Except every time I do, Chucky's at it again, hacking someone up with a knife. She flinches but I can tell she's no wussy. So I can't be one either. This is my chance.

I lean forward to whisper her name. She turns her head around and looks at me like I'm a stranger.

"Fruit snacks?" I whisper.

"What?"

I hold them out to her. "Want fruit snacks?"

Someone shushes me and she says, "No, thanks," and turns back to the screen.

I sit back. My fingers get awfully sweaty as I gobble up the rest of them fruit snacks. I dry my hands on the extra socks in my hoodie pocket. It was a dumb thing to do. She already has popcorn, why would she want fruit snacks? But at least now she knows I'm there. Only the movie could end any minute. I better get it all out. If she isn't afraid, I shouldn't be. I tell myself, Go on, wussy-pants.

I lean forward again.

"Monica," I whisper.

She don't seem to hear me.

"Monica."

This time she turns her whole body so she's almost facing me. She looks real pretty but also pissed. I'm no stranger now. I'm Heath and I have something to tell her. Something to ask her. To beg of her. I lean even closer. She cocks her head back and glares all angry and waiting.

"Do you want ...? Maybe will you come with me and we can leave this dump and I'll show you everything ...? Things as beautiful as you are ... So, when the movie's done ... Uncle Bob can help us, too, remember ... And we'll never come back because we won't need to because we'll have one another for always ... You and me for always ... Do you wanna come with me? Please. Please."

The same guy from before tells me to shut the hell up. I look at Monica and she looks at me and there's nothing on her face to tell me if she's decided. When she turns back to the screen I get a queasy feeling like when Miss Bonnie drives fast on hills. Only it's kinda my whole body now but mostly where my heart is. I sit back and they whisper and giggle and I'm red and about to cry and I really, really, really don't want Monica to see how red and about to cry I am.

So, I put my hood up and walk out of the theater into the light of the hallway. It's empty. The front doors by the registers are all glass. Outside, the rain looks cold and plus I'm suddenly hungry. There's popcorn and Raisinets sprinkled all over on the carpet. I pick out the popcorn and eat it and fill my hoodie pouch with whatever I don't eat. Then I eat what's in the pouch. I leave the Raisinets because they have raisins in them. In the bathroom I sit on the toilet in the stall that don't smell so much like poo.

Uncle Bob could be anywhere, maybe even Canada, and how far even is Canada? The tiles are gritty and not as white as they're supposed to be. But I'm sleepy and it's raining, and Canada is a ways away, I bet. I curl up on the tiles.

Thunder wakes me up a bit later. I wonder if maybe she's still there. Maybe she's changed her mind. Maybe she's waiting for me. So I run out of the bathroom.

There's no one around. Even the raisins are gone. The door to the theater is open. I run inside. It's empty. The movie screen lights the room with a dark blue glow. There's a red Exit sign but the exit door is locked. I run back out to the front doors by the registers. There's a big chain over the handles. Those bastards, even the display case is locked up so you can't get the candy inside.

For the longest time I sit with the back of my head against the glass door. I'd sleep if I could. Only now I'm thinking about the movie screen glowing dark blue like it's bruised all to hell from something trying to make its way through to me. Chucky or Michael Myers or the *Scream* guy or Freddy Krueger or Murphy who's snapped out of it and ready to whoop on me again. And I'm thinking maybe Monica couldn't find me because I hid in the bathroom. Maybe she didn't want her friends to know about our plans. Maybe she just don't want them to know how much she loves me.

Or maybe the whole plan was stupid, and she don't know me from Chucky.

I march into the theater. March right up to that screen. In my head I taunt them, Do it, fight me, grab my neck and twist me until my head pops off.

Nothing happens.

From then to the end of time I'm walking back and forth in front of the screen as it gets brighter and brighter and brighter and I'm thinking and walking and walking and thinking and running my fingertips over the scratchy screen. Fine. Fine. Fine. And I gotta make sure the way my right fingers feel on the screen when I'm walking to the left is the same way my left fingers feel when I'm walking to the right, or else I'll die in a car crash or Murphy and Dorian the Mute will die in a car crash and I'll survive or Miss Bonnie will die or Monica will die or she hates me or loves me or hates me or loves me or ...

"Heath! Heath!" A shout from the back of the theater.

A lip-sniffing scowl. Miss Bonnie stands between a cop and some guy with a nametag. I'm antsy but there's nowhere to run and they'll catch me.

So I walk to her and she meets me in the middle of the row and I wish so bad she'd pull my ears off my head. Something. Anything. But she don't. She squats down and pulls me in and hugs me like she missed me the whole time I was gone. Hugs me and kisses me on the top of my head and she's real beautiful then loving on me, Miss Bonnie.

"Let's go home," she says. She takes my hand and it's good, I think. It's real good, monsters or not, the way some of them love.

Dorian

Ten years later ...

A text from an Unknown number. 2:00 a.m.

So sorry Dorian.

I don't respond. I don't sleep.

At 6:00 a.m. I drive to the house my crew will shingle today. I get started and my workers arrive soon afterward. Weeks of Canadian forest fires have tinged the September sky a sort of salmon-pink. It's sickly-looking. The sun beats down on me. It can't pick a color. Neon-orange then vermilion, strawberry then ruby. As if confused or pulling a prank. Another shiny, hot, itchy day. Good for further staining the pits of my knitted long-sleeve shirt a brackish blond. Every new hire I've ever had has asked about it. "What's with the shirt?" "Not hot enough for you?" I smile. Maybe I laugh. He learns what the others have learned. Not to ask because I won't answer.

I work on the eaves since they demand more skill and focus than the rest of the roof does, long, monotonous. After an hour or so the crewmembers quit those smutty stories they know I hate. Sex, bloody knuckles. Embellishments at best. Then one of them turns on the hard rock station on a portable boombox and the only sounds are electric guitar and nail guns, kneepads scraping against shingles and extension cords tapping against the side of the house. The afternoon stretches on. The sun is a spoiled grapefruit. My shirt clings to my torso, my wristbands drip with sweat. If I'm to have just one addiction, it must be this. One sultry habit, a punishment for the others I've quit. At the end of the workday my shirt will dry on the wooden railing of my apartment balcony, and I'll once again be too tired to remember shit I'd rather not. Mercy.

Hours later I stand in the grass, inspecting our work. The sunlit shingles twinkle. I fill the bed of my truck with nails and scraps and remind the crew where to meet me on Monday.

Once they're gone, I stare at the text.

Who's this?

I know who it is. I know why she's sorry. A day like this, never mind that it was a long time coming. For some reason you always think you'll have more time. That you deserve more time. Hardly anyone deserves the time he gets. Five years coming, this one. A man can conjure any excuse he wants. Whatever fits the day, month, year. Excuses only add to the shame that had him making excuses to begin with. Five years of shame. I'd think to myself, "Five years, huh? What's six, then, what's ten, when I could drive to Sibley any time I want and thank her for mothering me when no one else cared to try?" The way a person thinks. What'll happen to all those kids, orphaned again?

My truck reeks of cigarette smoke, stale and fetid. Back at my apartment, I shower and change into shorts and a clean long-sleeve. I comb my hair neatly, drape my drenched shirt over the balcony railing, pin it down with a stone to keep the wind from blowing it into the street below, and grab a Coke from the fridge. I sit on the edge of the grimy tub, squeeze until my fingers throb.

My phone buzzes.

It's Emma. How you been, Dorian?

Good. What happened?

Miss Bonnie. She passed away. I'm so sorry.

When?

A month ago. I thought I'd let you know in case you hadn't heard.

I hadn't. Of course I hadn't. Who's around to tell me but Emma?

I get back in my reeking truck, the odor redolent of shame. It's the least I can do, go back to my childhood home, pay my respects. The least I can do.

Sibley is forty-five minutes from Walker. I drive with the windows down because the air conditioner's broken. I hit the highway, turn the radio on just in time for the top-of-the-hour news. A woman reports that radical combatants have killed two American military service members in Syria or Iraq or Yemen or Afghanistan. I don't catch exactly where.

"You got it all backward, stupid," Murphy said when I told him America's unending drone wars seemed like a mistake. He reminded me that terrorists use women and children as human shields. That when they have no more use for the civilians, they execute them. This encourages survivors to "make themselves useful."

"Not that the tyrants aren't worse," he said. Syrian jets bomb hospitals and rebel-held facilities housing civilians. When emergency units scramble to tend to the dead and dying in the rubble, the jets swing through again. Assad gases his own people with sarin, tortures them in prisons. "Turn your enemy into something subhuman and it's easier to kill him."

"You mean, like, with drone strikes?" That's what I should've said. He'd have liked that. He acted disgusted by my "ignorant fuckery," but he enjoyed it. Made him feel smart. Sometimes it was as if in his mind we'd stopped arguing about whether Americans ought to accept so much civilian collateral damage in the Middle East and started arguing about whether his first tour was pleasant and whether oppression and massacres were actually good things.

He told anecdotes about the war. By the time he finished chattering about improvised explosive devices, roadside and car bombs, and rigged animal carcasses. About captives drugged, vested up, and pushed out into crowded markets. About places in Kabul so poor anyone wearing shoes or holding a cellphone was trouble. About fellow soldiers killed in suicide attacks, "thrown from a car, severed spine, died two days later." About ambushes, "sniped, bullet entered the forehead and left through the brainstem." After all that, I'd have to leave him alone, so he'd cool off.

Blood brothers are different, half or not. Murphy and I shared a room at Hotel Bonnie, as we called it. For a while we hated her together. Hated her stink, cigarettes and orange-scented perfume. Hated the coats of makeup on her face. Her rosacea-scarred brow and nose, zigzagged from a water-skiing mishap, so she told Murphy. Her gray eyes like two dimes, the faces of Roosevelt worn off by decades of circulation. Hated that she went to church. Hated that she didn't drag us along, that she not only deep-down-in-her-gut believed in treating others well but was actually capable of pulling it off most of the time. Somehow, we got a kick out of her dabbing up sick kids' vomit, swabbing bathroom tiles after potty-training mishaps, washing fistfight-bloodstains out of volleyball uniforms. And I didn't rat Murphy out after he snuck beef broth into her precious Bugsie's and Dookie's dishes. The dogs had sensitive stomachs.

Murphy was capable of real savagery. He chased our brothers' and sisters' beloved pet rabbit around, wielding a stainless-steel potato-masher. And there was talk of dousing her raspberry bushes with industrial-strength brush-killer. Luckily, I convinced him not to. The best raspberries you'd ever had.

Why'd we hate her? Murphy had a theory, one I waited a long while to hear and even longer to understand. That's how he was, wilder than I was, more brutal, more childish. But somehow wiser too, in his own way.

He and I were lab partners in Mrs. Morgan's tenth-grade biology class, and he pulled my weight whenever I was too depressed to lift my head from my desk. One day Carissa Masters was annoyed I'd missed the party out at Gravdahl's parent's place. After a half-mile hike out into the woods there was an acre of knee-high grass. Right in the middle, a steel burn barrel for bonfires, sun-bleached maroon. Miss Bonnie had grounded Murphy and me for coming home stoned one night the weekend before, so we couldn't go to Gravdahl's. When Carissa made out with Joseph Thomas at the bonfire, I was the first to hear about it on Monday morning. I napped in biology, depositing puddles of drool on my backpack.

Thomas skipped class that day because I suppose he had nothing to learn from organisms as simple as he was. He probably couldn't read, whereas Carissa not only read but well and often. Her father was a pediatrician. He clipped out newspaper and magazine articles about women's issues, left them on her bedroom dresser. That day, she sat in the front corner of the class and stared at the Bunsen burner racks lining the wall. The kiss wasn't the thing that made me jealous. It seemed that way at the time. But that wasn't it. The real crux was that she felt about Thomas the way I wished she felt about me. That Mr.

and Mrs. Masters asked him, not me, over for dinner. Invited him, not me, to their weekly movie nights. I can't blame them, the Masters, Thomas, Carissa. He had two regular parents. I lived with eight other foster kids. He was the starting varsity running back. I sulked in the corner of the gym during pep rallies. He escorted her to prom junior year and after he dumped her at the beginning of senior year, I escorted her to the clinic. I was the only one she could confide in. There are good things too in all the shitty things that happen.

Blood brothers. The summer after graduation, in the days leading up to his deployment, Murphy followed me from job to job, drinking Jack-and-Sevens from the can, and handing me shingles as he stood on the top of the ladder. He badgered me about why I stayed friends with Carissa after she started "fucking" Thomas. By lunchtime he was too hammered to use the ladder so he just lay in the grass below, hollering up at me.

"Wasn't even your baby."

I said nothing. No one was supposed to know about that. He said she told him what had happened, told him she was glad she had me. I asked if she wanted him to tell everybody else.

"No. Duh."

"Then quit yelling about it, you fucking idiot!"

He knocked the ladder over. "And what does that snooty bitch Emma want, anyway?"

I'd already told him a dozen times. He didn't buy it.

"A poem? A poem?!" he yelled.

"Don't call her that, either."

"A *bitch*?"

He left to drink at home. He was awfully good at it, drinking at home.

50

It was because of Carissa that Emma came to see me the day after high school graduation. This was back when she was Emma Strumph and, though far from boy-crazy, looking forward to the day she'd be Emma Anything-But-Strumph. It's possible that for a minute she might've even thought, "How about Mrs. Smith? Emma and Dorian Smith?"

Coming into Sibley, I pass the dealership. A glistening row of new trucks faces the highway. Directly above the vehicles hangs a string of massive red, white, and blue flags. Between each flag are individual letters that spell S-P-E-N-C-E-R-S. In the open lot between the trucks and the pristinely white dealership building loiter fifty or so people, a block party.

I drive into town, park across the street from Miss Bonnie's, and open my Coke. The street is dead, the block's residents likely either still at work or shut in for the weekend, getting drunk in front of pedestal fans.

The two-story, Hotel Bonnie, is in bad shape. Squirrels have ransacked the bird feeders, now shattered and strewn atop bits of grain and suet on the sidewalk. The lawn is patchy wherever the purple flowers of Creeping Charlie haven't encroached. Vegetation fills the gutters, furry mold stains the faded grey siding, sunlight has bleached the horizontal blinds fossil-white. In the back yard, raspberry bushes hug the veering picket fence that divides Miss Bonnie's back yard from her neighbor's. Those tart, saccharine berries. I used to fill my mouth, tip my head back, let the juices roll down over my ticklish back molars.

Tasting them, I clear my throat.

Emma answers on the second ring. She sounds overly cheerful, like she's had more than a couple of beers.

"I'm gonna be in Sibley for a couple hours," I say. "Just letting you know."

"You should come by the dealership! Gavin and I are grilling out with some family and friends. It's the Spencer reunion but we're also having a big Labor Day sale starting tomorrow. Have a drink with us!"

I pause long enough to convey a "No, thanks." I say, "I didn't wanna run into you somehow. You know, have you wondering why I was around. Why I called, is all."

My precaution seems to amuse her. "It'd be great to see you. And you should meet Derek. Busy. So busy. Running in circles. Throwing his food at me. Breaking his toys. Good fun. No pressure but I'd love to catch up with you. By the way, sorry I texted you so late. I'd been meaning to. I know how much she meant to you."

"I hadn't heard anything. How did she die?"

"Suicide," she whispers.

"No." My answer is instantaneous and absolute and furious, as if it's up to me to decide what happened to her and how and why. Suicide? Beyond inconceivable. It's preposterous. A woman like Miss Bonnie, so devout, so invested in the lives of others, killed herself in the kitchen where she fed those who'd have gone hungry without her? Killed herself in my childhood home, a home for so many without homes, much less child-hoods? An impossibility.

"I was surprised, too." As if to head off the question, she adds, "Gavin's dad told him they found her in the kitchen."

"The kitchen? How'd she do it?"

"Hung herself."

"*How?*"

"You'd have to ask him for the details."

Clearly, she doesn't care for my line of questioning but what am I supposed to do? That kitchen ceiling with those sheets of ornate tin? How'd she reach the studs? What, a rope around the oven door handle, something slick on the floor, vegetable oil? Please.

"From the ceiling?" I ask.

"I guess."

"But—"

"You'd have to ask Gavin." She's had enough. "Why don't you come on out? There are few people here who could fill you in."

I'm about to decline again, light a cigarette and sit in the truck until I'm ready to knock on the front door, when I spot something. A flicker of movement inside the house. Someone peeking through the blinds to the left of the door. Then the blinds snap back into place.

"I gotta go," I say. "Sorry."

"For what?"

I end the call.

I smoke, watching the door for some time, clicking my jaw. Has the house been sold already? Are some addicts squatting there until someone kicks them out? I'd call the cops if I didn't know who'd show up and what they'd do about it, as close to nothing as they saw fit. Apparently, most of them are getting tuned up at a barbeque, anyway.

Done with my cigarette, I flick it into the gutter, cross the street, and climb up the front steps below the tin awning. Before I can knock, someone inside shouts, "I got a gun!"

The quavering voice is artificially deep. A boy trying to sound older than he is. I can't place the voice just yet. It's familiar and for some reason I'm certain it belongs to someone capable of a whole lot of deviance but not shooting a stranger for merely standing on a porch.

I freeze, put my hands up like I'll catch the bullets.

The boy says, "I know who you are. I know why you're here. You'll have to kick the door down if you want in. I've got a Model 870 Remington. Pump action. It'll put a hole through your chest big enough for me to walk through."

"My name's Dorian Smith. I used to live in this house and I knew the woman who died here. She was my foster mother."

The boy doesn't reply.

"Just came back to see where I grew up. I didn't know anyone was living here."

Silence.

It's getting hot on the stoop. "I'm not gonna hurt you," I say.

"I know you're not. Because I'll tag you worse. I'm not leaving town without her, so fuck off!"

"I don't know what you're talking about. But if this isn't your property, you're trespassing." I put my hands down, back down the steps. "Fair warning if you wanna run. I'm calling the cops," I bluff.

"Don't!" the boy screeches, his voice cracking as it takes on a more natural tenor. "Come back for a second. Please, dude. Let's talk before you rat on me."

"Rat on you for *what*?"

"You knew Miss Bonnie? Me too. I used to live here with her. Even after she quit fostering, I stayed."

"Wanna let me in? We can talk this through. Maybe I can help you."

"All right. I'm sorry for losing my cool," he says, suddenly friendly, too friendly.

He unlocks the deadbolt, twists the doorknob, and opens the door a few inches.

I slowly push the door in, glancing around. It stinks. BO, animal feces, rotting produce. When I step inside he charges at me, grabbing me by the collar and shoving me into the door, slamming it shut. I clutch his shoulders and we stare at each other. A cigarette juts up out of his grimace like a freakish bottom tooth. I recognize this boy. I know him.

I'm slightly taller so when I knee him between the legs, I lift him off the ground. He tumbles backward, holding his groin with both hands, yelping. His cigarette scuttles across the entryway rug.

"You're fine," I tell him, looking for the shotgun. I can't find it. He cusses me out as I have a look around.

To the right, the living room. Crusting up the mangy lilac carpet and threadbare sofas are cat and dog shit, gooey macaroni noodles, moldy bread butts, a hunk of bird guts, a dead mouse. Pictures, paintings, and newspaper cutouts cover the faux-stucco drywall. They're frameless, pin-pricked into the walls. Finger paintings, pastel nature-scene watercolors. Team portraits, senior photos. Polaroids of kids shoveling snow, swimming at Sibley beach, sledding, ice skating. Between a girl's softball picture and a diploma from the University of Minnesota Duluth is a picture of Emma and me taken the summer before she left for college. Her complexion, tan, a tad oily, glistens. Her walnut hair spirals down to her shoulders, her navy eyes match the color of her shirt. We look unrecognizably young, skinny, frail, happy.

To the left, the dining room. Miss Bonnie's olive linen couch butts up against the street-facing windows, its padding bursting through cushion cracks. A cellphone and headphones lay atop a sweat-yellowed, case-less pillow.

Beyond the dining room, the kitchen. The chintzy kitchen table is jammed up against the counter. Splayed newspapers cover the linoleum floor. The sheet of tin on the ceiling is dusty but otherwise unchanged from the last time I was here. The suicide (suicide?) didn't happen in the kitchen. Not like they say.

"Suck it up. I barely got you," I tell him, taking a seat on the couch.

He slaps the carpet and makes his way to stand. Lanky, no more than a foot wide at the hips. He wears moccasins, black jeans rolled up at the ankles, a hemp belt whose tongue has been cut off, and a plain white muscle shirt with a mustard stain over his heart. He sits across from me on a vinyl chair belonging to the kitchen set.

"You asshole," he mutters.

"Don't run at me again."

Blistering acne covers his neck and cheeks. Unwieldy cowlicks churn atop his cropped amber hair. His right eye bulges out, relish-green, its obsidian pupil dilated, while his left is swollen shut. His left cheek is fat, glossy, sangria, like a plastic-wrapped plum.

"Where's the gun?"

"What gun?"

"You said you had one."

"I don't."

"You sure? I'm gonna be real pissed if I find a gun lying around."

"Fuck you."

"I'm having a looksee, then I'll be out of your hair."

Bitter, he mutters to himself. Heath is his name. That's right, Heath Reynolds.

At the top of the stairs is the bathroom with its grand porcelain tub, clawfoot legs silver. I pass by, head to the bedroom Murphy and I shared. I don't go in just yet. Inside there are memories. I know this because I've kept them there. Or tried to and failed badly. I'm alone, still I make sure my arms are covered. Forearm scars from roughhousing. Etchings from my adolescence, achieved with a straightened paperclip. Elbow-pit track marks. Four years' worth of needle-pox, like spider bites. Inside this room are memories. I intended to keep them there, believing that without me, they'd die. As though they couldn't get by without me remembering them. For many years I maintained that excuse. For many years it did well to blunt the shame.

One thing at a time. First the memories. Then Heath and this suicide bullshit.

I open the door. The room is as I remembered it. A quilt-covered cot under the window Murphy and I used to sneak in and out of even when we weren't going anywhere forbidden and could've just used the front door, which was rarely locked. One of us boosted the other onto the awning. One of us pulled the other up from there. There's another cot against the wall to my right. Grey wallpaper with patterned baseball gloves, balls, and bats. But now there are animal sketches on the walls, done in colored pencil, freehand. And there's no oak desk pushed against the corner to his left. Now the room, like the house, is quiet. That's the biggest difference time has imparted on this place, the silence.

Emma knocked on Miss Bonnie's door the morning after graduation. She'd dumped Gavin Spencer for the second time in a year. I was in bed, right there under the window. Murphy and I were hungover, again. It's an awful lot an eighteen-year-old has to drink to be hungover. Miss Bonnie belted my name from downstairs. She wasn't happy. I'd been awake for a bit. Murphy woke me up every day by slamming the toilet seat down in the bathroom down the hall. I threw a blanket over my shoulders, pulled the ankle cuffs of my sweatpants up over my calves. I thought I was hallucinating. Emma was in the doorway, on crutches, a cast on her leg. She wore jeans and tennis shoes. A turquoise tank top. There was a picnic table on the lawn and we sat. My siblings stood in the window, watching. Murphy was making faces in the bedroom. She didn't seem to notice any of it.

I hadn't the faintest clue why she was there. Her mom was a financial advisor with an office in Brainerd and her dad sold upscale furniture and cabinets to people with seasonal lake-side homes. My mom was in prison for drowning my dad. One Tuesday morning he ate a watermelon soaked in vodka and fell asleep in the bathtub. Mom didn't need to hold him down, just let the water run. It was an accident. That's what she said in court, anyway. She just wanted to "scrub him good." After-ward I lived with Grandma, Dad's mom, then bounced around before landing at Miss Bonnie's. Plus there were only eighty-five in our graduating class and somehow Emma and I never so much as made eye contact throughout all of high school. Everyone but me seemed to care about what she was up to. She became the all-time points scorer in Sibley Patriots basket-ball history and would've carried the team to State her senior year if she hadn't broken her leg. I never saw her play. I knew nothing about the crutches, the cast, until there she was in Miss Bonnie's doorway.

As I dug in the soil with my kid sister's plastic beach shovel, Emma talked about how everyone wanted her to try to walk-on to the U of M girls' basketball team. She said she wasn't good enough, shattered shin or not, and anyway, she hated basketball.

"What I want is to be a poet. Will you read something I wrote?"

I asked outright why she couldn't get somebody else to do that for her and she said she knew I wouldn't "butter her up." "You hardly ever look at me," she said.

I didn't know anything about poetry. I still don't. But I knew hers wasn't too good. I told her so the next time we met, and not because I wanted her to go away so Gavin Spencer would stop rolling down Miss Bonnie's block with his shirt sleeve rolled up over his shoulders, his left biceps pressed flat against the side of his truck, his heavy-metal blaring, his cousin Jordan standing shirtless in the bed, rippled abs flexed. If Murphy had his way, he'd have unloaded our brother Emmitt's paintball gun on Gavin's truck. Then, assuming the cousins didn't peel out, he'd have pulled Gavin out through the driver's window and kicked his ribcage in. He could've done it too. I had to calm Murphy down. He didn't need to confront Gavin. Gavin was scared shitless of him, which is why Gavin never did more than drive by slowly. Same with Jordan.

Gavin wasn't afraid of me. Never had been. But even if I didn't have Murphy with me, I wasn't the easiest to mess with, the smallest or weakest. Colton MacGee and Danny Turnhauser were, so Jordan and Gavin pushed *them* into track hurdles, drenched *them* with frog-jar formaldehyde in the back of the classroom. Murphy laughed. I didn't. But I did nothing to stop it. You can't take credit for not giggling at something you don't think is funny. And disliking a shitty person doesn't make you a decent one.

Emma sat on one of those sofas in the living room, gripping the paper like she was paranoid the wind would take off with it. She'd written a poem called "The Orange Glands." It was about her mother. When Emma was a girl the two of them shared an orange. Her mom pulled the orange apart "tiny swollen gland

59

by tiny swollen gland." The taste was "sweeter and tarter than that of any fruit" Emma had ever had. Emma later put two and two together and realized that her parents were having marriage troubles at the time of the orange incident. All this in the poem. I told her I liked it because it had more heart than her other works. She thanked me, then read another, this one in a whisper sort of like the one she used on the phone with me a bit ago.

This poem was the whole secret. It was about leaving for college in the fall, being inexperienced and "not knowing how it's done," "not wanting him to be the first," "not wanting him at all." The paper quivered in her hands. "Are *you*?" she asked when she finished. I had no idea what she was talking about. She seemed miffed by this. She leaned closer, her head down. It was like she was reading the question from the page when she asked, "I mean, you've had sex, right?"

I was thrown off, embarrassed. I felt like the townie scum most people took me for. I nodded. She wanted to know who the girl was, and I told her she didn't know her. She asked if the girl was from around here. I said no. Her eyes lingered on mine when she bowed her head and lifted her eyebrows like I was as dense as they come.

The poetry ruse had come undone. She didn't wanna head to college a virgin. I wasn't going with her, I wasn't part of her circle, I wouldn't gab about it, and even if I did, who'd believe me?

I asked if she'd thought about just lying instead like most kids did.

"But *I'll* know the truth," she said.

That's plenty of remembering. Plenty for now. I back out of the room. I'm about to go downstairs and talk to him, but I pause at the top of the staircase. I see the van now. In my mind, I see it.

What dumb luck that Heath was one of the last people to see Grandma while she was sane. Hell, he may've been what broke her. His siblings rescued him by escaping in their mother's van. Then they parked in the woods outside of Crosslake and survived on gas station food. For warmth they ran the vehicle an hour on, an hour off. Grandma and I happened to be at the gas station near where their van was parked. She bought me giant sunglasses and a slushie. The cup it came in was bigger than my head. Grandma was buying cigarettes and lottery tickets when I walked out of the gas station and found Heath sitting alone in the back of the van. The others were still inside the store.

I knocked on the window of the sliding glass door. His eyes were puffy and I asked if he was on drugs. He shook his head, said he was sick as hell. I asked where he was staying. He said, "Here."

"In Crosslake?"

He shook his head again. "In this van."

I went into the gas station and pulled Grandma out by the wrist. She was in a good mood since she had her smokes on her now. She dragged so hard on her cigarettes you'd think she might suck them up into her throat. She screamed at Heath. She wasn't mad. That's just how she talked.

"Dorian says you and him lived together."

"Who's Dorian?"

"My grandson," she said, pointing at me with her cigarette.

"You mean *Bunkie?*"

"What the fuck's a Bunkie?"

"*He* is," he said, nodding at me.

61

It took some explaining. All about the bunkbeds. After that Grandma's lips were turned down sharply and trembling. It looked like she was trying to close them but couldn't, trying to keep what was left of her senses from slipping out of her mouth. Using her cell he contacted his case manager, who set him up with another home. And over the next several months Grandma's health declined. Then she went mute, as mute as I was when I got to Miss Bonnie's.

Rescued him? Rescued him. Robbie (was it?), some brother to one of Murphy's foster moms, beat the hell out of Murphy and took Heath under his wing to lure him up into the garage loft. That's why his siblings ran off. They saved him. Just now Heath and I acted like we didn't know each other. Like he and Murphy didn't live together before coming to Miss Bonnie's. Like the three of us didn't live here together for a couple years. No, actually the pretending between Heath and I didn't start today but when I first arrived in this house so many years ago and couldn't bring myself to look at him, to comfort him. A hell of a thing to know it could've just as easily been you up in the loft.

I know him. I know this boy. I guarantee he remembers me. I'll go downstairs. In a sense there's nothing unusual about what'll happen then. Two strangers thrown into an arrangement that isn't familiar, that resembles but isn't family. The trick is knowing that by and large, whether we show it or not, we're all ashamed. It's pity that tells on us. So, the most courteous thing you can do is pretend you don't know what you know and hope others return the favor.

Downstairs, it now stinks of weed. He's still on the vinyl chair, his back to the kitchen, to the newspapers splayed out on the floor and the tin ceiling, unchanged since I was last here.

I return to the couch. Pinched between his middle finger and thumb is a slender metal cigarette case that he's absently spinning in circles. With his other hand he holds a joint. Smoke springs up from the tip, curling upward, disappearing. He closes his eyes and tokes like it's his last gasp on Earth. For half a minute he holds his breath, chest puffed out. When he finally exhales, he offers me a hit.

"I'm good, thanks."

"See what you needed to see?"

"I did. Appreciate your hospitality."

"Don't mention it."

"What's your name?"

"Gert," Heath says, solemnly and without hesitation.

"How old are you, Gert?"

"Eighteen."

"What happened to your face?"

"You don't wanna know."

"Why didn't you want me to call the cops?"

"Cops are all corrupt here," he answers. "They hate me."

"Did they do that to you?"

He shrugs.

"I'm actually pretty goddamn tired. I worked all day and I don't have time for—"

"You don't know what happened here."

"Why I'm asking."

"I mean, to Miss Bonnie." He pulls a shotgun shell from his front pocket and tries to balance it atop his knee. It falls, makes a flicking sound when it hits the newspaper below. He takes another hit, picks the shell up, and tries again. "Paper lied."

As he examines the tip of his joint, I ask, "The ones who hurt you the same who hurt her?"

He nods.

"And it was either the police or someone close to them, that's why you don't want me to go to them?"

"It wasn't a cop."

"Who was it?"

"I can't say who because I'm gonna get my ass murdered next. I'm not lying to you."

"Just sounds that way, huh?" I slouch down into the couch, fold my hands over my breast. "I'm not leaving without the truth, whether I get it from you or the cops or whoever else. I know a lot of people in this town."

He scoffs.

"Don't believe me?"

"Cared about her so much, huh? So much you never came back to see her?"

"I was too small of a man to thank her."

"But now you're gonna sort it all out?"

He snuffs his joint out on his pant leg, crosses his arms, and rocks forward, staring absently at his moccasins. "I really loved her, dude," he says. "You gotta know that Miss Bonnie was ... I had nothing before she took me in. She saved my life. They were gonna send me away when she quit fostering and all that. But she let me crash here. And now she's dead because she cared about me when nobody else did. I wanna tell you everything. I wish I could. I wish I could tell everyone. He said he'd kill me if I talked."

He flings the shotgun shell into the living room and it lands silently behind a sofa. He stands. Skittish, moping, he paces back and forth across the living room. There's a bald patch on the back of his head. It looks like he trimmed it down to the scalp after someone ripped out a handful of hair.

"Say, Doleman still chief of police?" I ask.

He stops and looks at me, conflicted. "You gotta promise me. You can't tell nobody else about what I tell you. Not a soul. That's the only way to keep me safe. The only way to keep *you* safe. Trust me."

"All right, I trust you. You're like every other foster kid who's never told a lie before."

"'Other kids have toys.'" One of Miss Bonnie's many sayings.

He's back to pacing. "It was all about this girl that I really, really, really love. She's amazing. Like, the smartest person alive. She used to come to my shows. I play guitar and I'm really good. I mean, I slay *super hard*. We go by The Concrete Nipples but our fans just call us The Nips. I'll show you if you want ..."

"The girl."

"What about her?"

"That's what I'm asking."

"Let me finish."

He's in no hurry and wants me to know it. He likes an audience and it must be a while since he's had one. This performance is just getting started.

He blabbers a bit more about his band. I try not to interrupt. Sooner or later, he'll talk himself into a corner. After a few minutes, summing the opening monologue up, he adds, " ... and '*the girl*' is Monica. Monica Spencer."

I flinch at the name. Noting this, his good eye bulges out in excitement and with a hint of jealousy. "You know her?" he asks.

"No. Last name, though. I know those people."

***

Sweat trickles down the middle of my back. I bite down hard on my inner cheek.

"If you went to school here you know the name for sure," Heath says, returning to the kitchen chair, sensing my captivation. I can't hide it. I'm not sure I even want to. He might really know something. "Jeremy ... That's Monica's older brother. It started out he didn't like I was dating his little sister. He'd follow me home from school, hold my face down in puddle water until I almost drowned. A psychopath. He's got a scholarship to play hockey in Duluth next year so I guess he's okay at it. Who gives a shit. One day we're walking past each other and out of nowhere he runs at me and checks me up against a locker. Principal was standing right there when it happened and didn't do shit about it. He just looked at me. Waiting for me to hit Jeremy back so he could expel me. Assholes all of them."

"Jeremy did all that to your face?"

"This isn't even the worst of it. You want some coffee?"

"Coffee? It's pushing ninety out there."

He's stalling. He pounces onto the kitchen table and crawls toward the coffeepot on the counter.

"You might consider moving that table out of the way."

"I don't wanna walk where she died. I've wiped the blood up a hundred times but I still can't seem to get it all. Especially in the corners. I checked the attic for a rug. No luck. That's why I put the newspaper down, see."

He can't find a clean mug. He resorts to pouring coffee into a soup bowl. Full to the brim the bowl spills as he crawls back into the dining area, scorching his hands. "Goddamnit. I can't stand this house. I'd have left town already if not for Monica. But, like, if not for her I wouldn't be in this situation. It's not her fault. That's not what I'm saying. It's just—"

"What was that about blood?"

"Hold tight, big guy," he says, lest I forget he's in charge. Then he sips his coffee too quickly, coughs, curses, squeezing his eyes shut.

"You okay?"

"Wrong pipe."

"The blood."

"Almost there. See, when I'd had enough, I quit school. What was the point? I could hardly walk from class to class most of the time, anyway. That's when Monica told me she wanted to leave Sibley with me. I didn't want her to leave her family. Plus, she's gonna go to college next year and I didn't wanna screw that up for her. I could wait. I could leave and get situated and when she went off to school, I could live nearby. We could even live together then. We talked it all out one night. Miss Bonnie was willing to drive me to Brainerd for school so I could graduate this year. We were just starting to figure it out for ourselves when Jeremy found out about me and Monica. You have any cigarettes?"

I toss him the pack. He takes three out, lights one, tucks the other two behind his ears, and tosses the pack back.

"Should've known if I stayed here I'd put Miss Bonnie in danger. She opened the door for Jeremy and he busted inside. Brushed right past her. I was sitting on the kitchen counter. It was different from the other times he attacked me. There was a look in his eyes. Like, I was about to die, dude, and before I knew it Miss Bonnie grabbed him by the shoulder and spun him around and clocked him in the jaw. I'd never seen her so angry. He fell down on one knee, holding his chin. She had him in a headlock so fast. She hollered at me to call the cops. I was fumbling for my cell in my pocket. I should've never left the kitchen. Should've stayed and helped her ..."

He shakes his head. He's already sucked his way through the first cigarette and used it to light the second. He pinches the first out, flicks it onto the newspapers behind him.

"I don't know, dude, maybe he would've killed me too. Why'd I hide in the living room? We could've held him down together. My hands were shaking like crazy. I couldn't dial the cops. I looked over just as he threw her down. I can still hear her head cracking on the ground. I was paralyzed. Suddenly he was up on his feet, staring down at her like he'd forgotten why he'd come in the first place. Like I wasn't even there anymore. A second later he was gone. Left the door wide open. Craziest thing I've ever seen. I went to her to see if she was alive. She wasn't breathing. There was blood all around her head. For a while I just held her. I didn't know what to do ..."

Scornful, tearless, he stares at me. With his good eye he says, "You believe me so far. You buy all this."

If I don't believe him, it isn't because the alternative (suicide) makes more sense but because it's foolish to trust someone who'd lie about something as trivial as his first name. And I don't put money down on something I can't afford. This, no less, is an expensive thing to be wrong about.

"Go on," I prod him.

"I started thinking about what the cops would find when they came here. Me and her. No one knew I lived here, and she'd just been murdered. Would they believe me, especially when I told them that the Fire Captain's kid did it? I was scared. But I decided that I had to do the right thing. My nerves had settled some by then, too. I'm not sure how much time had passed. It must've been a bit because right when I was about to call, someone started knocking on the door. Not banging hard, just tapping. I figured it was Jeremy coming back to finish me off.

I grabbed a knife from the silverware drawer, looked through the blinds. It was Travis, that's Monica and Jeremy's dad. He was alone. I cracked the door, and he asked if he could step inside. He said Jeremy had told him what'd happened, that he wanted to check on me. This guy hated me more than anything and so I didn't trust him. But what was I supposed to do? I let him in. He went to the kitchen, saw what his son had done, and just scowled. That's it. Like Jeremy had totaled his truck. Like 'look what he did this time, that darn Jeremy.' My hands were covered in her blood. I couldn't talk. I thought that was it for me. He had me. He'd wanted like hell to get me out of his daughter's life, and this was his chance. Then he looked me over, told me to go wash myself up good. I did. When I got back from the bathroom, he said, 'Go out and wait in my truck.' Said, 'If you don't get out of this house right now, I'll leave you with her.' So, I ran out the door as fast as I could. But there wasn't a chance in hell I'd wait for him in his truck. What, so he could drive me to the boondocks and kill me? I ran as far as I could. I even passed Police Chief Doleman in his police car on the way. No flashing lights or nothing. Like it was any other day. Cruising around. You know, Travis and Doleman go golfing all the time, vacation together, all that bullshit."

He lights the third cigarette with the butt of the second, which he snuffs out on his pant leg. He gulps down the rest of his coffee and drops the butt into the empty bowl. Then he paces in and out of the living room again, his hands on top of his head, his elbows sticking straight out on either side of him.

"I hid out in the woods for a few nights before I came back. There was blood in the kitchen, but her body was gone. I waited for them to come arrest me. Nothing happened. No calls, no texts. It was a while before I realized what was going on. I think they wanted to pin it on me, but they couldn't do that without risking a bigger investigation. The investigation might involve people Doleman and Travis couldn't control. County or feds. Maybe someone would find out there was a third person there. Then it would come back to Jeremy and why the Fire Captain was the first person on the scene. Doleman got the body over to the funeral home the night she was murdered. By the time I got the nerve to go over there and ask about her they'd already cremated her. The easiest way to cover it all up was to say it never happened, that it was an accident, or better even—a suicide. Even if that meant they couldn't lock me away. That's what they did."

"Okay..."

"But I didn't know that right away. I went to Travis myself. Met him at the fire station because I didn't want Monica knowing what was going on. What if they started a real investigation and I'd said something to her? She'd wanna lie for her family, or they'd make her. I thought it over a billion times. I had to talk to Travis. I went to see him at the fire station, and he acted like he had no idea what I was talking about with Jeremy. Like it was obviously a suicide and he'd never even come out to Miss Bonnie's place. It was the only time he'd ever been decent to me. He might've even felt a little shitty that I'd lost her. I kept telling him that I knew what'd happened and that I wanted justice for her. He acted all confused. 'Maybe you should get some counseling, Heath. Maybe someone at the school will talk to you about what you're going through. I'm so sorry, kiddo.' When he called me kiddo, I knew he was fucking with me. I wasn't sure what to do after that."

He drops his third cigarette into the bowl on the floor.

"That night Travis came to the door with some meathead who slammed me up against this door and pulled my hair out and smashed my face to a pulp. Afterward Travis told me that if I kept barking up the wrong tree he'd come back. So, I've just been here since then. I'd have already left Sibley if not for her. Like I said, I love her. I love her, dude. I don't know what to do. We were supposed to leave town last weekend but she up and changed her mind at the last second. I'm trying to talk her into it again."

He plucks another joint from the case, his non-swollen eye tired, glassy, emotionless.

"Spencers are everywhere. Like a cancer. A lot of them volunteer for the fire department and work up at the dealership. They all played hockey here. That's all they talk about, the glory days. They got the town in a chokehold. Whatever you got, they'll take from you. Where you going?" he asks as I rise and start toward the front door. I've heard enough. "You can't ..."

"Can't *what?* Gonna shoot me with your imaginary shotgun? Anyway, I'm not telling anyone you're here. I need to get some fresh air and think a little."

"You leaving town?"

"Maybe."

Heath steps in front of the door. He must really not want me to go because he hasn't lit his joint yet. "Don't talk to anyone."

"We'll see—"

"You gotta believe me."

"I don't, actually. I'm gonna figure out exactly what happened. If it's like you say I'm gonna raise hell all over. Miss Bonnie meant the world to me."

He points the joint at my face. "You think you're special? Another one of her big tough foster boys? You're no different than me. You'd have stood in that living room while she died, just like I did."

"Move."

Suddenly, with some amusement in his voice, he says, "I know you. Murphy's half-brother. The Mute. Daddy died in the bathtub."

I look him over. "You're thinking of someone else."

I shove him aside and open the door.

"Make sure you follow the news!" he yells. "If you hear about how I hung myself, you'll know just what happened! Once Jeremy finds out you've been talking to people, I'm dead! You don't understand—!"

I shut the door in his face. I cross the street, climb into my truck, start it up, and take one huff of rank cab air before starting for the dealership.

It's ten minutes away. I have ten minutes. Ten minutes to think of what I'll do when I get there. I came to pay my respects. Now I can't leave without the truth. Without helping a boy who lied to my face. About what exactly, I'm not sure yet. Gavin, Jordan, the like, they'll be there. Remember, they're no better than me. More importantly, they're no worse. Just people. Not devils, just sinners. They are what in my darkest moments it's apparent I am too.

Emma is there. Minutes away. I'll talk to her alone if I can. Talk *only* to her if I can. Gotta wrap my head around seeing her, lifting the lid off that rotting coffin not knowing much about what's inside except that it wasn't dead when we buried it.

To my shame, I thought her virginity proposal over. Meanwhile, Murphy kept at it. "Snooty bitch," he'd mutter. It almost came to blows on my day off. That sweltering, cloudless afternoon at Lake Sibley beach. The half-mile path down, narrow and boggy, teeming with flies, mosquitoes, poison ivy. We drank Hamm's on partially inflated floaties in the shallows. I'd have gotten a swing or two in before he drowned me. Assuming he spared my life, he'd have never let me forget how wound up I got defending her. Almost as wound up as I got denying that I cared about her at all. Suzie and Jane from the grade below came out to the beach. Two-pieces thready. He and Jane went back to her car. Suzie and I eeled around in two feet of water. She kept bugging me about the long sleeves I wore to cover up my handiwork. She ran her cool, pruny fingers up my chest because she wanted me to do it back, as I'd done before. She unzipped my cutoff jean shorts and reached inside. She kissed me. Her top was tied in back like a shoelace. I tugged loose a string. She'd already pulled her bottom aside. I stopped it all, wishing I didn't know why.

One afternoon that summer Gavin parked his truck on the street and walked toward the house alone. At first, I didn't recognize him. He was wearing a collared shirt, tie, black slacks. Like a Bible salesman. Murphy watched from the window, a sentinel. I met Gavin at the picnic table, he shook my hand, and for half an hour he jabbered about how he didn't wanna be the asshole he was in high school and how much he respected me and how he wanted to be better and how he wanted to change and he was sorry he'd driven by so many times but he'd been gaining the courage to sit down with me and apologize if he ever did or said anything to make me feel less-than. He said he'd already talked to Danny and Colton and Joey Fisher and Jeffer Splutze. He said he wanted to earn Emma back. He might've been warning me. If so, he must've believed his warning was working because I just sat there straddling the picnic table bench and staring down between my knees, mute. Not a word.

As soon as Emma came clean about her designs on me, I should've told her she couldn't change how she felt about herself, much less improve it, with sex. But I didn't. Not right away, not for another month, when Miss Bonnie went on her weekly grocery run and my siblings were out back playing tag and so I had the basement to myself. Her tank top straps were already hanging near her elbows. Bare shoulders broad, lean, bronze. Her lips were already on mine. Plump and firm and damp and warm. Her exhales these wafts of hot, moist peppermint. She asked again and again what was wrong.

The insult didn't hit me until then. Until then I somehow didn't see myself the way it seemed she did. A rite of passage. Sterile. Disposable. Afterward I'd be even less than that. But that's not what I told her. Instead, I gave a better reason not to lose it to the foster boy townie. She'd feel like shit about herself later. I told her I didn't mean anything to her, that if I did she wouldn't have arranged to lose it to me for no other reason than to know she'd lost it to someone. She didn't respond at first. Her shoulders slumped. She didn't bother to put her straps back up. I'd embarrassed her. I shouldn't have let it get to that point, the kissing and all, but I did. She talked about Carissa then. About the trip to the clinic. Emma told Carissa about her summer plans and Carissa told her she could trust me. Here I didn't ask for clarification because I figured it'd only get more complicated. Trust me to what? To be respectful? To keep the secret? To be good at it?

She left for college. She studied accounting and took a poetry course and lost her virginity to a Rastafarian who planned to pay tuition by playing ukulele in Twin Cities coffee shops. They dated for a while. Her parents weren't excited to hear about him. She emailed me poems about everything. About the campus' "gorgeous brick buildings" and her "beyond pretty" roommate and coursework and infected nose-ring and "ragtag" intramural basketball team. About finishing school and having children and working from home as an accountant. About breaking up with Chaz and quitting the team and dropping out and coming home again. About how immature the boys were and how bummed she was. How grateful she was that I called her out "for trying to use" me. How special our summer together was. How she missed me. How she daydreamed about my body. Two or three emails a week.

I never replied. I wished she'd stop writing. I wanted the strength to not read them but I always gave in, as eager to hear that she cared about me as to ensure that she didn't, couldn't, never would. So there was never a moment when thinking of her didn't torture me. Hope and despair both. The last one I received, before she came home for Christmas break, wasn't an update. It was a confession. The subject: "How it could work." It gave me that gut-drop dread I get sometimes. I deleted it before it could entice me further. Over the break I ignored her calls. Then she came to my new place. The unfinished basement of Kenny Benson's duplex, three blocks from Miss Bonnie's house. It was his former private mixed-martial-arts dojo. Grey rubber jigsaw tiling on the floor. A boxing bag hung from the ceiling. I sat there staring at it as she slammed her open palm on the egress window behind me and yelled, demanding an explanation for why I never emailed her back, what was so wrong with her in my eyes, how I could be such a dick about things. Rage, bewilderment, exasperation. Rage.

Supposing I could speak, who was I supposed to say? The truth? That I was a lot more like Murphy than whatever she took me for? Not as loud as Murphy, maybe. Not as vulgar. Not as violent. But closer to his type than it might seem from the outside looking in. The broken cannot explain their broken-ness to the unbroken. At least I couldn't. Not then. It's more than imperfection. Deformity. Metal coat hanger wallops on the neck. Mommy napping with bags of frozen vegetables on her mushy face. And me rooting for Daddy because I hated underdogs. Curling up on the sleeper-sofa in Grandma's base-ment while she guzzled mouthwash and hallucinated for hours on end, telling me stories about the goldfish in her scummy tank. Grandma with her brittle black teeth, always screaming because her voice couldn't go any softer. Dementia got so bad she turned to spitting on me when I visited her at the nursing home in Saint Cloud. Things actually got worse when I real-ized all in all it would've been better if my dad never hurt my mom and my mom never hurt my dad, if nobody ever hurt anyone, because then there was the embarrassment of knowing it was once all so everyday. How normal, how mundane it'd been once upon a time, before I knew I was broken. Cruelty felt and cruelty dealt.

She left Kenny's duplex. The emails continued, one per month now.

After his first deployment, Murphy crashed with me. The room reeked of Murphy's no-sun-for-days BO. He brutalized the hundred-pound bag for six three-minute intervals, handed me the gloves, and sat pretzel-legged with his elbows on his knees, panting. He said he expected to die during his next tour. He pulled out his kit, said he needed to tar up to escape the desert, like that wasn't all he ever talked about when he wasn't too stoned for talking. The numbing warmth mellowed me. I could see it, what he described. Fields of poppy plants that from a distance looked like squat cornstalks but that up close were otherworldly. The bulging tips of the plants stretching skyward like the arms of so many beggars, flowers brash red and pink and orange. He told me it was easier to get heroine than morphine, something both here and there have in common. He walked through the fields, head down, watching his steps carefully, enraged because though drug profits supported the enemy, he couldn't bring himself to step on one single plant, snap or crush it. Not because it would've been futile or because his superiors said not to but because those plants were the only beautiful things to see in the whole desert.

"Why'd we hate Miss Bonnie so much?" he asked then, out of nowhere. The question wasn't for me. For a moment the silence was the type that makes your ears ring. The punching bag hung there, the uvula of a suicided man. He cackled, his voice throaty, weak. "Whatever the government paid her, it wasn't enough. Her job is a fuck-ton harder than mine." "We're fucked, you know that, right?" he asked. "Totally fucked. Thing is, we didn't have a clue about how fucked we were until she showed us." He said, "Like learning you got cancer because the chemo started. We were used to cancer. But chemo, her love? That's what set us off."

The night before he was supposed to leave for his third deployment, he called from Santa Fe. He was with a girl. I said I was worried about him. He said he was worried about me. We had a good talk about not tarring up anymore, about treatment. His flight was early the next morning so he couldn't talk long. He stayed in a hotel room for three days. According to the girl who called Miss Bonnie on the morning of the fourth, a maid had found him dead. Overdose.

Gavin and Emma were back together by then. He'd found her emails so Jordan and Gavin and two of his college buddies came to Sibley, smelling of dirt and vodka. In high school Gavin had a receding hairline. Now he'd shaved it all off. I climbed down off the roof I was working on and sat down on the lawn. Just sat there. His nose points upward, so I could see into his nostrils even when he squatted down on his haunches to look me in the eye. I didn't listen to what he said. They held me down while Jordan choked me. I blacked out, woke up with snapped ribs and a bruised cheek. They probably would've done worse if the rest of the crew hadn't scrambled down to run them off.

I'm almost at the dealership. Heath's full of shit. But which part is the lie? Which part is the truth I can't leave without? And what am I gonna do about it? Heath, the boy who once adored me, the boy I couldn't look at once I learned he'd been the victim of something I just as easily could've been.

Gavin and Jordan will be there. I'll talk to Emma alone and won't give her any reason to suspect I know about the emails. To suspect that this is about me and her.

***

I park in the customer lot beside the main dealership building. I call Emma but she doesn't answer. The crowd is still there, blaring country music. Some of them wear jeans and matching cobalt polos, others shorts and button-ups, many of the women flowery sundresses. Scattered across the lot are charcoal grills, kegs, picnic tables for chips and buns and fixings, patio tables with umbrellas, and lawn games. There are clusters of women with babies on their hips and beers in their hands. Teens toss horseshoes at iron stakes in the ditch, shouting after every throw. The dealership belongs to Fire Captain Travis's brothers, Jonny and Stevie. They laze on folding chairs, wearing matching bucket hats. Seated on a folding chair to their right, cashing a bottle of beer and reaching for another, is Travis Spencer.

He has a salt-and-pepper handlebar mustache and sideburns, a buzz cut, and a receding hairline. He's dressed in denim overalls with the legs rolled up. No top on underneath. No socks or shoes. When he laughs at one of his brother's jokes he sticks his tongue out and bobs his head up and down. Atop his knee is a gaunt teenage girl in short-shorts and a yellow tank top, chin-length brown hair cupped around her face. She's texting, her lips puckered into a pout. That must be her, Monica.

I don't see Emma. I get out, cross the lot to the building entrance. Windows cover the bottom quarter of the façade. I have to squint to peer inside. There are only a few customers. Reflected in the windows is the party behind me. Two men in oversize sunglasses leave the party and approach, a small boy accompanying them. As they near, I recognize them.

I turn to face Jordan and Gavin. They're holding plastic cups. Jordan isn't wearing a polo but a forest green flannel shirt. A nest of curls creeps over the top button, chestnut brown as the high-and-tight wave of hair atop his head. Gavin is in uniform, his gut bulging beneath his polo, his bald head shiny, his black chinstrap beard crisp and neat. Their cheeks and veiny foreheads are tan. Derek stands in front of his father, driving the back of his head into Gavin's thigh.

"You in the market?" Jordan yaps.

"Just got off work," I said. "Haven't been back to Sibley in a while. But, no, I'm broke."

"Heard you've been hitting it big up at the casino—"

"Dorian, how you been?" Gavin interjects, sneering at his cousin. "I hope you can stay for a bit. Help yourself to a brat and some beers. We should catch up."

"I ate. Actually, I thought I'd stop and see Emma. She texted me yesterday about Miss Bonnie. I wanted to check out the house one last time before the bank sells it."

"Emma, huh?" Jordan asks.

When Jordan tips his cup back for a gulp, Gavin flicks the bottom. Beer spills onto Jordan's cheeks. He keeps smirking as he wipes his cheeks dry with his shirt.

Gavin says, "Sorry to hear about Miss Bonnie. Emma's still working on some things. I'll take you to her."

He grabs his son's hand and leads me into the building. I glance back at Jordan, who raises his glass to me and winks.

Inside is a popcorn machine and a refrigerator full of complimentary bottled water. We walk between a new truck, claret, glossy, and a small putting green with synthetic grass and a pin with a flag bearing the dealership logo, two grinning brothers with their arms around each other's shoulders. We pass a reception desk and enter a long hallway.

Midway, Gavin stops in the doorway of a side office. "Honey, someone's here to see you." He smiles at me, pats me on the shoulder as he and Derek pass by on their way back to the party.

I step into the doorway. Emma sits on a leather swivel chair behind a desk, wearing the company polo. The carpet is grey, the walls white. There's a two-foot tower fan on one corner of her mahogany brown IKEA desk. On another, a little shelf with slots for paperwork. In the middle is a computer monitor. A large claw hairclip holds her hair behind her head. She's loosed a few tufts on either side of her face. Her hands rest on her pregnant belly.

"Dorian," she says with a quick glance up. She looks down at her phone, points at the swivel chair opposite her. "Please sit. I just saw you called. I've been so busy trying to get ready for the weekend. It's been a zoo here."

She sounds the way she did on the phone earlier today, stilted, unnaturally cheerful, as if to counterbalance the despair in the diary that, like her belly bump, I must pretend I don't know about. This for both our sakes. I sit down. I'd like to look comfortable. I have too much adrenaline, so I sit stiffly upright.

She says, "I'm used to accounting, but this weekend we're all sales associates. Hopefully we're all needed. It's been a little slow lately." She sighs. Softly, she adds. "God, Dorian, I'm so sorry for your loss. Such a sad thing."

I nod. On the walls are pictures of her family. Her framed diploma from the U of M. "Congratulations, by the way," I say.

She rubs her belly. "Thanks. Derek will have a little sister this December."

"That's great." I say this like I didn't know.

"You get something to eat?"

The merry small talk grating me, I say, "I stopped by her house." My voice is gruffer than I mean for it to be.

"How was that?"

"Strange."

"I bet." She sighs again, nodding sympathetically. She looks down at her belly. "How long has it been since you were there? Seems like a lifetime ago."

"It does. That's not what I mean, though. There are a thousand places I'd rather be than near this barbecue."

She squints, turns her attention to her computer screen like she's reading some pressing document. "I'm sorry to hear that, Dorian. Maybe we can catch up another time."

"What I'm saying is that I wouldn't be here if it wasn't important."

"If *what* wasn't important?"

"I'm so sorry to ask this of you but can you do something for me?" For the first time since I entered her office, her eyes lock onto mine. I listen for footsteps in the hallway. Hearing nothing, I cross my arms, lean toward her. She cranes her head forward. "Please don't share what I'm about to tell you with anyone else. Did you know there's a kid living out there?"

"A foster kid?"

"His name is Heath."

"The Reynolds kid? He's a piece of work."

"I picked up on that."

"Last I heard, all the kids left last spring. When I kept seeing him around town, I figured he was staying with a friend."

"He said he never moved out. He said a lot more than that, actually. I'm embarrassed to get into this. It's not pleasant to think about."

"Okay?

"Miss Bonnie. You said she died in the kitchen."

"That's what I'd heard, yes."

"From who?"

"Gavin's uncle Travis told Gavin's dad, I think. Travis is still real close to Chief Doleman."

"I was there today. The kitchen ceiling is made of tin. Sheets of tin just like when I lived there. I don't see how she could've hung herself there."

"Maybe I misunderstood him."

"Heath has a different story."

"That doesn't surprise me. I only met him once, around the holidays last year. We got to talking and he claimed he was building a 3-D printer that could make assault rifles. He was gonna sell these on the black market and make five hundred thousand dollars in the spring. His plans must've fallen through, because he still owes Monica two hundred dollars for the stereo she bought him. I'm not sure I'd take is word on anything."

"I don't know what to make of it all. He was all beaten up."

She looks at her screen, clicks a few times, looks back at me. "Sorry, I'm listening. What are you getting at?"

"It was real bad. Was Gavin's cousin Monica dating Heath?"

"They broke up. Why?"

"He didn't mention that part. He made it sound like her family was standing between them. Said they all hated him, and nobody wanted him around."

"Right. After she broke up with him, he wouldn't leave her alone. He's always calling and texting her. Twice last week he came by the house. He's delusional. He still thinks she's leaving town with him. So he said my in-laws roughed him up?"

"That Jeremy did."

"Well, Jeremy is … You remember how Jordan was in high school? Jeremy is the same way. He got kicked off the hockey team. I still can't believe he … Anyway, it was absolutely disgusting. I was shocked he didn't get suspended. I don't ever leave him alone with Derek."

"What'd he do?"

"We don't need to talk about that," she replies with a wave of her hand.

"Mind if I close the door, Emma?"

She shrugs.

I peek outside the door. The hallway is empty. I pull the door shut. Too anxious to sit, I stand behind my chair, rubbing my hands across the top. "I'm sorry, Emma. I don't wanna cause any drama. I'm embarrassed that I never made it back here to thank her for everything she did. I keep thinking that if something happened to her I gotta make it right. I know Heath hasn't been completely straightforward with me. But he's scared shitless, I can't deny that. And there are other things I saw while I was there, the kitchen was covered in newspaper like something happened to the floor."

"Newspaper ...?"

"He said that Jeremy came to Miss Bonnie's in a rage. Miss Bonnie tried to intervene to protect him. Jeremy pushed her and she hit her head. He might be full of shit, Emma. But if she killed herself there it didn't happen in the kitchen, or at least not the way you told me it did. All I'm saying is that something's off."

She's motionless. She gazes down at a stack of papers for several seconds before making as though to speak. She says nothing.

I wait for her. Finally, she says, "Heath is saying that Jeremy killed her, then Travis got Chief Doleman to cover it up for them by calling it a suicide—"

"Before you say any more, please know that I'm not asking for help. I just wanna know whether you think it's possible. You know the family better than I do. If he's telling the truth, I'll handle everything from there."

"What'll you do?"

"I don't know yet. Maybe I can talk to the county sheriff."

"The county sheriff?" she replies in disbelief.

"I'm gonna do *something*."

She clears her throat, shakes her head, and pushes down on the arms of her chair so she can stand. She pulls her polo down, stretching it flush over her swollen stomach, then slides her hands down onto her hips.

"Dorian, what you're saying is ... I think you need to take some time to think. Miss Bonnie was very important to you and she died in a horrible way. You haven't had a chance to grieve yet. I thought about you so much when I found out. I didn't tell you right away because I figured you'd learned somehow. Then I wasn't sure you had and I couldn't get it out of my head and so I finally messaged you last night. She told me you were clean and that's the best news. I hope it stays that way. Please get help if the cravings are too much. I imagine this will be a vulnerable time for you. I wish you the best."

When she walks around the desk, glowering at me, I start toward the door. "I am upset ... you know what these people can be like. *Gavin's* family."

"*My* family. They're not perfect and Jeremy's a shithead. You're not talking about being a shithead. You're talking about ... I'm not even gonna say it, and a cover up. It's ridiculous, frankly."

"Emma—"

"You need to leave now."

"That's fine. Just please don't tell anybody."

"Why not?" she snaps, standing in front of me now, wounded. "You think they'll come for you next."

"I promised him I wouldn't tell anybody."

"Did it cross your mind that he didn't want you to tell anybody what he told you because he didn't want anyone to tell you he was bullshitting?"

"It did. But you should've seen his bruises."

"I don't doubt it and I'm sorry that happened to him, whoever did it. Truly, I am. You're a good person, Dorian. I've always thought that. And you've always been more sensitive than you let on. I'm sure you want like hell to keep him safe. That doesn't mean he's not trying to trick you into doing something stupid, like pick a fight with Jeremy. From what Monica's told me, Heath can be very manipulative."

"How so?"

"Never mind. I asked you to leave."

I put my hand on the door latch, "I was hoping this would go better than it did. I wish you and Gavin well. Can I please ask you one thing before I go? What'd Jeremy do?"

"You'll promise to not bring this up again?"

"Fine."

She talks to the carpet, her words rapid and terse. "He held an underclassman down in the shower and urinated on his face. If he were my kid, I'd have made sure the other boy's family pressed charges. Instead, Jeremy's fought like hell to keep him in school. They even got him back on the hockey team. To this day they act like it never happened. There, now you know."

"Thank you."

When I grip the latch, she places her hand on mine to stop me from leaving just yet. We look at each other for several seconds. The way she grimaces it seems she's long known that the messages she's sent me these past years haven't gone unread. She looks away but doesn't release my hand. She squeezes my fingers for an instant, grinding my knuckles together, the pain she causes some sort of rebuttal to the pain my silence has caused her.

She removes her hand and I turn the latch and briskly leave the office, then the building. Outside, Gavin stands alone out front, holding a paper plate of chips, coleslaw, pickles, and a hamburger.

"In case you're hungry," he says, offering me the plate. "You mind if I talk to you for a minute? I swear I won't try to sell you a new truck."

I'm starving. I devour the food as we walk to my truck. When out of earshot he removes his sunglasses and tucks them into the V of his polo. Wincing, he says, "I'm real sorry about Jordan. He's a ... degenerate. I try to avoid spending time with him when I can. Nothing good ever comes of it. In his defense he hasn't had it the easiest lately. His girlfriend took his daughter and left for Indiana. He hasn't seen them in six months or so. Not that I blame her for leaving. But that's not why I wanted to talk … I need to apologize for what happened a few summers ago. When me and Jordan came out to Benson's place. What has it been, four years? I don't recognize the kid who did that. I quit drinking liquor after that. I'm not trying to blame the alcohol. I shouldn't have let it happen. I should've done a lot of things I didn't do and I wish I'd never done a lot of things I did do."

"Don't worry, it was a long time ago."

We reach my truck. He runs his fingertips over the top of his head, takes a deep breath through his nose like he has more to cop to, stuff that may or not be any of my business.

"It's good to see you. I hope you're doing well, and I am truly sorry about Miss Bonnie," is all he says.

He takes the empty paper plate from my hands and hustles back toward the party. Over his shoulder he says, "And that's a lot of rust, too, Dorian. I bet you're damn-near two hundred thousand miles. Come by when you're ready for a trade-in."

I start my truck, stare at the steering wheel, trying to sort it all out. I'll go for a drive. I'll clear my head and get back to the house.

I'm about to put the truck in gear when a young man comes toward me on rollerblades. He's stout and muscular, wearing only jean shorts. With a hockey stick he's pushing a rubber ball across the lot. Fifteen feet from the truck, he flips a wrist-shot that whacks my door. The ball bounces back to him. He stops it with his stick and keeps gliding forward. His face is long, his cavernous mouth hangs open. His grungy, straight copper hair reaches his shoulders. His eyes, light blue and immodest, seek out mine. He rolls to a stop next to the window, which I slowly crank down. Up close, the boy looks no older than sixteen. He stinks of liquor.

"I was looking for you. I'm Spencer. What's up, man?"

In the distance, Gavin watches us, baffled.

The boy taps his stick on the hood. "What's up?" he repeats. "Why are you here?"

"Who are you?"

"Spencer."

"You're all Spencers."

"What were you doing out at that house?" he asks.

"What house?"

"You stupid?"

"I used to live there."

"One of hers, huh? I heard you and him were in there talking for a while. What was that all about?"

"He told me he's been having some problems with people."

"He always has problems with people," he says, tinkering with the loose bit of hockey tape near the heel of his stick. "That's why I keep an eye on him. Wanna make sure he doesn't do anything silly, you know. He doesn't believe it but I'm actually on his side. Sometimes he just needs the sense slapped into him. I bet he told you about Monica. He probably made up a bunch of lies about how he and my sister are soulmates and how our dad and me are keeping them apart. I'm sure he didn't mention how he made her do stuff with him after he got her baked. I'd hear her crying in her bedroom. My mom would have to go in there and talk to her for an hour or two every night just so she'd go to sleep. God knows what all he did to her. They're not supposed to be seeing each other at all. I'm making sure they don't. The best thing for him would be to get the hell out of here, you know. Same goes for you."

"Did you know the woman who lived in that house?"

"Nope."

"Do you know what happened to her?"

Jeremy, it must be, shakes his head no, still preoccupied with the loose lip of tape. He resorts to rapidly unwinding it from his stick.

"What I heard is that she offed herself," he says. "No surprise, spending all that time living with him." He balls the tape up, tosses it into the cab of my truck, pulls a roll from his back pocket, and begins to re-tape his stick, eyeing each swath.

When he notices me staring at him, he stares back. "What about it?"

"I heard something different," I say.

"What, from Heath? No shit you did, he's a goddamn liar."

"He said someone killed her."

His eyes constrict, then he laughs. "He told you I did it, didn't he? How'd he say it happened? Did I smash her head in with a big rock? Strangle her? Stab her fifty times? I *just knew* something like this would happen. One of my buddies lives not far from there so I told him to be on the lookout for someone coming by the place. See who's coming and going. Heath's so predictable. I knew he'd try to pull something. That's who he is. Too much of a pussy to come talk to me man to man. Got some piece of shit to do it for him."

He bites the tape to tear it off. He puts the roll back in his pocket and turns his stick heel-down again.

"Chill out."

"*You* chill out," he spits back. "What the hell would I kill someone for?" He turns and points back toward one of the grills. "You see that guy in the apron flipping burgers? That's the Police Chief Judd Doleman. Me and his son have been playing hockey together ever since we could skate. If you got information bring it to him."

Cussing under his breath, he rollerblades back toward the party, passing Gavin on the way. His eyes on his stickhandling, he avoids Gavin's gaze. The conversation has drawn the attention of the entire party. Even Emma, standing in the shade in front of the building while Derek punches her hip, watches Jeremy, who cocks his stick back and fires a slapshot at a grill thirty feet in front of him. The ball misses Doleman's head by no more than six inches and soars to the other end of the lot. Doleman jumps up, checks Jeremy in the shoulder as he skates by. Jeremy briefly loses balance, spins once, and speeds off to retrieve his ball, skillfully weaving between lawn chairs and strollers.

I pull onto the highway in the direction of Sibley, thinking it all over. Within a mile I find myself driving fifteen miles above the speed limit. After deciding to return to Miss Bonnie's before I do anything else, I feel I need to get to Heath as soon as possible. That feeling of dread I get sometimes returns. It's abrupt, total, dire. I blow by a dawdling minivan that keeps veering onto the rumble strip, step on the gas. Still the drive feels longer this time.

I was recovering in bed when Miss Bonnie came over to tell me my brother, my blood, Cameron Murphy, was dead. She wasn't crying. She was trying hard not to. She didn't ask me what happened to my face or why I wasn't at work, so I didn't have to lie. She had Murphy on her mind. She'd checked into some things and learned that he never showed up to camp for his first deployment. Never spent a minute outside of the

States. He'd been living with some vagrants out in Santa Fe. She didn't ask the girl if there would be a funeral because she couldn't leave the other kids behind and couldn't afford to go to Santa Fe anyway.

"I suppose he'll be buried out there," she said, at last breaking down. "See, Dorian, make sure you don't die some place where you don't wanna be buried."

I was in denial. "He's such a liar. How do you know he's really dead?"

"A mother knows."

A few weeks after Miss Bonnie's visit Emma came home for spring break. She stopped by Kenny's first. It was dark. Whistling blusters swept over the house. Air so frigid it cuts your lungs like there are bits of glass in it. I invited her in because I didn't have the energy to argue about emails I supposedly hadn't read. I'd gone long without eating or showering. Too tired to get high. The swelling had gone down but there was still blood in my urine. In the moonlight the darkness was an eerie patina of day. The healthy flesh looked bruised. The yellowing bruises looked healthy. The vertical window slats glinted burgundy, the comforter on my bed pistachio. I told her I fell off a roof. I think she believed me.

Miss Bonnie had told her about Murphy. She wept. Her sage green irises looked like oil on the water of the whites of her eyes. She said she was coming home for good. She hated the city. Hated the smell. Hated the noise. Hated feeling stupid and shallow. The old nightmare didn't seem so bad to her anymore. Being a former high school basketball star, coaching her kids' sports teams, helping some small businesses in the county with their taxes. I nodded along like her drastic change of plans made total sense, and I had no objections.

But before I had the chance to not voice them, she bit my lip. I kissed her. Her flesh was somehow paler for the lighting, sleek tallow. I rubbed my cheek against the hairs on her tummy. She scissored her thighs open, knees bent. Her skin caramel. A dab of molasses the birth-mark mole an inch to the right of her bellybutton. All the syrup. My jaw grew sore. She stroked my hair, asked for me. I didn't wanna go just yet. I wanted to stay as long as she'd let me. Then she pulled my hair, drawing my face to hers. She told me she hadn't accepted Gavin's proposal just yet but she probably would. She wanted to start having children as soon as they got married. She didn't mind working at the dealership if she couldn't find something better. When she pushed me inside of her, the talking stopped. It was the first and only time we made love.

I haven't seen her since. When she and Gavin came home that spring, I left for Walker. The emails didn't stop. She must've assumed they went unread. She grew bolder, less guarded, with each message. After a while my inbox became her diary. I learned about her pregnancy before Gavin did. I learned the name she liked for Derek before she told Gavin. I learned about her marriage problems, about her bitterness toward the life she'd chosen, toward the "roots" she'd put down. "Greedy, growing roots. Roots you can't pull out without the risk of killing the flowers they nourished."

Naturally I feel guilty each time a new email arrives. Still I read them. A strange thing, how learning better ways to love teaches you how the old ways weren't good enough, weren't love at all. Back then my silence ensured she wouldn't know I was chasing oblivion every day after work, playing solo drinking games that involved my nail gun and a bullseye poster stapled to the wall, which I punctured, spackled, sanded, repainted again and again until I needed new drywall. Ensured she wouldn't know I was daydreaming about driving as far as I could into the Mississippi. Wouldn't know about the casino, the fifty-dollar-an-hour woman, the mouthy college kid whose arm I broke.

Now my silence keeps her secrets safe. Now there is no torture, no hope, no despair. Only love. More powerful for the fact that it has no existence beyond the scope of memory.

My own secrets I saved for Miss Bonnie. She was the one driving to Walker, her car full of groceries and cleaning supplies. She was the one calling to make sure I went to work. And I never, not once, thanked her. For taking me in. For feeding and clothing me. For never mistreating me. I wanted to. I wanted to. I wanted to. The longer I waited, the more embarrassed I was. The more embarrassed, the worse I treated myself. The worse I treated myself, the more sarcastic the thought of thanking her seemed. She might've thought I was making fun of her, that I didn't mean it. And I sure didn't wanna hurt her anymore. So I hid instead. And by the time I got clean and upright again, I thought, three years? What's four? A man always has excuses. Conjures them up. The simple fact is it's always easiest to just hide.

Easier now yet since she's gone.

Parking in front of the house again, I look for him in the window. The drawn blinds are undisturbed. I knock on the door, call his name. No response. The door is locked. I check the back yard, empty aside from the rotted picket fence, the bare clothesline, the raspberry bushes. For a few minutes I sit in my truck with the door open, glaring up at my old bedroom window, wondering if he ran off. If so, where did he go? And if so, why'd he lock the door behind him?

For the next forty-five minutes I am only adrenaline and urgency.

From the moment I decide to drive all the way to the front door, climb from the hood onto the awning, and wriggle through the dusty window, until I hand the boy's body over to the emergency room physician at the Brainerd hospital twenty-five miles away, it's as if I'm not in control of myself. Only after catching my breath and relaxing my taut shoulder blades and sinking down into a sofa in the otherwise empty waiting room do I feel the weight of Heath's frame, hefty with insensibility, wrapped in Miss Bonnie's crusty beige bathrobe. Only then do I see his slackened body in only a pair of boxers, in the pink and suds-less bathwater, blood coiling from his thighs. Only then do I hear from my childhood bedroom in Hotel Bonnie the sound of a distant bathtub faucet dripping *plunk plunk plunk* into water.

Pocket Full of Posies

Emma

After fixing myself a plate of food, I return to the office and stare at my reflection in the black computer monitor, sweating, yawning, pouting, rubbing my belly, which Marybeth kicks and slugs, quite a riot for one little gal. I eat out of a sort of animal necessity because I'm nauseated while she of course isn't. Sometimes I envy her, not a care in the world, queen of the seas, adrift in amniotic fluid, yet faintly aware that the ocean is a dream and she's in fact captive, warring with the walls of her prison like she has any idea what she'd do once she escaped. Good girl, keep fighting.

When you love someone, it doesn't matter how selfish they are. You always wish they'd ask for more. Derek is easy to love. He'll cry for my affection, whine, beg, stomp his feet. Gavin's the same, though less theatrical, usually. A man like Dorian asks for nothing, yet I've never met someone so selfish.

I *had* to overthink it. I *had* to tell him about the party. I couldn't imagine him actually showing up. Then there he was, thick shoulders, sunburnt cheeks, widow's peak, clear and stern auburn eyes, wearing his nicest knitted long-sleeve like it's picture day. As ever, stubborn and self-righteous, moody and cut up and principled. Principled on account of his moodiness and cut ups, moody and cut up on account of his principles, principles I respect entirely although not as much as I do the fact that he upholds them so stubbornly and so self-righteously. And what have those principles dragged him into, what with Reynolds in his ear, dishing him some incredible dirt that gave his visit a purpose beyond admiring the algae-like mold on the back yard fence, or the front lawn gone to seed, gave his visit serendipitous purpose? As though he can finally pay her back for all the times his principles failed him, all the birthdays and holidays on which he couldn't possibly have called her since he was too busy shooting up, emptying bottles, brooding. Now he's on a mission to create more trouble than Reynolds could alone.

Jeremy's violent and it's no wonder why. He was no more than thirteen years old that time he'd gotten into dad's booze. Gavin, our friends, and I were sitting on overturned logs in Delia and Travis's back yard. S'mores. Campfire sparks dying in the dark. Jeremy came out through the sliding glass door wobbling and giggling. Travis and Chief Doleman duct-taped him to the hood of Doleman's Ford and took him for a spin down the block. He threw up all over the truck, all over himself. They brought him back. He was bawling and Delia was shaking and Travis was saying, "That'll learn you, you shit."

I left early and haven't been back to Delia and Travis's since and Gavin never asked me back there either. "That's not right," he said on the drive home. "No way to treat a child. No way to treat anyone." He doesn't talk about his childhood. Perhaps there's nothing of note to mention. Perhaps there's too much. He's good with Derek. He's patient, more patient than I am at times. What more can a woman ask of her husband?

Jeremy wouldn't kill someone he barely knows. And despite Doleman's friendship with Travis, Doleman couldn't have covered up the crime and certainly wouldn't have for Jeremy, whom he despises as much as everyone else does, that is except for Travis, Delia, and Mr. Delacroix, the hockey coach. Then again, people are capable of unimaginable horror. Just give them a reason, a little girl's flower to protect, and anything is possible.

I can't bother Monica. She's been through enough already. I can't risk harming her over nothing, picking at the scab, because all that matters is not wrecking the children's lives. Or wrecking them less than the generation before us did ours. Miss Bonnie, knowing this, never questioned whether she ought to do everything she could for these kids bumming around outside the school with black-ringed eyes and dirt-stained mouths and cracked lips, all that snot. Kids showing up stinking of soiled clothes. Even after all she lost. One of her foster sons put his baby girl in an oven and skipped town. The baby's mom found her. Another son fell into an Everglade swamp and drowned. They never found the body, only the strap of his backpack.

It was with Miss Bonnie in mind that I first noticed Monica lolling about with more than the standard teenage blues. More than the awkwardness of looking like a child when you're trying to play an adult, of looking like an adult when you're trying to play a child. With Miss Bonnie in mind, I called Delia and asked about as point-blank as a person can in this Midwestern den of passive-aggression and monastery-like concealment whether her daughter was or had been carrying a child. "A special burden," the words I chose. She denied it a tad melodramatically, proof to me that my instincts were correct.

Like this: Jeremy found out about the baby. He went ballistic and confronted Heath. Miss Bonnie intervened, and Jeremy accidentally killed her. He then called Travis, who convinced Doleman to rule it a suicide because he doesn't want anyone else finding out about his daughter's abortion. They threatened Heath into silence. Heath told Monica what happened. Now she's stuck between living with a murderer for a brother and co-conspirator for a father or running off with a boy she doesn't like anymore.

It's far-fetched. And why would Doleman go along with it?

Most likely: Miss Bonnie committed suicide and Heath wants Jeremy in trouble so he can see Monica more often and more easily and maybe convince her to get back together with him.

Dorian *just had* to show up, *had* to stare me down with that baleful gaze of his. Only he can pity me so pitifully. And I *just had* to spend the past six-odd years depositing my secrets into his inbox, praying he wouldn't read my entries, or would, depending on the emotions I felt the moment I hit Send. Except I knew he read them. Otherwise, why the giddiness, the school-girl tizzies? Why bubble baths, Merlot, cigarettes beneath a cracked window? And why else omit mention of Gavin's affair and focus instead on the sadness that began to overtake me back when a recently widowed Henrietta Sampson sold newly wed Gavin and me her three-bedroom, two-bath. In my defense, the sadness predated Gavin's infidelity, the latter a gut-punch to which the former had inured me.

Sadness. Middle-class Americans have produced every type of distraction from it. Dopamine, all our dreaming. For several months—so I told Dorian—distraction took the form of mortgage officers and retirement planners, of inspectors and realtors and appraisers, of mutual funds and Roths and 401ks and charity receipts, of perforated documents in three-ring binders that I organized alphabetically on the bay-windowed side-kitchen bookshelves. Took the form of retaining walls and water heaters and HVAC units, of dandelion herbicides and aerators and grass seed, of eaves leaking snow melt, of chandeliers so fragile it seemed they'd shatter at the touch of a duster, of cords of fruitless grape ivy strangling the walkway arch, of sheet-metal sheds housing Henrietta's plastic flower-pots and backless Adirondack chairs in the fenced-in back yard, mosquito-infested and reeking like a lagoon. A not too subtle "Can't you see what an accomplished and well-rounded woman I am, Dorian? Can't you see what you're missing?" He has to suspect that if my sex-life were anything to write home about (so to speak), anything more than a minute of tugging and grinding in the shower or under the glow of matching Target nightlights, he'd have heard about it by now.

Gavin was not a cautious adulterer. Doleman's niece Rose left a big red thong in the glovebox of Gavin's truck. It looked like a slingshot. Must've been some tasteful goings on between them. I found it while searching for my registration after I'd been pulled over for speeding between Brainerd and Nisswa.

"Do you know how fast you were going, ma'am?"

"What the fuck?!"

Noticing the garment, the officer seemed more embarrassed than I was. He let me off with a warning.

But Dorian knows everything else. After all my emails, he knows as much as anyone about the dealership's insolvency and the reasons behind it, the growing poverty in Cass County, the rise in alternative sales models, the advertising strength of the dealerships in Brainerd, the Spencer sister who had my job before she and her husband ran off to Costa Rica with an embezzled thirty grand.

Dorian can probably sketch my house and property from memory, can probably relive that spring Saturday which began with the innocuous task of situating the back yard shed and ended with my lying to Gavin that I was fine, just fine, totally and eternally fine. That morning, I put coffee in a thermos, threw on my U of M sweatshirt and sexiest gardening shorts, hot pink, grubby, loose at the hips, showing off my unshaved legs, and went out back. After arranging hundreds of various-sized pots in tidy rows on the bare ground in the shed, I replaced the citronella containers in the bamboo torches. Then I attempted to repair the Adirondacks. I bought two-by-fours at the lumberyard and pulled rusty nails from rotted slats using the claw end of a hammer, only to realize I hadn't purchased enough lumber. Tireless, I painstakingly dismembered every chair plank by plank. Then my sweet, sinless boy walked into the shed. He hugged me. He told me he loved me, that my "thumpy" heartbeat scared him. He asked again and again and again what was wrong.

Gavin asked the same thing that night after dinner as I gawked at a sink full of unrinsed dishes, roast beef flecks and bread-slush and whole cherries denuded of their glossy supermarket sheen. "Nothing. I'm fine," I said. Eventually he walked away, perhaps convincing himself I meant it. I could've grabbed his arm. I could've come clean. But I didn't because I'm lazy with him, even too lazy to resent him for not reading my mind. What good would it do him anyway? What luck would he have in understanding me when I confuse myself. What luck would Dorian have, for that matter?

So, I wiped down the dinner table at least six times, the counter at least four. Then I sat on the living room couch, gawking at other things, the lamp, the ceiling, the dusty, blank living room television screen. Gavin ran the trash out. It took him fifteen minutes. My dad used to do the same thing and he'd return stinking of weed. Gavin wasn't a pothead. He was out in his truck, probably wondering what happened to his trophy panties. When he came back, he was parched and a bit short of breath from romancing Rose on the phone. I swear sometimes I half-expected him to still be humping the air like a dog. That's all in the past now, thank God.

It wasn't the infidelity that saddened me. It wasn't the house. It wasn't Sibley. What saddened me was that there was nothing behind the sadness and the more I wished it meant something, the worse I felt. Sure, the karats with which we weigh the world are nothing more than sunlit shit, and this filth is the beautiful all-we-have. Why, then, if it's beautiful, can't I just accept it, the all-we-have? These thoughts would hit me, and I'd soon have blood in my mouth from chomping down on my tongue. I thought of talking to my parents but they'd have been no help. Sadness never seemed to affect them the way it did me. Anyway, they're not decent people. Kind, yes. Cultured, yes. Intelligent, yes. Generous, absolutely. But decency is a way of seeing the world. They never noticed the black eyes, red lips, purple cheeks the way Miss Bonnie did. I want so badly to be as decent as she was. So I went to see her.

She was wearing denim overalls, sitting on the kitchen counter, ankles crossed, waiting for her rhubarb crisp to bake. She asked me to sit at the dinner table with her, then she smoked cigarettes, lighting the next with the butt of the last. As I tried to explain what was bothering me, she frowned, her face scrunched up, her puckered lips lifted to her nostrils in that peculiar way of hers. I couldn't find the words just then. I was too tired. So I bitched about Jesus, asked rhetorically, sardonically, why God made some people without faces, with a head but no mouth, a nose but no ears. Forget about cancer or heart disease or stray bullets, where empathy is possible.

"Imagine being the only person on the planet with webbed fingers and a beak," I said.

She replied that this is what Jesus is for, to suffer with the individual sufferer, the one with whom no one suffers, and I told her that Jesus was not a duck, that the Gospels couldn't finesse any sense out of the fact of the hoofed, cleft, mush-brain crazed, convulsive.

Saintly, she patted me on the head and offered me a cigarette because I "needed it more" than she did. I smoked and she talked about suffering the children, about the kingdom of Heaven. Her eyes lingered on mine, casting out that despondent signal which the intelligent will from time to time, a question you can answer, ignore, or miss entirely but cannot ultimately silence.

"I told Dorian this same thing once," she said. "I'm sorry, you can't kick Jesus out of your heart."

"Bullshit."

She let out one quick, dusty scoff-huff.

"And why can't I?" I asked.

Not until I asked the question did I realize she'd posed a riddle. She replied, "How you gonna kick out someone who you haven't even invited in yet?"

It was my turn to scoff.

"But you will," she said.

"Maybe I prefer godlessness to the god that made what we've got here."

"You will. You've already begun. Otherwise, why think about the duck people?"

This wasn't a real question, though, because she didn't stop talking. Didn't even pause. Sure she was right, she didn't allow me the opportunity to dig a deeper hole. She talked about her vegetable garden, her neighbor's yeasty piss-elm stump and its slimy roots, while the other conversation reverberated. That's what I heard, what I saw in her impassioned and flabbergasted expressions, her rigid, ruddy face proof that were Christ to return, he'd probably work in a fast food kitchen, stigmatic grease lesions on his skin. And if Jesus were a woman, he wouldn't have been such a coward as to die just once.

"It won't stop," she suddenly said.

"What won't?"

"The darkness you're experiencing. You could medicate."

"I do."

"Me too," she replied, lighting another cigarette.

Before I left, she showed me a postcard she once received from New Mexico. It was from Murphy, whose overdose upset me despite the fact that I never had much affection for him and could never wrap my mind around the idea that he and Dorian were related. He wrote that he was "sorry for being such a shit" when he was younger, that he was grateful she took the time to teach him about kindness.

"You never really know about people, Emma. It's true. Believing in them, that's how I medicate."

Decency. Look where the world says not to, the dimly lit corners of public libraries, the mall coves outside of restrooms. Look for the children. They feel more than the rest of us do. They sense more. So their pain is greater. Look for them. Listen to them. Even if doing so reminds us of the days when we felt and sensed more than we do now. Even if it forces us to feel and sense things we'd hoped we never would again. Do all you can do. All you can do: wreck their lives just a bit less than yours were.

I shouldn't have been so cold to Dorian. It's not his fault I've given him a spare key to my journal, which is why I was short with him to begin with. I tried not to be, so as to pretend there is no spare key, no journal, that the internet doesn't exist.

This: Jeremy killed her. Travis convinced Doleman to rule it a suicide and they threatened Heath into silence. Travis not only doesn't want anyone else finding out about his daughter's abortion but wants to protect all the jobs at his brothers' dealership. Doleman went along with the reasoning, certain that the dealership is essential to the community's welfare, and Travis might've also convinced him Jeremy's a good kid with an excellent future who acts out every once in a while only because his dad is a bit too hard on him at times, that no one cares about an old lady who housed troublemakers with foul language and baggy pants, with bloody scabs and lice.

If Heath is telling the truth, there will be hell to pay. And Gavin, for all his faults, will help me see to it.

All that matters is the children. So go on. Maybe I can help Monica. Maybe she and Heath are what I ought to have been looking for. Maybe he can be saved.

I grab my plate and, clutching my belly with my free hand, waddle out of the office, down the hallway, past the front desk, and onto the curb by the entrance. Cupping my eyes from the sun, blotted with haze, I scan the parking lot for Monica. She's sitting cross-legged at the edge of the ditch, a friend on either side of her. Her friends are both thin, both wearing jean shorts and tank tops (one purple, the other pink), both staring at their phones.

I text her, *I have a surprise for you.*

What is it?

Look over your shoulder.

Monica turns, squinting from the glare of sunlight on the building windows. I wave her over. Her friends don't notice when she stands, brushes grass clippings from the seat of her shorts, and starts across the lot. She slips her phone into her pocket and sneaks a beaming, blushing smile at me. Her caramel eyes are kind yet doleful. Halfway across the lot, she lowers her gaze and doesn't raise it until she reaches the curb. She grins sidelong up at me. "What is it?" she asks.

"Ice cream. You want some with your favorite cousin-in-law?"

She talks to the curb. "My mom said I gotta stay at this stupid thing all day."

"I'll bring you right back. If they have a problem, they can talk to me. What do you want, a cone or a bowl?"

She's expressionless. She keeps her head down, bites the corner of her bottom lip like she's mulling the choice, like she's been caught.

"Can Sandra and Julie Ann come?"

"Let's make it just the two of us today."

She wiggles her toenails, painted the same yellow as her shirt. I'm about to wave a hand in front of her eyes to bring her back to the conversation when she nods.

"I'm going inside. I parked out back. Wait five minutes and meet me out there."

I slip inside before she can change her mind.

The ice cream shop is in town, two blocks from the school. I buy two waffle cones with enormous scoops of cotton candy, and we sit on the same side of a picnic table, apart from the other customers. I ask about school, her friends and classmates, her plans for the future. Her replies are concise, not quite rude. She eats her treat deliberately, one hand balling a napkin beneath the table, careful not to let any ice cream drip down the side of her cone. Everyone is "good." Everything is "okay." She has no plans.

"I have to admit something, honey," I say.

The instant I scooch closer and attempt to put my arm around her she looks up at me, her eyes filmy and pink, her jaw tight, and her cheeks rouged with shame. The tendons in her neck tense up as she swallows. "Who told you?" she asks.

"No one," I stammer. "Actually, I guessed it. I asked your mom because I was worried about you. You seemed so different. You were depressed and quiet—"

"I don't wanna talk about it." She taps her nails, looks around to make sure no one's listening, then continues in a whisper. "Sorry to be mean but I'm tired of thinking about it and I'm tired of my parents watching me so close. It's driving me totally insane. I didn't want any of this to happen. I made my decision. It's over now."

"You're right, it's none of my business. It's yours and yours alone."

She drops her napkin, crumpled into a ball, damp with sweat. She flattens it on the table, rests her cone atop it, and stares down at her lap. Her silence is the sort you keep so as not to say anything mean, regrettable.

"Did you see that guy who swung by the party?" I ask. "He was wearing long sleeves."

She frowns, nods.

"His name is Dorian. He's an old friend of mine. He actually lived with Miss Bonnie for a long time, back when we were in high school. He said Heath is still living at her place and that Heath told him a story. He said something happened to her, Monica."

She's silent.

"You know anything about—"

"She meant the world to us."

"I had no idea you spent time with her."

"I didn't really. Not until around the time Heath and I broke up."

Again, she looks around the seating area. She clears her throat, abruptly stands with her cone, and walks away from the table. I dip back inside the shop for a handful of napkins, then follow her.

We toss our half-eaten cones in the trash and walk down a residential street that leads to the school, her flip-flops slapping against the gravel. When we reach the chain-link fence around Sibley High School's deserted football field and track, she begins to whimper, to tremble, then to sob. We stop and I wrap my arms around her and hold her snugly.

After several minutes I escort her down to the track, faded hoary. We sit cross-legged. The track is scratchy and hot, and Marybeth is on a rampage from the ice cream. I hand over the stack of napkins and Monica plucks them up one after another, dabbing her face dry and blowing her nose. When the tears stop, she flicks pebbles into the endzone grass for some time.

Finally, she pinches her eyes shut, opens them, and begins, "You can't tell anyone about this, Emma. I really did like Heath for a long time. We broke up, right, but it isn't because of how he treated me or whatever. Jeremy's been telling people that he tricked me. That's not how it happened. I wanted to do it. I mean, now I wish I hadn't but only because of what happened after that. Heath cares about me. It wasn't about trying to do stuff with me so he could brag about it to his friends. Jeremy only sees it that way because that's how he thinks. When Heath and I started hanging out, everyone gave Jeremy shit. So he bullied Heath, which was easy because Heath doesn't have many friends. Like, his only real friend in Sibley was her. Now he has no one. And I abandoned him too. I feel terrible about it."

She blows her nose.

"Our family hates him, and they keep telling me how much I'm supposed to hate him, but he's actually a good person with a good heart and he cares about me. He really cares. He's respectful and he always wants to talk to me about what I'm thinking, like, the future, my plans, my dreams. I guess that's why I felt comfortable, you know, having sex with him. I still like him. It's just that we can't be together now because of the baby. He doesn't know what I did. I didn't want anybody to know, but definitely not him. I can never tell him. It'll totally crush him, Emma. Because he doesn't hate our family back the way you might think he does. He's never had what we have. He used to tell me how lucky he felt to date me, because I have such a loving, like, normal home. I kind of think he liked our family more than he even liked me—"

"But what about—"

"I know, I know. It's just, you gotta understand how important Miss Bonnie was to him. She was everything. And she's an amazing woman. You could actually talk to her about anything, and she never ever got annoyed. I only really spent a little time with her but I loved her so much."

Scowling, she pauses to remove a flip-flop, which she uses to smash a nearby colony of ants. *Thwack. Thwack.*

"When I took the test and learned about the baby, I told my mom and she just had no time to talk about anything other than 'you gotta keep it, you gotta keep it.' I was so scared and I didn't know what to do and it wasn't like I for sure wasn't gonna keep it but I needed to talk it through. I didn't have anybody, except I knew if I absolutely needed to I could talk to Miss Bonnie. She wouldn't tell anybody. That's when everything went wrong."

Thwack. She wipes ant specks from the bottom of her flip-flop and puts it back on.

"She didn't tell me to do this or that. She just supported me. She was the only one who supported me. I mean, it was my decision and I'd have made it even if I hadn't talked to her about it first. My mom couldn't believe I'd even been considering an abortion. Jesus, I don't wanna be stuck here my whole life just like her. No offense, Emma."

"No worries, honey."

"I wanna go to college and maybe I'll come back and visit and all. But I won't live here, I promise you that. And if I went through with it, if I had the baby, then what? Forget about the rest of my life. There's more for me than this place. My mom, though. She didn't get it. She needed to know who I'd been talking to. I shouldn't have told her. That's where I fucked up. I mentioned Miss Bonnie. From then on, my mom blamed her for everything. She still says nasty things sometimes and that pisses me off, you know. I mean, Miss Bonnie is ... She can't defend herself now. Emma, we can't tell anybody about all this. Please don't. Not your friend or anybody else. Promise me, please."

"Keep going."

"Promise me."

"I can't do that, Monica."

She tucks the napkins into her pocket, gets up, brushes loose the little nuggets of track imprinted into the bottoms of her thighs, and heads onto the field. Slowly, I stand, dizzy, my clothes sticking to my skin. I walk after her and she stops, waiting for me to catch up, a gesture from which it's obvious she'll tell me more with or without my pledge to keep her secret.

She explains, "I need you to understand why it went down the way it did, because you'll see why I haven't talked about it to anyone. But ... Okay, here it is ... I don't know how he found out."

"Who?"

"Jeremy. Someone told him. It could've been only one of two people, my mom or Miss Bonnie. It wasn't Miss Bonnie. For a long time, I couldn't understand why my mom would've done it. But I know now. She couldn't stomach shaming me about it anymore than she already had so she had Jeremy do it. And he went further than she did. A lot further, even though he was also ashamed, I guess, and that's why he didn't tell anybody else. He pushed me up against the bedroom wall and had his hands on my stomach. He kept pushing and pushing. And he was shouting at me ..."

"Shouting ...?"

"He knew all these details about what'd happened. I couldn't have denied it even if I tried, even if he'd been making it all up. You should've seen his face, like he wasn't even there in his head anymore. He knew when the procedure happened and how my mom and I told people I was sick when I stayed in my room that week recovering. And he knew Heath was the father and that Miss Bonnie ..."

She trails off, sniffling.

"He knew Miss Bonnie had listened to me while I talked through what I should do about the baby. And I shouldn't have told him. I should've tried better to lie. He'd have kept pushing me. He'd have held me down and shouted and cried and God knows what else he'd have done. But still I shouldn't have said anything. But I nodded along out of fear. The next thing I knew, he was out the door on his way to Miss Bonnie's place ..."

She trails off, nibbling on her bottom lip. Her tears are single streaks on her cheeks, replenished with each blink. I take her hand.

"Jeremy was gonna kill him and ... I think that's why my mom told him. She wanted Heath dead just as much as Jeremy did, just as much as my dad would've if he'd found out when she did. The rest I learned from Heath afterward. She'd stepped in front of him, and Jeremy threw her on the ground. Then Jeremy called my dad, who talked to my mom and called Doleman, and before you could blink they'd taken her body away and filed whatever reports they needed to."

She begins to sob again. I hug her as tightly as possible, as tightly as my belly and the suffocating heat will allow. Her tears, sweat, and snot soil my polo, her words coming in sputters.

"After my dad learned ... Learned about the abortion ... He quit looking at me. Like ... he babies me more than I can ever remember ... And he kisses me before bed ... But he doesn't look at me anymore ... Not in the eyes ... Like, I know my mom and dad are covering for Jeremy but ... But I sometimes think that, you know ... Sometimes I think they're actually covering for me more than anyone ... They don't want ... They don't want people to know their son killed a woman ... But they'll do anything to make sure people ... To make sure people don't know I killed a baby ... I'm more of a murderer than he is because ... Because my baby was their grandchild ... While Miss Bonnie didn't mean shit to them ... That's not right ... That's not right ... That's not right at all, Emma."

She steps away. Out of napkins, she bends forward to dry her face on her tank top. After she gathers herself, we head back to the ice cream shop. At one point my phone buzzes and she grabs my arm.

113

"Emma, you gotta promise me you won't tell anyone. Not your friend. Not Gavin. Not a soul. Promise me. I don't want anything to happen to Heath. Or to Jeremy. He made a terrible mistake but if word got out about what he did it'd be all over the news. Please, Emma. It could destroy the family. It could destroy the dealership and everything our family's worked for. That's how I gotta look at it. Otherwise … I wish it would all just go away. Can you promise me?"

I don't reply. I'm burning up and hungry again and my bladder's full. After using the shop's bathroom, I dab my forehead with a paper towel dampened with cool water.

She's waiting for me in the SUV. Before starting the vehicle, I say, "I won't patronize you by telling you what the right thing to do is. You're a smart young woman. You already know. And you're asking me to do the wrong thing, are you?"

"But Emma—"

"Honey."

"Just, people can't find out. They just can't, Emma."

"I can't live with knowing what I know now and not doing something about it. I'm not gonna let you do that, either. If what you said is true, he needs to be held accountable. *Our family* needs to be held accountable. You can be mad at me if you want. No one needs to know about your decision to end your pregnancy. But, Monica, you did the right thing talking to me. You can always talk to me."

The car ride back to the party is quiet. She examines her reflection in the visor mirror, sniffles, then flips the visor up and leans her head against the window.

I park in the lot behind the dealership, and she jumps out without a word and hustles inside.

I have a missed call from Dorian. I text him, *You still at the house? I have to talk to you.*

Call you in a bit. I'm at the hospital with Heath.

Dorian, what happened?

Surgeon is trying to save him. He hurt himself bad.

On my way.

***

There are only a few other people in the waiting area outside the emergency rooms. The nurse at the front desk has a crooked smile and one honey-blonde braid slung over her shoulder. A badly sunburned child moans. A middle-aged woman holds a blood-soaked paper towel around her pointer finger. A spindly teen whines about the hornet stings on her legs. Dorian and I sit side by side on a plush green bench in the back corner of the room, where no one can overhear me telling him what Monica told me. I apologize for my rudeness, for being so defensive of my family. He nods yet doesn't reply, his gut smeared crimson, his face sickly, dour. Gavin calls twice. I don't answer. Dorian's eyelids are heavy. He perks up only at the trill of the front desk phone and the whir of the opening mechanical double doors behind the desk. There've been no updates regarding Heath.

In the silence something occurs to me.

"It was a little odd, how Monica opened up. At first she said she didn't wanna talk. But as soon as I brought your name up, she really spilled her guts. I don't know what to make of it."

He's deep in thought.

"What are you gonna do, Dorian? Tell me. I wanna help you."

He sits up straight, folds his hands over the blood stain on his stomach, and shakes his head. "I have the strangest memories. I mean, because there was nothing strange about it at the time.

That's just the way it was. Nothing weird about it. Now, I can't imagine opening up my apartment to a bunch of kids I only just met."

"She was an extraordinary woman."

His voice is urgent and stern. "Before Miss Bonnie's, I was at this place. One of the older boys there used to pick on this tiny little foster sister of ours. One day he sat her down on the gas stovetop. I couldn't have been ten, I'd say she was eight. He turned the burner on. Maybe the whole house was there watching it, or maybe it was just me, I don't remember. I wanted to do something to stop him. I should have but I didn't. Half a minute in, you could smell her jeans burning. He held her down until smoke came up from below. Not much. Enough to see and smell. He didn't even help her down. He just walked away, and she hopped down on her own and ran out of the kitchen. It took me over a decade to realize how goddamn insane that was. I knew it was wrong when it happened, I wanted to put an end to it. But just how sick and horrible it was. I didn't understand."

He fills his lungs and continues.

"I went to see the girl later. I'd found out where she worked. At a hotel in Walker, not far from the casino. Heard she went by Sally, so that's who I asked for. I recognized her right away, even though I hadn't seen her in years and she'd dyed her hair pitch black and pierced her eyebrow with a bolt. She knew who I was too, except she didn't say anything. I apologized for not doing anything and I told her how mad I was that it'd happened. I *was* mad. I still am. I'm furious. She was caught off-guard. She said that it wasn't her and that I was mistaken. 'Let's just do this, huh,' she kept saying. She was naked by then, kissing my neck, hushing me. It wasn't in me to ... I just paid and she kissed me on the cheek, and she hugged me hard because she was grateful, I think ... I think she was glad someone remembered what'd happened that day and had at least told her it wasn't right. What else could I do for her after all those years?

"I felt good after that, though. I was ready to get clean and clear my head and start over. But the only way I could do it was if I forgot about Sibley for a while. Forgot everything. You, Miss Bonnie, Sibley, school. So that's what I did. It worked. I *am* clean and my head's right. But I never came back home to thank her for all she did for me. To see if there was anything I could do for her. I had these daydreams of helping her with her house. The shingles look like hell. Who was there to ask her if she needed anything? Maybe she had some demons she wanted to talk through. Maybe she had nightmares and withdrawals of her own. When you're wounded you take time to heal. And all that time you take healing you can't help anyone else get better."

"It's okay, Dorian. She understood all that. I promise she did."

He frowns as if awaiting the right words. "I get to thinking sometimes that the world is horrible. But it's not true. Just, the worst parts are loud about it. All the good stuff is quieter. Harder to notice. That's what I think of when I think of her."

He reminisces about Miss Bonnie, how she sang along to the radio, how she washed the little ones' faces with a wet, soapy washcloth after meals, how she drove everyone to Murphy's football games in the fall. She'd back her van up to the fence, open the trunk lid, and lay a blanket down in the cab for them to sit on. She packed plastic baggies of tuna sandwiches and barbecue chips and cubed watermelon. And she'd drink boxed wine from a thermos and munch down graham crackers half a sheet at a time. Whenever the front desk phone rings he pauses and raises his head expectantly.

All the while something pesters me, something I do and don't wanna say, an impulse I do and don't wanna act on. Chalk it up to Marybeth and the extra blood in my veins, the heat, my exhaustion, the torrent of information Monica rained down on me. To these circumstances, a family, *my* family, involved in some plot to aid a privileged boy in evading justice while a deprived one fights for his life in a room down the hall. To Dorian, shoulders thick, cheeks sunburnt, auburn eyes clear and stern, knitted long-sleeve bloodied up, with his principles, his stubbornness, his self-righteousness. Dorian, whose way of seeing the world has proven him right so many times he must be awfully tired of his own decency, who asks for nothing and empties me all the same, who'd leave a woman wondering whether she'd still love him were he to finally accept that love, because who'd he be without his commitment to never breaking up a happy home? Who'd I be, for that matter?

Chalk it up however I please, it's as if I were someone with scarcely a past, the trajectory of my future awaiting these moments here in the waiting area, that I might amend its course. It's an eerie thing, to be unsure not of what to do or whether you have the stomach to do it, but of what you'll be in your eyes afterward, courageous or spineless, despotic or powerless, sinful or pure. Right now, I can't think of a reason not to do as I please.

Fighting this impulse, I ask, "Is that why you never wrote me back? You were taking time for yourself?"

"I didn't write back because I thought I wasn't good enough for someone like you."

I know this. I've always known this. What good is a truth like this? I'd rather be bullshitted, if only he could manage that for me. "You know better now, yeah?" I reply.

"Most days, I do." Abruptly he adds, "If he pulls through, I'm taking him home with me where he'll be safe. He and I can talk to the county sheriff, call whoever else, I don't know what. We'll do something. If he doesn't, then I'll do what I can on my own. It could get ugly here and I'm sorry about that."

"I understand." Gavin is my husband. I'm married to Gavin. "Please let me talk to Gavin first, though. He'll help us out. He might even know who we need to talk to at the sheriff's office."

He clears his throat.

"Dorian, he's not like he used to be."

He lowers his voice to a hoarse whisper. "I only care about the kid, and I won't put him in any more danger than I have to."

"I don't wanna endanger him, either. I was insensitive back at my office and I'm sorry. He'd told some lies to our family, to Monica, so I didn't believe him. Now that I know he's telling the truth—"

"You might not have been so casual if this was about another kid, not a foster child."

"Why do you think I'm here now?"

"Same reason I am. Guilt."

"Fine, 'I'm callous white trash, just like everyone else, and I don't give a damn whether he lives or dies. He's an orphan after all, so fuck him.' I was wrong to be glib back at my office. I was shocked by it all. But I'm here now. Here for you. I'll pray with you if that's what you want. Or I'll just sit here and shut up or wait in the car or go back to the barbecue and tell them I had an errand to run. It's your choice ..."

"Fine," he says, grinding his knuckles into his eyes.

"Fine *what?*"

"Sit with me until the doctor comes."

"I can do that."

He yawns. "Thank you. I'm sorry."

"What the fuck for?" I ask.

"For despising you all so much."

"After this I can't blame you. Gavin called me a few times. I'm sure he's wondering where I am. Dorian, let him help us. Whether you like him or not, his family has a lot of respect for him, even his uncle Travis. Doleman, too. Gavin didn't know Miss Bonnie well but I promise, promise, after I talk to him he'll be as upset about it as I am. Please, Dorian. Why don't you come by for dinner tonight? When Derek goes to bed, we can talk things through."

"I can't leave the hospital. I need to be here when he wakes up."

"What about breakfast at our place? Is seven too early? Actually, if you need a place to stay ..."

"I don't."

"What, you're gonna sleep here in the waiting room?"

"Maybe."

"The offer stands. Either way we'll see you at breakfast?"

"Fine, breakfast."

"Okay, then. Good."

We fall silent. For the next few hours, we converse little, how much and how little there is to say. The impulse stays with me, with it these laden moments, that eerie feeling. I can't shake them. Twice I trek across the hospital to the cafeteria, returning with coffees and muffins on the first trip, with chicken noodle soup on the second. Every twenty minutes he crosses the waiting area to speak with the nurse, who sends him back without additional information. Soon he doesn't seem to notice the phone ringing or the doors to the emergency room hallway opening. For some time, he seems to be on the brink of sleep.

"And you three are ... You're happy?" he asks.

"Four. Yes."

"Four, right. That's good, Emma. That's all that matters. A name for the baby yet?"

"No. Still thinking."

"Derek's a nice name."

"I love it. What about you?"

"What about me?"

"How are *you*?"

He leans forward, resting his elbows on his thighs, his hands hanging down toward the floor. When he senses me glancing at his forearms he sits up, crosses his arms.

Fuck it, I tell myself, fuck it. I whisper, "Let me see."

We remain out of earshot of the others in the waiting room, so there's something conspiratorial about the request. I turn his hand palm-up, tug his sleeve up to his biceps, and touch him. I'm cautious, my movements close to but not quite sensual. Braille that I might read his soul. Mutilation, needle pricks and haphazard slashes, impromptu tattoos poorly crafty and arbitrary and heinous, so unlike him. Nor are these scars the ones I felt by moonlight so many years ago. Today there are more. Yet they're old and healed, which is reassuring. Good, I think, now we're even. And no sooner do I think this than say, "I used to wonder if you'd ever stop breaking my heart."

He just bites his bottom lip.

Then they're over, those grave and vital moments are gone. I am a married woman, a pregnant wife.

I'm grateful for this new present. As grateful as I've been in some time, grateful in a way that recalls me to the past, my home, my family, my life. It's over.

When I release his arm, he pulls his sleeve down to his wrist.

Minutes later the nurse waves at us. Beside her, a man with curly black hair and bushy sideburns rubs his hands together. Dorian rushes over and I trail him cumbersomely.

"You're the one who brought Mr. Reynolds in?" the man asks.

"Yes."

"I'm Rory and I'm the nurse who'll be looking after him tonight."

Rory leads us through the double doors and into a long white hallway. After a few feet he stops and explains, "We need to keep him overnight. We moved him to Recovery so we can look after him."

"He's gonna make it, then?"

"We believe so."

"That's great news. Thank you. Thank you."

"Is he your son? Brother?"

"Brother," Dorian replies.

"You found him?"

"Yes."

"Just in time. Fortunately, he missed the femoral artery, but he severed some smaller arteries in the thigh. Lacerations were severe enough to cause significant blood loss. And you must be the sister-in-law?" he asks me.

"Just a friend of the family."

"Can I see him?" Dorian asks.

"He's asleep, so you can't talk with him, but yes. We have some resources here at the hospital that I think you might be interested in. Psychiatric and psychological out-patient services, social workers. Has he exhibited self-harming behavior before?"

"I ... I don't actually know," Dorian says.

"He's never been treated for anything, as far as our records indicate. It might be worth checking with your parents about that. Anyway, he's a minor. We need their consent for ...?"

"He doesn't have parents, as far as I know. We're foster brothers, actually."

"I see. You're his guardian ...?"

"No. I've been checking in on him, though."

Rory shifts his tone instantly. "I apologize. I should've clarified your relationship to Mr. Reynolds earlier and I shouldn't have told you about his status without first ... I need to ask you both to please return to the waiting area."

"I don't need any more information, Rory. I just want someone to be there with him when he wakes up. There's no one else."

"Excuse me, sir, ma'am. You—"

"Rory, you must have a supervisor we could speak to about this," I interject.

"George Walters is his name," Rory replies, haughty now, "and he'll tell you the same thing I just told you."

"Why don't you go ahead and get Walters anyway, Rory? Tell him Emma Spencer would like to talk to him. If he doesn't recognize that name, tell him that my uncle is Travis Spencer, the Fire Captain up in Sibley, who's best friends with Judd Doleman, Police Chief in Sibley. Tell him Judd Doleman is best buds with Chief Carter here in Brainerd, who knows Mayor Puntzer quite well. If he doesn't know already, tell Walters that Puntzer meets regularly with the administrators at this hospital."

"Ma'am—"

"Or maybe you want your name to come up at one of these meetings? Because it seems unavoidable at this point since you've either disclosed confidential patient information to someone you shouldn't have, or are withholding viewing rights from an authorized loved one. Not to mention the stress you're putting Mr. Spencer's pregnant niece through."

"Are you threatening—?"

"I am. Take me to Walters so I can threaten him too. Or just let Dorian see his little brother."

Rory's cheeks redden. Finally, he scoffs, smiles nervously. "Let me see what I can do."

"Thanks so much, Rory," I tell him as he turns and scurries down the hallway.

Dorian takes my hand, squeezes it once firmly, and lets go.

Minutes later, another nurse escorts Dorian further down the hallway to the hospital wing in which Heath is recovering. I decide to leave Dorian alone with the boy.

I head home. Though frantic, I drive slowly on account of Marybeth.

At the house, Gavin and Derek sleep on the living room sofa, the lights on, a children's book splayed out on the floor beneath them. I'm careful not to wake Derek along with Gavin.

"Where you been?" Gavin asks groggily.

"The hospital."

"Honey..."

"Hush. Don't wake him up. I'm fine."

"And Marybeth?" he asks.

"She's fine, too. Let's get him to bed. We need to talk."

"About Dorian?"

"About everyone."

Gavin

Before I know it, it's that time in the morning. Too early to get up and too late to fall asleep without waking up more tired than I already am. Biggest day of the year and I couldn't sleep worth a jack. Emma didn't used to be this way. It's the family that made her batty. Now it's always something. Granted, she doesn't give a fuck about the dealership. But it's the biggest day of the year! Uncle Travis likes to brag about all he accomplished without making it past sixth grade. A shame. Seventh might've done him some good. Hell, how about a little junior high, Travis? His kids are smarter than him, even his glue-sniffing son. Monica running all over town, knocked up at sixteen and everyone saying she was raped by that vagrant. Jeremy with a foot in prison. Yep, another year or two might've taught Travis something. Maybe he'd have been a little quieter on the phone in the firehouse office last month. He's half deaf but won't bother with hearing aids. Yelling about "the woman!" and "Did we take care of it?!"

After he hung up, I went in. "What's going on?"

"Nothing!" he said. Lately he'd been rubbing his mustache so hard it was thinning out.

"Better tell me."

"It's nothing, Gav!"

Next day he needed me and Jordan's help straightening somebody out. Never nothing, always something.

I have a piece of toast and drive to the gas station and grab a coffee and head to the firehouse to see Travis. Delia told him he snores like hell when he's had too much to drink. So, for twenty years now he's slept on a recliner in the firehouse lounge. Watches late-night reruns of whatever until he dozes off.

The dealership is gonna sink or swim. If it'd just choose one or the other, I could move on with my life. It won't, though. Too many people believing it's not already sunk. Whatever, by spring I'll be selling furnaces in Brainerd. Rose Doleman will set me up. Said she would and seemed confident she could pull strings. Okay, we were both blitzed that night so who knows. It was raining hard after the concert up at the casino. We got back to the car before the others. Got to talking. Kissing but just pecks like schoolkids do. I hope the furnace offer stands even though she put my fingers in her mouth and tried to slide them down her pants and I said no because I can't keep doing that with her, I just can't. She'll get over it.

Sooner the dealership goes, the sooner I'm gone. Problem is, I can't leave early because they'll get pissy, Jordan, Jonny, Stevie. Everything seems to be of one mind. 'Burn it down but don't get caught with the matches.' With any luck, what Emma said is true and everyone will be at each other's throats, we'll close the dealership by midday, I can give Rose a call. Better money selling furnaces, anyway. Me and Emma can go to Disney World with the kids. A man sees his wife that upset, he's gotta do everything he can for her.

Couldn't sleep a damn wink. Emma springs all this on me like she forgot what day it is. She tells me don't go to Travis and don't confront Jeremy and don't tell a soul about it. Tells me basically, Here's a big problem that's gonna destroy the family and everything we've worked for but please, pretty please, don't do anything about it. Tells me to get some sleep because tomorrow's the biggest day of the year and all the while I had to act surprised. "Goddamn, Emma, that's terrible!"

Jordan and Travis needed a ride to the house. Not really, though. "We been drinking," Travis said, like that'd ever stopped them before. What they needed was to rope me into their business so I wouldn't tell on them. They were gonna visit the kid who raped Monica. I thought she was awfully nice to him for him being a rapist and all. Travis said Monica was a good girl who he'd never so much as heard a curse word from so "you do the math." That's something, a guy who can't count to twenty telling me to do the math.

"Fine, but you gotta tell me more about that phone call," I said.

"It's nothing! I swear!"

Whatever, I sat in the car. Took five minutes.

That's what's wrong with Jeremy. And Jordan and Stevie and Jonny and Travis. They can't see anything past their next beer, screw, or ribeye. It's why our name doesn't mean half of what they think it does. Why nothing we do impresses anyone with a last name different than ours. The Perhams take their kids to museums, the Grand Canyon, shit like that. Most Spencers couldn't handle leaving the county for a night. It's all one long, sad, late party, selling cars and going to church and watching the kids play sports. Why the dealership's shot.

Then there's Dorian. Must be lonely in exile, running out of casino sluts, so Jordan heard. If he's here much longer he might get to poking around and asking questions and putting his hands on her. That's what this is all about. Not his foster mom. Not the vagrant. Emma said she "needed to be sure" about me. "That's all it was, Gavin. And just the one time." I said all the right things because I wanted to believe them. Sometimes I even do. It doesn't matter. It doesn't. Derek and Marybeth, that's where my mind stays. I'm so scared they'll grow up to be like me and not like their mom. But if they're shit out of luck when it comes to their genes, I figure I ought to be better than what I've been at times. Ought to fix what's broken, be good to my wife, tell myself that her fucking Dorian doesn't matter. Believe it too.

I park my truck in front of the firehouse and head inside. AC is on the fritz and so Travis kicked his quilt off in the night. The pant legs of his overalls are rolled up to his thighs. The top is unhooked and flopped down onto his crotch. Bottoms of his feet black as soot. All in all, he looks like a hobo on a coal train. And he's still snoring. The sound of water bubbling.

I gotta flick him on the forehead eight times before he opens his eyes and pushes my hand away.

"Last night my wife told me that your son killed a woman."

"What?! Who, Jeremy?!"

"You have another?"

"Not that I know of!"

"You gonna tell me what happened, or do I need to ask him myself?"

"Ask him about *what*?!" he says.

He's laying it on thick. Yawning and shaking his head and groaning and slapping himself on the cheeks.

"I'm losing patience real fast, Travis."

"It's too early for all this! Any coffee made over there on the counter?!"

I pour him a cup of day-old mud. When he reaches for it, I splash it on his face. I liked doing it, just not that I did it. How it goes.

"Shithead!" he croaks, wiping his eyes with his palms. He doesn't bother getting up to do something about it, though.

"Quit dicking around, Travis. That boy we visited is in the hospital. Almost killed himself yesterday."

He slicks his wet hair back. "Almost?!"

"Doctors stitched him up. I need to know what I'm covering up."

"Nothing, Gav! It's nothing at all! This is a misunderstanding!"

"Jeremy at home?"

"Don't bug the kid! He's been going through some stuff with college! Might not get in where he wants to go! Don't put anything more on him now!"

"He's an idiot. He's not going to college. He's going to the show floor until we shutter the place."

"At least can you give it the weekend?! Then you and I can talk!"

"You really aren't gonna tell me, huh?"

"What's there to say, Gav?! An old lady got hurt bad! Some people might know what happened, but they aren't talking!"

"It's not done. Emma knows. That guy who came to the party yesterday knows. The kid's talking."

"What are you gonna do about it?!"

"It's always up to me, isn't it? I'll tell you this much, Travis. I don't care about you or Jeremy or Monica or the boy or that lady or the dealership or anything. Only Derek, Emma, and the baby she's got inside her. If she's upset, I'm doing something about it. The rest of you can go to hell."

"You won't like what you find!"

"Something tells me you'll like it even less." I head toward the door. "Your son at home?"

"I don't know!"

"That sounds about right. And your daughter?"

"No question!"

"How can you be sure?"

"Delia would've told me if she wasn't!"

"Take a shower, Uncle Travis, you smell like ass."

It's sticky-hot. All smoggy from the fires Canada can't seem to put out. I roll the truck windows down and blast the AC. I put my hands on top of the steering wheel to air my armpits out. Only thirty minutes before me and Emma are meeting Dorian for breakfast.

I drive to Travis's place, call Delia on the way. She answers the house phone on the fourth ring.

I'm all pep. "Good morning, Aunt Delia. How are you? I'm looking for my buddy Jeremy. He and I had plans today."

"Plans? Aren't you busy at the dealership all day?"

"Right, that's why we were getting it out of the way early."

"Getting what out of the way, dear?"

"Boy, I'm not sure. He asked to speak with me. I think it's about cleaning up his act and getting into fewer fights."

Aunt Delia's just delighted to hear this. "Wonderful, Gav!"

"Have you seen him?"

"Of course. He's still asleep. Came in late. Always messing around. I'll get him."

"Tell him I'm waiting out front. Got breakfast waiting."

"Gav, thank you so much. Let me know how it goes with him, okay? You have no idea how grateful Travis and me would be."

"Will do, Aunt Delia. Love you."

"Love you too!"

County Road 29 is two miles out of town. After half a mile I turn left onto the long dirt driveway that leads to Travis's single-story ranch house. Fields of wildflowers and grass all around it. On either side along the driveway, there are post-and-rail fences made with thick beams of timber. I turn around and park facing 29 again, the front door in my rear-view mirror. I drink my coffee. I wait.

Fifteen minutes before breakfast with Dorian and Emma.

It's simple. If I let Dorian and this vagrant get their story to the right people, Jeremy's screwed. As much as I wouldn't miss his mouth-breathing, Delia and Travis would put all their money into his defense. Do everything they can to keep him free. Stevie and Jonny right behind them. Until the dealer-ship is depleted. Might even ask me for money, ask me to keep lying. Ask me not to admit what they know I know. And if I let Dorian and the boy destroy my name, the family will convince themselves it was fate. They'll tell themselves it wasn't their own doing, tell themselves they were smart, and they worked hard all the time and they went about things the right way. It'll be "poor Jeremy couldn't catch a break," "the kid wouldn't hurt a fly," "judge had it in for him since the get-go" from now to the end of time.

Granted, might be no different if the dealership collapses some other way. Say there's a fire. But I got no choice, really. I can't let it be this way. Maybe if Dorian hadn't fucked her, I could let him have this one. If he wasn't such a smug, two-faced ass emailing back and forth with her, trying to break up my house. If he hadn't fucked her and I hadn't asked if it was good and she hadn't answered, "You really wanna know?" all snide and vengeful like how she gets sometimes. What all I've done to deserve that, I'm not totally sure. Maybe if she hadn't demanded that I apologize for whooping his ass and I hadn't lied and told her I already had since, Lord knows, I was never gonna see him again. If he wasn't here all of a sudden, crashing my family's barbecue, acting like he didn't fuck her, wouldn't have even dreamed of it. If I didn't have to apologize for real to cover my tracks because Emma snaps these days when she catches me lying.

Might be the baby messing with her brain. Might be she suspects something about Rose in the back seat after the concert even though I said no and did the right thing. Seems the more I do the right thing, the more fucked things get. So, Emma spends the evening with him hearing sob-stories about his dead "mom" and pitying him again because his dad passed out in the bathtub and his real mom held the guy's head underwater and his grandma went insane. There at the hospital last night he's reaching for her face and she's saying, "No, it's over," and he's saying, "No, it isn't, Emma. No, it isn't." I can't lose to him.

Just gotta make sure Emma's satisfied with how it plays out. Gotta scratch her pregnant-brain itch. Gotta play nice with Dorian. She and the kids are what keep me from being like the rest of them. I'm not like the way they are. I'm not.

Finally, Jeremy comes lurching out of the house and starts toward the truck. He's wearing sandals, a white wife-beater, and sweatpants he cut down to shorts with a utility knife. Part boozehound, part athlete-in-training. What a shitty feeling, wishing I didn't wanna knock him around. And say I do, I don't wanna enjoy it. And say I enjoy it, I wanna be able to stop when I've done enough. Because say I can't stop, then I'm not man enough to deal with any of this.

"What's up, bro?" he says, climbing into the truck.

I give him a nod and drive back to 29. I ignore his questions. "Where we headed to?" "Do I need my wallet?" "Everything cool, bro?" Every time I look over and get a glimpse of his hair in a bun on top of his head and his mouth hanging open and his giant wet lips slack and his too-long ogre face staring at me blank as a cow's, I envision my hand smashing his head against the glove compartment.

Halfway back to town, I pull over and tell him to get out. I meet him on his side of the truck. He leans back against the passenger door with his hands in his pockets, frowning down at the edge of the gravel. I cross my arms and mean-mug him.

"I don't have time for this today, Jeremy. I need it to go as quick and easy as it can. Can you help me?"

He's sheer hangdog. "Sure, bro. Anything, bro. I don't know what's going on lately. Everyone's just been ganging up on me."

"Did you do it?"

"Do what?"

Blood rushes to my fists. I try to sound calm. "Did you?"

"No."

"You didn't do it?"

"No, bro. I swear, bro," he says, looking up at me.

"People are pretty-damn sure you killed that lady, Jeremy."

"I got no clue what happened to her. I didn't touch her. Why would I?"

"Jeremy, don't lie to me. I can't help you if you lie."

"Okay, yeah, that boy who was living there with her, me and him got into it a few times. Maybe I went too far once or twice. Monica was mad at me about that, whatever."

"What'd you fight about?"

"I was standing up for her. She's my little sis."

"Then what?"

133

"What do you mean, Gav?"

"You went over to that lady's house to confront him ..."

"I never ... Bro ..."

His mouth is still open but now his lips are quivering. He keeps rubbing his shoulders. Hugging himself like he's cold. What does it say about me that I'm this idiot's hero?

"Jeremy, you didn't snap for a minute, accidentally crack her skull open?"

"Is that what they say happened? I mean, I smacked *him* a little ... His nose was bleeding and he was moaning like he was hurt inside. Okay, I did go to her place once. I didn't go inside, though. He met me out back. I was giving him a chance to back off. That was it."

"Where were you on August 2nd?"

"I'm not sure."

"Think hard. It was a Friday afternoon."

"Home, probably. Watching a movie or playing video games or helping my dad with something."

"Jeremy ..."

He's onto me. My arms are limp at my sides, but still I can't hide it anymore. He puts his fists up, closes his mouth, and purses his lips. "How many free swings you want before I start on you?" I ask.

He huffs like a bull.

"I'm trying to help you. We both know you did it and neither of us wants you in prison." I lay it out for him slowly: "If you have an alibi, A-L-I-B-I, it'll be easier for us to say you had nothing to do with it. But if you act crazy like this, it'll be harder."

"Bro," he threatens. He's sizing me up, confused because my arms are still relaxed.

"I wish you would. I hope to God you try it, Jeremy. You think I wanna do this for you? I don't give a damn about you. I'm trying to protect the family. Our family. You and Monica and your parents. Will you help me protect them? Who's your best friend?"

"Huh?"

I knee him in the gut. He falls and I stomp on his ribs a few times. It's nothing. He squirms around like he survived an explosion.

"Don't worry," I say, "I won't mess with your face. Who is he? Who can you trust?"

"Brett, bro. It's Brett," he grunts.

"And you were with him all day and night, is that right?"

"Yes."

"Were you?!"

"Yes!"

"See, it's not complicated. You just gotta tell him the same. Can you remember all that?"

"Yes, bro. Shit."

He grabs my legs like he might try to tackle me to the ground, but he just hugs them tight. I feel so bad for him I don't kick him away.

After a minute he says, "I was with Brett all day. We were drinking some beers and listening to music and throwing the football and chilling at the beach and driving around and that's it."

"Good boy. Stand up now. We gotta go see some people."

"Who?"

"Emma and her friend. You're gonna tell them what you just told me. Anyone who ever asks you about this, you'll tell them the same thing. I'll take care of everything else. Come on now. Get back in the truck."

He whimpers. "I'm hurt."

"Let's go, *bro*," I tell him. "It'll only take a sec."

It takes him two minutes to get back into the truck. The whole ride over he's growling and grumbling and tearing up, so I crank the radio. Audioslave. "Show Me How to Live." His face is flushed. His eyes are swollen and pink. I get napkins out of the center console and toss them on his lap.

"We're almost there. Calm down, would you."

"I'm gonna kill you. I'm gonna cut your neck."

"At least give me Labor Day, we need to move units this weekend."

He sits up straight again.

"This'll go quick. Then you can get back to causing mayhem. How's the football team look this year? You gonna have a good year?"

"Fuck you, bro."

I park in front of the house, next to Dorian's beater. The kitchen blinds are drawn. He's probably in there rubbing her shoulders, Derek in the other room eating cereal.

"Now, where were you on August 2nd?"

"Hanging out with Brett all day. Just messing around, not killing anybody." He's snorting breaths, his mouth clamped shut.

"Do you have any idea what I'm trying to do for you?"

He stares ahead absently. "Let's just get this over with."

"My thoughts exactly."

I lead him into the house, find my wife and Dorian sitting opposite each other at the oak dining room table. They're drinking coffee from the "his" and "hers" mugs we got as a wedding gift. She's in pajama bottoms and a U of M sweater. He's wearing his jeans and knitted shirt from yesterday, blood on the stomach. Derek's feet patter on the hardwood as he runs over to me. He jumps onto my leg, and I walk into the dining room with him clinging to me.

They spot Jeremy coming in behind me. Dorian scowls at his folded hands and Emma starts in on me.

"This wasn't the plan, Gavin,"

"Honey, it's fine. Got it all ironed out this morning. Jeremy—"

"Why didn't you just listen to me?"

"Emma, relax. Jeremy and I had a chat—"

"You weren't supposed to tell anyone!" she cries.

I'm steady and calm as can be. "But why all the secrecy? Ever since Dorian showed up, it's been secret meetings and sneaky conversations. I don't like it, Emma. It pisses me off a little bit, to be honest. Why can't the four of us sit down and figure this whole thing out? I think once you hear what Jeremy has to tell you, you'll feel much better, both of you. The boy, too. How is he? Dorian, were you there when he woke up, like you hoped to be?"

Dorian doesn't even raise his head. Emma replies for him. "Heath's gonna be okay. He was too groggy to talk. Went right back to sleep."

"Terrific! Jeremy, you want coffee? Why don't you sit down? Derek, buddy, go watch cartoons. Put the TV on loud."

Derek scampers off into the living room. He turns the volume up high. I pour two more mugs of coffee, hand one to Jeremy. Me and him sit across from each other at the table.

"I apologize for going off-script," I tell Emma. "You're right, I messed up. I was only trying to speed up the process. That said, I'm glad I did it. I learned something interesting this morning. Jeremy, tell them."

Emma and Dorian look at Jeremy. He'd been looking down at his coffee. He flicks his menacing little eyes up at me, probably imagining how he'd beat me to death. I nod, encouraging him. He sneers back, smirks. "I did it," he says. "I hated that crusty hag."

"That's not funny."

"I'm not joking."

"Tell them what you told me in the truck."

He frowns, acting confused. "I told you I did it. Then you said I should come up with an alibi instead. I don't know what for. I'm getting away with it no matter what. Haven't you noticed, I can do whatever I wanna to whoever I want?"

Dorian stands but I jump to my feet. "Bear with us, Dorian. He's just acting silly."

On my way to Jeremy, I put my hands on Dorian's shoulders and he sits back down. I stand over my cousin.

"Quit messing around," I say.

"Dead serious," he says to Emma, smirking.

I won't let him smirk at her again. Already I'm popping him in the side of the head and my knuckles are burning and he thuds down on the floor and then everyone is shouting for me to stop. Dorian grabs my arm to keep me from swinging and I shove him away but I can't get to Jeremy because Emma's crouched over him and she looks into the living room and there's Derek watching it all. Everyone freezes.

Sweat tickles the small of my back. I touch my slimy forehead. Today of all days! Now I'll have to take a goddamn shower before I get to the dealership.

Jeremy's chair is on its back. I put it upright and plop down into it. Jeremy sits up, his back up against the dishwasher, threads of blood on the side of his head. Emma sits next to him, and Dorian stands behind her empty chair. Derek runs into his mother's arms, sobbing, howling.

Dorian won't look at me. Instead, he keeps glancing at Jeremy, like he's not satisfied after all me and Emma have done for him.

"Well, what are we gonna do?" I ask them. "Should I call his dad? Doleman? Dial 9-1-1 and see who the dispatcher sends out?"

No one replies. Everyone's breathing hard.

"Jeremy," Dorian says, "why'd you do it?"

"I hated her old ass."

"But why?"

He looks especially confused.

Emma and Dorian look at each other, then at Jeremy. Emma says, "When did you find out about the … operation?"

"What?" I butt in.

They ignore me.

"What operation?" Jeremy says.

"The *operation*, Jeremy. When did you—"

"Operation?"

"Monica had an abortion?" I ask. "You didn't say anything about that last night."

"Shut up for a second," Emma tells me.

Jeremy shakes his head in disbelief. "She was gonna have a baby?"

Before I can ask them anything else Dorian rushes out of the house, Emma right behind him, Derek in her arms.

I run to the door. They left it wide open. "Where you going?!" I keep shouting as they get into their vehicles. But it's like I'm not there.

They drive off. Then Jeremy brushes past my shoulder and sprints down the driveway.

It's just me now. Derek's cartoons blasting from the living room. I shut the door and go to the kitchen and drink two cups of coffee and eat four scrambled eggs. She doesn't answer her phone or respond to my texts. All that time to figure out what in God's name is going on. All that time, but I can't.

Monica

I love Heath so much I hope he's dead.

I'm listening to Radiohead on my phone. *In Rainbows* is me and Heath's favorite. The basement guest room is cool and bare. It's boring as church down here. This is where I've been since the procedure. This is where I belong. The walls are robin's egg blue. The carpet is the color of bourbon. The closet has two cream white doors that fold in half when you pull the knobs in the middle of them. Through the egress window I can see the sun. It's being such a weirdo. It's purple, almost black, and the sky is pink, so it looks like a little tiny lifeboat in this big ocean. A big ocean dyed pink one drop of blood at a time.

At first Mom told Dad and Jeremy that I'd had an ovarian cyst removed. This was smart because they don't know what cysts are. Or ovaries. After the procedure, I moved from my bedroom on the second floor down here to the guest room because it was easier for me to go downstairs than up. Mom brought me everything. Food, painkillers, clothes, fresh towels. She was a nurse and a maid. So I'd have something to do, she put the basement TV on the chest at the end of the bed. Some church lady upholstered the chest with happy daisies before she went blind. I didn't watch TV. I texted while listening to music on my phone. When it died, I was too lazy to charge it. Instead, I stared at the daisies until they danced. Mom charged my phone upstairs so she could look over the texts. I deleted anything that might tell on me for what I've done, my shitty doings, and I always warned Heath not to message me when the battery was low.

I still haven't brought the rest of my things down. Basically, I'm a guest in my own house and I'll keep it this way until I leave for good. Mom hasn't offered to bring them down, either. Maybe she thinks she's punishing me by keeping me in my recovery room forever. Maybe she doesn't know I like the punishment.

Oh, Heath. The pain he goes through every day is more than I can stand to watch. I've always known it would end like this. Still, he talks and talks. A million tiny lies are nothing to him, how smart he is. I always listened. I told him things and he listened too. It was like meeting the devil in the confession booth.

How I'll tell it to the authorities will be different than how it was. I'll be honest, only there's just too much to tell. Like how Sandra was being such a brat about me and Heath having sex that I decided to take the pregnancy test at her house and leave the pee stick in the bathroom trash bin for her mom to find. It was Julie Ann's idea. It was funny, then it wasn't. I took the stick home to show Mom. Her shifty, far-set hazel eyes bugged out so far, I thought they'd never go back inside her head. She wasn't breathing normal, either. Little sniffles. Like if she didn't take regular breaths, she couldn't yell. She was trying not to yell. And she didn't, not until after I decided not to keep it.

Maybe she told Dad out of spite. Three years ago, Mom was excited because her second-grade classroom was finally getting new desks. They were donating the old ones to a school in

Minneapolis. The next day she was mad because they weren't gonna donate the old ones after all. They were gonna trash them. So, she brought two of them home from work and told me they were the desks me and Jeremy used when we were in her class. A tiny schoolhouse unit. The desktop was connected to an arm that was bolted to the back of the chair. It was too small to sit in. She had plans to put it in her garden but she tucked Jeremy's into his bedroom closet and mine into mine.

I forgot about it until one day, a month ago now maybe, when I found it in the corner of my room next to my nightstand. I think when Dad found out about the baby he went to my room and stood there for a long time and got all weepy and ashamed of his tears and so he busied himself by poking around in the closet like he was fixing a shelf or looking for studs in the wall. Then he found the stupid desk, pouted for a while, and dragged it out into the bedroom where I'd find it. He figured it'd make me feel enough remorse for him to accept me as his little girl again, at least until I meet another boy.

Anyway, officer, that's why I stayed in the basement.

Snobby Emma rubbing her belly like it's good luck. I called Heath after she cornered me. I had to warn him about what I told her. I knew something was wrong when he didn't answer his phone. That morning he wrote me two thousand texts about how he just couldn't take it anymore and we needed to leave for Minneapolis right away and he'd get us a hotel room for a couple nights and we could make plans from there. *No way they track us down, Monica.* He went on and on, texting me that I needed to keep my eyes open for a guy coming by with questions. *He'll get me killed.* Then he got super sad again like it's all over for us. He was *feeling crazy.* The *bad thoughts were coming* for him again. I was all, *Oh baby don't say that stupid shit. I'll come see you soon. We'll talk it out.* And he was all, *I love you! I love you! I love you! I love you! And keep your phone on you please! Please! Please!* Then he ghosted me.

Julie Ann was the one who first told me he tried to kill himself. I was shocked, no shit. Shocked but not surprised. The way his mind works, if I won't escape with him what else is he supposed to do?

Fucking Jeremy. If I had the chance, I wouldn't use Dad's pistol or utility knife. I'd knock him out somehow and tie a skate lace around his neck and cinch it tighter with quarters until his veins popped out and his cheeks turned the color of wet lavender, the same way he used to look before he held me down and rapped his middle knuckle on my breastplate, that bastard. Julie Ann would get over it. She could get over anything but losing her texting thumbs. She's been texting me about how she was texting Poppy Rudd that she's a skank with chlamydia and texting Jeremy that he shouldn't sleep with Poppy because she's a skank with chlamydia and texting her mom about can she push curfew back tonight because she wants to smoke a bowl with Jeremy even though I told her fifty times not to since he probably really has chlamydia because he really is a skank. Ugh!

And Julie Ann wants to hang out with his crew tonight, so I texted her that he and his friends are insane and there's no telling what they'll do to her once they get her alone. She says she wants to find out, but she really doesn't. She's just acting tough. Just like how she and Sandra used to brag about how they'd done this and that with some guy at camp or in the townball field dugout. So, duh, I didn't think it was the biggest deal to have sex with Heath, especially since he's so sweet and thoughtful and he wrote me that song that he played on his guitar, and he made me that wreath of wildflowers. Then I told them what'd happened, and they got quiet before admitting that they're both virgins and didn't I know they were only kidding about what boys like and how to do this or that to enhance my orgasms? No, I didn't! Like, if I'd told them I was pregnant, would they have said, "That's crazy! We don't even have vaginas!"?

This morning Mom came downstairs to tell me about Heath's suicide attempt. She had on that gigantic butterscotch shawl over her white Vikings t-shirt. Her hair was up in a butterfly clip. Her eyes scanned the room for clues to the many mysteries she hasn't solved just yet, angry little pupils like I's dotted with a black gel pen. She was holding a roll of toilet paper. She wadded up a couple dozen sheets and stuffed them in the pocket of her shawl, for my tears.

"Why, Mom? Why'd he do it? If only I could've been there for him ..." She didn't even furrow her brow or give up some crocodile tears, but I put on a great show. I mean, no duh, it's sad. Except if Heath's dead I won't have to keep stringing him along with plans to leave town, elope or whatever. If he's really dead, it won't matter whether Emma believed me when I told her he didn't know about the baby. With all the other things we talked about she probably doesn't remember that part anyway. If she remembers, she believes me. I couldn't let her get ideas about him. He'd be the first to go down for what happened. He was always gonna be the first. Not Jeremy. Not Doleman. Not Dad. I tried hard for Heath. I really did. I had to remember all those itty-bitty details on the ride over to the ice cream shop. One big lie always becomes a million little ones. One lie is easy to tell. A million? Fuck, only Heath can manage that.

The night she died I got home and put on the raincoat that was in Mom's trunk. It covered my shirt and shorts. I went inside and Jeremy laughed and said I looked like a stripper. Mom was in the bedroom. I hurried down to the laundry room to throw a load in because that's what Dad told me to do. I'd called him just before that. I said, "Daddy, I killed her."

I knew it would come to this. If someone asked questions. If someone learned something they weren't supposed to.

"What do we do, then?" Heath asked me, a frantic little boy that night. The night she died.

"We tell them it was Jeremy."

That was the plan.

Months ago, we didn't need plans like that. We didn't need anything. We had everything already. Me and Heath were parked in the Pfeiffer's Drugstore lot, drinking malts, and he was so excited to be a father he started drumming on the glovebox of Mom's car and shouting out names. "Gordon. Perry. And … Melvin."

"And if it's a girl, you sexist ass?"

"Lauren. Cheryl. And, um … Whitney. I know, Gwen or Bonnie."

Nothing that comes from his lips ever sounds made up. He's so funny like that. "I can do cars," he'll joke, pretending to sell Mom's to me, rubbing his hands on the dash and bragging about the low mileage and explaining the finer points of the latest tire rotation, oil change, and total-body inspection. "All of them, by the way, have been performed by me or under my supervision." If I'm not already dying, I always crack up at that line.

I was happy then, too, there in the car, thinking about our baby. So happy I almost forgot how badly I wanted him to be the one to say we needed to get rid of it. It was like a dry run for the happy I'll be when I actually have a baby someday. When I'm lounging on one of those sprawling summer Twin Cities' patios, sipping a drink with an umbrella in it, ordering food from the kids' menu, mac-and-cheese or corndogs. While everyone else is still back here, still being stupid, still throwing parties to celebrate their stupidness. Because I won't be like these women. Smug like Mom and Emma, who just wouldn't stop rubbing her belly in front of me. I won't work at that dumb carbon plant. I won't pretend I'm fulfilled by gardening projects and home catalogs, blah. I'll go to college and work a good job. Work for good people doing good work for good pay.

The hiccup was that I had to tell Heath. Sometimes, like when I have to break plans, he goes silent for five whole minutes. He bites his arm and saliva oozes from the corners of his mouth. One time he drew blood. So I tweaked my argument a bit and told him that we'd be stranded in Sibley from now to eternity if I went through with the pregnancy. But this didn't work on him, either.

Somehow, he still doesn't hate my family. Even though Mom and Dad wouldn't let me invite him to dinner. Even though Dad refused to come to the door when he stopped by to introduce himself, pitting out in his too-big white button-up. Even though Jeremy and his goons took turns pissing in his locker before the janitor finally put a new lock on. He didn't hate them the way I figured he did, God knows why. Sometimes it was like he enjoyed how shitty they were toward him. Just a little bit, anyway. At least this way he was part of the family, and what could've tied us all together better than a child, even if it meant endless punishment and harassment from Dad and Jeremy and even Mom?

"Where'd you sleep, Heath?" I asked him this one time.

They caged him up in the winter, so he loved spring, summer, and fall. He dozed under trees, on stoops, beneath bushes, in the ditches of dirt roads hoping someone would come along thinking he was dead so he could jump up and run off laughing.

"Weren't you scared, honey?"

"Always," he said. One older brother, Martin, Merlin—it started with an M—liked to finger his girlfriend, then give Heath wet willies. He'd slug Heath in the cherries and push his head against the bedroom window. "I held off as long as I could," Heath said. It was worse than pissing his pants, the tears leaking out, he said.

"Honey? Honey? What happened with that guy? Did he hurt you?" It wasn't always the homes. Wasn't always the kids, either. Uncle Bob, crashing at his sister's place. Heath didn't wanna talk about him and that's how I could tell it was bad. Because if he couldn't lie about it, that meant he couldn't handle telling himself the truth.

"Doesn't matter," he said, "because my sister, Cynthia the Rat, came with the heavy machinery and busted us out right quick." Cynthia the Rat. These ridiculous names. He said she had buck teeth and hairy cheeks and matted down redhead braids. She walked hunched over with her hands in front of her. He said he liked to drop bits of mozzarella on the floor in front of her. He wanted Uncle Bob's help building a trap for her. Back then he loathed her because she was always talking about France and fancy coffee and famous scientists. Her favorite topic was how there are more planets like Earth in our galaxy than grains of sand on Earth. Drove him insane, the thought itself as much as her never shutting up about it.

"Looking back, though," he said, "she was my first mother. She could've left me behind when she split." Instead, she took all the kids with her.

The "heavy machinery"? One day after school, middle of winter, innocent little Heath was in the garage with Uncle Bob, his hero at the time, when in ran Rat holding a handsaw in one hand and a hammer in the other. Their sister Jill Koozie had broken a pair of scissors. She clutched a blade in each hand. Someone had a tire iron. Skink, his brother, a screwdriver. Everyone was yelling at everyone else and then Heath started crying so hard he couldn't hear. He crawled out of the garage and ran up the driveway and hid behind an oak trunk. "The oaks were big there along the driveway. I thought they were giants." It was snowing good. His tears turned to "scabs" on his cheeks. He thought everyone was dead. Then his Mom's van rolled down the driveway, Rat driving. She leaned on the horn and the side door slid open and they yelled at him to get in. Finally, Rat jumped out and wrestled him to the ground and dragged him into the van.

They stopped in some back alley so they could swap license plates with a vehicle parked in an open garage. Rat had a bunch of dollars rolled up in a rubber band. They drove for a while, then parked in the woods. "Living was just being cold and trying to be warm. Just arguing about everything and climbing trees and finding somewhere off in the woods to piss without nobody watching." Being hungry so long you're not hungry anymore, how can there be such a thing? "Eating heat from the van vents. Drinking snow." They were all sick, too. "Throat choking down gravel, nose packed with gunk." "Stumbling from tree to tree some days just wanting to get kidnapped by someone better." Rat bought him cough syrup at a gas station. He drank it and she talked to him about the planets and outer space and God.

He ran into some friends at a gas station and got picked up by social services. Rat made sure he didn't go back to Uncle Bob.

Murphy, that was that boy's name. Murphy, the bully with those filthy fingers.

A few days after I told him we were pregnant, we met up again. It was ten at night. Rainy and cool. I told him my decision and he closed his eyes and hung his head and nodded, consoling himself or whatever, then he got out of the car and disappeared for a bit. While he was gone, I listened to the radio. I've always hated silence. I've always hated the silent-thoughts. I hate them even more now. He came back with wet hair and knuckles all cut up and gory from punching a tree. Idiot. I wasn't scared of him. I've never been scared of him. I felt bad, though, so I lied and told him I'd think about it some more. Later on, after the procedure, I called to tell him what I'd done. I didn't wanna tell him. I tried hard to think of a way around it. I could tell he was irate, only it was weird because he wasn't mad at me or was too distracted to lash out. By what I don't know, but his wheels were really turning. Maybe it's just that I could never do anything to make him hurt me. He loves me too much. And he thinks I'll never stop needing him, especially now.

He's wrong. I love him but he's wrong. He's the one who needs me. I don't need anybody. Like, after the stirrups and clamps and tubes. The numb and suction. Fetus, placenta. Cramping, discharge. After all that, I'll never be un-clamped, -tubed, -numbed, -suctioned again. Good, I've realized. I see that now. Good. That doctor cut out the part of me that is Sibley, that is Spencer, that is this house and the people in it. I don't need them. Not anyone. When I leave it'll be for good. Heath will understand. I mean, he *would've*. He's dead. I know it in my heart, and I love him, *loved* him, and I'm happy for him. He doesn't have a reason to come back, either.

The front door bangs open. Two sets of feet thunder down-stairs, Jeremy's and Dad's, I can tell.

Jeremy throws open the guest room door and Dad grabs him by the waist. I jump out of bed looking for something to defend myself with. My phone is a rock, my keys claws.

"You little slut!" Jeremy yelps.

"If this is about Julie Ann ..."

"You fucking whore!"

Ashes, Ashes

Heath

I'm not ready to open my eyes just yet. Something is waiting for me. I know it's not nothing, because at least the sun is here, the same disgusting blood orange from yesterday, blotting the fuzzy black of my inner eyelids with peach, scarlet, and lemon tones. It's not nothing, because at least I'm conscious. Consciousness just seems to be this infected wound that won't heal but won't bleed you out either. I sit up straight and open my eyes. The room is beautiful, like, sarcastically gorgeous.

It can't be meant for me, the glossy clean-white cabinets and prickly stucco ceiling and smooth, bright navy walls and neat tile floor and throne-like hospital bed and perfect IV bag on its perfect stand with its perfect needle in my perfect hand. My gown feels silky. It caresses my legs and arms and stomach and there's the soothing pressure of my thigh wraps and the crinkly paper sheet underneath me. Where the pain should be, it's not. If only it were there. Or better, I felt nothing.

On the counter across the room, in a plastic bag, is an off-white, bloodstained bathrobe. I remember everything. In the bathtub, blood serpents slithered up from my slashed thighs.

A woman (maybe thirty, no older than thirty-five) pokes her head into the room. Seeing that I'm awake, she enters the room. She wears heels and pantyhose, a cobalt blouse, and a charcoal pencil skirt with a matching suit coat. Her platinum-streaked beige hair is a cinnamon roll atop her head. Unbound tufts twirl down the sides of her face. She holds a clipboard.

"Hello, Mr. Reynolds. I'm Doctor Candice Granger. Please call me Candice." Her voice is calm, firm, prim, except her squinty, vigilant caramel eyes belong to someone fussier.

I nod at Candice, and she stares at me, pouting, poorly mimicking my helplessness. Her bedside manner needs some work. It's like she's mocking me.

She shuts the door and sits on the sofa beneath the window-sill.

"May I call you Heath?"

I shrug.

"Heath it is, then."

"Candy?"

"Candice," she corrects me. Polite but stern.

"You an investigator?"

"What would I be investigating?"

"I don't know."

"You aren't in any trouble. I'm a psychiatrist. I'm here to talk with you about the reason you're here."

"*You all* are the reason I'm here. If it were up to me, I'd be somewhere else."

"That is what I'd like to talk about—"

"I'd rather not, Candy."

"We don't have to talk right away. For now, know that we have a room available in what we call a Grace Unit. It's a safe place. We can run some exams on you, we can get you started on some medication, we can monitor you … It's an excellent facility. We do, however, need to ask some questions. Do you have any family members around who could assist us? Phone numbers, places of work. All that information would be helpful. I also have a bit of paperwork we need to fill out, insurance—"

"That all sounds nice. You should save the room for someone else. I'm actually feeling much better now."

"But—"

"Does anybody call you Candy?"

She lowers her eyes to her clipboard, makes a note. "No one," she replies.

"Ever?"

"Not that I can recall."

"But you could've forgotten if somebody had?"

"I suppose."

"But you didn't forget," I insist.

"Why do you say that?"

"Because it bothers you."

"I just don't like the name. That's all." A mannequin smile.

"Who called you that?"

"Let's talk about you, Heath."

"Do you know what death is like?"

Her eyes spring open. "Of course not."

"Then how can you be so sure it isn't better than living?"

"You're right, I suppose I don't. All the same I'd like to speak with your parents or guardian. Do you have their phone numbers? Are they in your cellphone?"

"I didn't plan on taking it with me. Sorry. Candy sounds like a dirty nickname."

"Perhaps. Happen to remember their cell numbers?"

"Maybe."

"You wanna call someone?"

"No."

"Your dad?"

I gaze up at the stucco, sigh, and begin to yammer about my dad like I was just thinking about him. Like I ever met the guy.

"My dad lives in a trailer park in Hackensack, about an hour north of here. You turn off the highway just past that sign that reads 'Jesus Saves', for some church, and just before the one that says 'dot, dot, dot, For Retirement,' for some bank. Last time I saw him was five years ago. He took me fishing up in Walker with one of his high school friends. The guy's wife, believe it or not, died in the Oklahoma City bombing. Very sad. Summertime, Dad went fishing every Sunday after church. He hated church but he liked having a reason to drive into town on Sunday mornings. His only other reason was the liquor store, except back then liquor stores were closed on Sundays. And he liked having an excuse to wear collared shirts. You see, he was a mechanic, if he happened to get out of bed, I mean. Anyway, he took me and Rod, his Oklahoma buddy, up to Leech Lake. Pulled his boat on a trailer. Boat was real nice. We had everything: seat cushions, life vests, lures, minnows. We trawled for sunfish. Dad sat in the back next to the motor. I went through two entire packages of sunflower seeds, drank six Mountain Dews one after another. I kept having to stand and pee over the side of the boat. Dad told me that my Dew-piss was poisoning the sunnies. I kept laughing and laughing and laughing. Long story short, he and Rod ran off together later that summer. Never saw him again."

"That's—"

"Mom was an angel. She taught me everything I ever needed to know. The most important thing I learned from her is that the worst shit in the world doesn't last forever. Pain and worry will outlive us all. It took me a long time to see what I needed to do, but figuring it out brought me so much peace."

"Suicide, you mean?"

"Uh-huh."

"And is your mother around?"

"She was murdered."

"I'm sorry."

"You have any children, Candy?"

"I have a son. He's six."

"That's nice. Who called you Candy?"

"I'm sorry?"

"I'm wondering who called you Candy."

"I don't see the point in—"

"Because you don't wanna talk about it."

"You want me to be uncomfortable?" she asks.

"I'm hoping to piss you off a little."

"Why?"

"If you hate me, you won't be so sad when I'm gone."

"Do you push a lot of people away like that?"

"Not enough of them."

She jots down more notes, looks up. "It was my grandfather who called me that. He was not a good man. He was violent with my grandmother. Plus, it's a rotten nickname, in my opinion. I find it disrespectful."

"I'll quit, then."

"Call me whatever you please, Heath. May I ask where you were living? Is there anyone you can call?"

"I'll think on it. But I need to get some sleep. Say, you know what this is for?" On my bed is a detonator-looking stick connected to another IV bag via a long cord.

"It's for pain management. Just hit the button if you're hurting. You can't overdose, it'll only give you so much."

I close my eyes, return to the fireworks in my eyelids.

"Thank you, Heath, for being so open with me. I'll be requesting that the nurses keep a close eye on you. We'll talk more later."

"You're the boss, Dr. Granger. Sorry your grandpa sucked so much."

"Thanks, Heath."

She's motionless for several seconds. No scribbling on her papers, no brushing lint from her shoulder. Then she stands to exit the room.

"I did it," I say.

"Did …?"

"Mom. I killed her. I need to sleep now, Dr. Granger. You've been very kind to me, and I sincerely appreciate it."

She asks a series of questions about the half-real, half-fictional woman she believes is my mother, becoming increasingly baffled and pesky the longer I ignore her, talking the way she might to her son when the boogeyman haunts him.

It's tricky because I can't open my eyes until she leaves the room but I can't afford to waste any time once she's gone. She might not be gone for long. I gotta get out.

I peek with one eye. The room is empty. I trigger the detonator again and again until my thumb cramps up, wait a minute as the numbing juices pour into my veins, then get busy untaping the syringe from my hand and pulling the IV needle out. I'm too woozy to climb down from the bed so I try to steady myself by staring at the sun, which looks ready to vomit. The hairs on my arms stand up. I swallow some acidic bile.

When did I last eat and what'd I just pump into my body and what floor am I on and who gave the doctors my name and where is Monica and does she think I'm alive or dead or barely-alive-almost-dead. And was it, would it have been, that put-on surprise from my classmates and teachers, "Oh my God, I can't believe he went and done something like this, no, he was such a happy boy always, oh no, maybe we should've treated him a tad better"?

I'm wobbly. My legs buzz. The thigh wraps are tight and the seeping from my wounds causes the gauze to stick. Each step toward the door tugs at the skin around them. On the way out of the room, I slip into the bathroom, turn the sink faucet on, step out, and shut the door behind me. I grab the plastic bag containing Miss Bonnie's robe and sneak into the hallway, eyes on the floor, avoiding the grout between the tiles because Monica could never love me again if I step on it, that old gag showing its face again. Still, what type of lunatic would risk losing the woman he loves over something as simple as accidentally stepping on grout?

I step into the next room over. An old man is sleeping, his handlebar mustache cloud-gray and thorny. In his own plastic bag are cowboy boots, a straw cowboy hat, and jeans stinking of manure. Must be he's one of those snus-gobblers collecting bailouts from the government whether the crop comes in or not. I put the hat on. It covers the top half of my head, fits clear over both my ears. My gown tumbles to the ground and I throw on Miss Bonnie's abrasive robe, tightening the belt around my waist. Then I slip on a pair of grippy socks. Candice and some dude return to my room. They call out for me, knocking on the bathroom door. The farmer mumbles. His eyes flutter open. Groggy, he says, "Who the hell are you?"

"An angel."

"My hat ..."

I dart back into the hallway and head in the opposite direction of my room, stepping on every gap possible. She'll love me again. She'll love me again. She'll love me again. No, she won't. She'll love me again. Just as I glance up and spot the exit sign at the end of the hallway, Candice calls my name. I move as fast as I can, a shuffle-almost-speedwalk, toward the door. Seconds later Candice is standing in front of me next to a cross-eyed behemoth in scrubs.

"Where you going?" she asks.

"I'm not crazy."

"I didn't say—"

"You can't keep me here."

"Heath, I really think it'd be wise—"

"Don't you get it, lady? I'm not sticking around."

"I'm pleading with you. Let us help you. Whatever's going on, we can fix it, you and I. Maybe not right away but in time."

"I'm going far away. Siberia or Somalia or maybe Toledo. Somewhere. Don't worry, you'll never hear from me again."

"Heath, you also need medical attention. Those injuries—"

"I have business to take care of, people I need to visit."

"I don't like the sound of that, Heath."

"You would if you ever met them."

"Heath—"

I'm already down the hallway and through the exit door. They follow me to the elevator, and I go in. When she tries to step in next to me the behemoth holds an arm out in front of her. The elevator door closes.

I get off on the second floor and take the stairs the rest of the way in case they're waiting for me on the first, scheming to snatch me up and strap me into a wheelchair. I pass the reception desk and shove my way through the revolving doors.

Freedom. It's so goddamn goopy-hot out the nurses are smoking right outside the doors so they can dip back in as soon as possible. I tilt the hat forward, right above my eyebrows, and start away from the hospital. I shuffle through the heat-haze of the parking lot, past some rundown single-family dumps, between two brick buildings (a dry cleaners and a salon), and reach the sidewalk along Highway 210, which cuts Brainerd in two.

There's no real reason why the things that happen happened, your fault or not. Most times they're your fault. Most times they are. But the *reason* something happened is really just another *something-happened* looking for another reason for it to have happened, onto infinity, all that. Whatever. So, like, long before Monica's decision, *the* decision, I was a boy who left Miss Bonnie's place to revisit the house of my childhood torture. And before that I was a boy who didn't know I needed to revisit the house of my childhood torture, because I didn't know quite that it was torture. And before that I was a boy who didn't know how much I'd someday love and hate and miss Miss Bonnie, because I didn't know her from any pack-a-day in the county. And before that I was a boy up in that cold grey garage loft, one of many probably, being tortured and not knowing it. These things happened.

He was tall and had a long brown ponytail and wore work boots, plaid, and jeans with oil-stained knees. In the loft was a cot, a bunch of quilts, a space heater, and a shade-less lamp in the corner. "Until I fix the truck engine," he'd say when I asked how long he was staying. He liked to laugh, his belly jiggling over the top of his jeans, his face contorting like he was having digestive problems. At the time, I was just taking the dare of drinking his "good-boy water" (vodka, I have to guess because the smell has always made me gag), then just waking up on his cot in the loft as the mini-fridge motor below groaned like one long pulled root, the groan just a whisper out of the frigid dark, "Hush," like even it was in on the secret. At the time, it was just a game like any other you can't win until it's over, when I spat and then chomped down on my tongue to rinse my mouth with the taste of iron, just a game I needed to win if I was ever gonna be as tough as he was. Real tough. Boy, was I lucky to have him.

The torture began long after I escaped it, when I finally put it together that Cynthia the Rat hadn't kidnapped me. She'd rescued me. Then the occasional musty odor of sawdust and clammy jeans began to stir up that *No, no, no, please don't, please anything but*, or the occasional *No, no, no, please don't, please anything but* began to stir up the musty odor of sawdust and clammy jeans, pick your poison. Then I could relive the event with a terror and rage that fit the experience.

I decided to return to that house, walk into the garage, beat him to death with the first tool I put my hands on. This was the only time I ran away from Miss Bonnie's and even this doesn't really count because I was only gone for the afternoon. It was August. Fourteen years old, a year away from my driver's permit, I stole her car. I imagined the garage walls at my former foster mom's house armed with mauls and hammers and chainsaw chains and shrub clippers. I imagined Uncle Bob old and feeble even though it'd only been four or five years.

Sure as shit, there he was in the garage. He wasn't alone. With him was some little boy then living in the house. Uncle Bob didn't seem to recognize me, at least not until he had the knife in his hand. Then it was like he'd been waiting for me, like I wasn't the first man to return to him with revenge on the mind, jaw taut, eyes narrowed. He bought me and the boy sunflower seeds and Mountain Dew, brought us fishing. I didn't drink the Dew. I didn't wanna pee over the side of the boat like he and the boy did, laughing about how they were poisoning sunnies. Afterward, he (the little boy called him Robbie) drove us back to his sister's house and parked the boat in the grass next to the driveway and carried the string of fish into the garage and slung them down on a card table and showed us how to filet them. During the demonstration, he called me Heath. I told him when I showed up that day that my name was Barney. Prick.

I couldn't bring myself to do it, not when he had his back to me as he monkeyed with the finicky boat motor, not when I sat in the back seat, right behind him, and stared at the seatbelt dangling to his left, an immaculate right-there-for-Christ's-sake noose, not when he handed me the filet knife and said, "Now it's your turn, Heath" like I wasn't thinking, You son of a bitch. And he: Stick me back if you'd like, it's only fair. And me: Son of a bitch. And he: What are you gonna do about it? Stab me if you're so bent up out of shape. And me: Fuck you, you nasty son of a bitch.

I just stood there, deader than the bass, and handed him the knife back so he could cut the head and tail off, grind the scales off with the dull base of the blade, and so on, saying, "Heath, pay attention. Pay attention, Heath. What are you looking at? The loft? I can show you what it's like up there later if you'd like."

I drove back to Miss Bonnie's. My siblings watched me and Miss Bonnie in the back yard as I buried my face in her sleeve and wailed. She didn't say a word about the stolen van. Not that I expected her to, the way I was blubbering, humiliated by how pathetic, weak and cowardly and stupid, I was. Her affection deepened the pain. Like, imagine a boy who's allergic to the peppermint ointment his momma rubs so tenderly on his sternum. Every kind word made me squirm. All those years with her and I still couldn't square her unconditional loving with my boyhood of park benches and back alleys and dive bathrooms and liquor-soaked sofas. My survival and contentment should've, by the rationale of everything I'd ever known, meant nothing to her, yet meant everything.

I've seen miracles. The first was that I told Miss Bonnie what happened in the loft, and over the next few months the terror and rage that accompanied those memories weakened. The second was that she treated me no differently after learning how pathetic, weak and cowardly and stupid, I really truly to-my-core was.

That should've been it. I should've turned the corner. I should've grown. Maybe I did, just a bit. But I couldn't stop the wheels from turning, my brand of consciousness too rich for my own blood. The terror and rage found new memories, new fears. An incessant mind. The fact that I desperately needed to find and kill Bob instead of find and thank Cynthia is all Dr. Granger would ever need to know about me.

The mall isn't far. I slog across town, slouching a few degrees deeper after each stoplight. Eight fast food places. Four liquor stores. Three grocery stores. Two pharmacies. One porn shop. Drivers gawk at me, truck engines rev, kids on bikes call me a faggot. The sky breathes into the coal sun glistening, and I stare at it because if I don't Dr. Granger's son will die in the Iranian War when he's twenty-three. I can save him from dying in battle if I stare long enough. If I stare long enough, he'll develop an aggressive form of prostate cancer later in life but the doctors will catch it early, never mind the farm boys in their mufflerless trucks or the bigots on bicycles. Still, there's a seventy-percent chance that Monica will overdose on prescription pills at some point in the next decade and she may or may not have the type of friends around who will call an ambulance or rush her to the emergency room to have her stomach pumped, so I must keep staring, staring, staring, at the sun until I have to close my eyes. Then I almost walk into the street. A horn honks at me, the honking and the burning of my eyelids two sensations paired together like a screeching demon yakking hellfire on me. Let's say Hell exists.

The night before the murder, Monica called. I took the call out on the sidewalk in front of Miss Bonnie's. For the past week Monica had been telling me she was sick, and I kept asking her how she was, if she needed anything, how her tummy felt. When she told me why she couldn't see me, what she'd done, how she'd come to her decision, all of it in one long, sloppy, stalling confession, I didn't say much. My blurry vision was a mystery to me. It turned out I hadn't blinked for at least a minute and was trying to see through tears. Eventually she said goodbye, claimed her mom was calling her name. I didn't hear anyone in the background. I dropped my phone on the concrete.

I couldn't go back inside. Instead, I paced around the block, whispering to myself, "She killed it. She killed it. She killed it," like I'd have forgotten about it all otherwise. This "it" had no flesh I could caress one last time, no final breath, no sex, no name, no heartbeat—according to those highway signs infesting the stretch of highway between here and Sibley, there to comfort moralizers with fish stickers on their cars and crucifix tats on their lower backs—had no essence except for what I dreamt up in the blood-black clouds that night, nothing for a eulogy but me whispering "She killed it," no proof of having lived save the fact that a thing like it can be killed.

I'm dragging my feet now. I'm starving but I might puke if I eat. It's not quite pain, except the numb isn't quite as numb as it was a few blocks ago. I smell the mall before I see it, fryer grease and popcorn.

Monica doesn't wanna see me again and doesn't wanna leave with me and doesn't daydream about me the way I do about her, and she wouldn't endure for me what I have for her. And later on when the man who will become her husband and who will father her children and who will drive them all back to Sibley for Thanksgiving and Easter asks her if she's been with anyone else, she'll lie and tell him he's the first or say it was nothing, say the boy was nothing, say the boy was just a mistake she made when she was a flighty child with a reptilian brain. I'd have done better to stay dead.

Now she has no reason not to rat me out and tell her dad that she, no shit, didn't help me kill Miss Bonnie and so Doleman will be free to lock me away and keep me from Travis's daughter just in case she changes her mind and loves me again, which she won't. She doesn't love me, she doesn't love me, she doesn't love me. And the only reason she hasn't already told her father that I killed Miss Bonnie without her help is that she pities me.

So how many could I take with me if I got back to the shotgun? She'd be mad at first but eventually (after ten or twenty or fifty years) she'd see the blessing of my rampage, that I'd unshackled her from her family. By then I'd be so far out of her life she wouldn't remember my name. Or maybe she'd remember me fondly wherever she is, remember the unshackling, cherish her liberty. Romance is dying a hero to the woman you love.

I yelp and slap myself twice, the flush smacks stinging. Adrenaline jolts up my spine and I open my eyes. On the bench in the shade behind the mall sits a couple. They're my age and they've been watching me. They've probably seen everything. Their disbelief disappears when they break into laughter. I walk toward them, and they stand hand in hand and scamper off to clear the bench for me. I sit down, lie on my side, loosen the robe's belt to let some air in, and tilt the hat down so it covers my face completely.

"You're a good boy, Heath, with a good heart," Miss Bonnie would tell me.

I was born for one purpose, to be the pastor and reader and sole mourner for that unnamed heart or beating nonheart or thoughtless, dreamless, faceless, screamless, fleshless organism whose soul existed only out of that lessness that proved it had existed in my own, that proved I ever had one to begin with, a soul.

"What'd I tell you? You can forget about all that now. All those old places where you slept," she said.

A gravedigger too. With my phone I butchered the anthill in the crack between the sidewalk and the lawn, gouged deep.

"You won't run from my place, sweet boy. Nope," she said.

It doesn't matter where you draw the line. Almost dead is the same as alive, almost alive is the same as dead, unborn, and you can't undo a thing once done any more than you can recast the hex to rid you of it, undo striking someone with a strength you didn't know you had, dropping her to the kitchen floor.

"Nope. You're gonna remember this one above all those other ones you didn't run away from for no reason," she said.

Home, home, home, home.

"Home," she said.

***

I wake up on the bench to Monica saying, "But why, Heath?"

"I killed her."

169

"Why?"

"I killed her."

"Why? Why? Why? Why? Why?"

My skin is clammy, my pain an achy pulse. Miss Bonnie's robe is open wide, and the breeze is hot and moist. I can't have been sleeping long because the shadows behind the mall are just as they were when I fell asleep. Some Samaritan tucked a ten-dollar bill into the pocket of the robe. Score.

As I stumble into the air-conditioned mall, I smell Groucho's Pizza, basil and sausage grease. My stomach groans. I go right up to the heat lamp where fresh pizzas steam and sweat and I tear off half of one and fold it over and walk out. A cook behind me yells, "Dude?!" I bumble as quickly as I can to Macy's on the other side of the mall, scarfing down gobs of cheese that scald my mouth. I hold the pizza behind my back when I think I'm gonna puke in a center island trashcan. I swallow the vomit, keep walking, devouring the rest of the pizza by the time I reach Macy's. I lower the hat on my brow. This way no one will get a look at my face while I'm perusing the men's section for a t-shirt.

Three years ago, Miss Bonnie spent the first weeks of spring talking up the majesty of the Mississippi River, then surprised me and my siblings with a day-trip to Itasca State Park. From there the river begins its twenty-five-hundred-mile trip down through the States. She drove us from one podunk scat-castle town to the next, crooning all twangy to the oldies station, disregarding Chubby, Ren, and me as we elbowed one another in the ribs. In the seats behind me Toby Genzel licked the window and wrote notes in her saliva and Mariah pen-sketched cruciform Jesus, shredded abs and all, on her thigh.

I must say, given all the hype, I was disappointed. It was like the headwater rocks and the squirrelly eddies between them actually decreased in size as I got closer. And the whole place stunk of rotting animal carcasses. Whatever, we took off our shoes and socks and walked stone to stone across the water. On the way back to the car for a hot nap in the van, I saw the doe, swollen, rotten. I couldn't fall asleep. It wasn't the van's scorching polyester. It was Monica.

She has this quality of seeming from a distance complete and graceful and in control of herself, exactly who she is, was, will forever be, though up close she's like me. She yawns and sneezes and coughs and farts and thinks thoughts as dumb as I do sometimes. The idea of Monica wouldn't have gotten me this far fucked up. And only the real thing can save me now, the thing that napped on the plaid living room couch at Miss Bonnie's, drooling onto Toby's baptismal blanket that Toby's grandma finished knitting days before she had her last stroke and that Toby left for Miss Bonnie as a token of her gratitude. I drew the shades and brushed Monica's hair out of her face and, using the blanket, dabbed away drool.

Three years ago, though, there was just the idea of her. When Valentine's Day came around, Miss Bonnie told me I was blushing. She asked how she was supposed to help me introduce myself to my crush if she didn't know the girl's name. I didn't want help. Anyway, Monica already knew my name, if little else about me.

"Does she like you?" Miss Bonnie asked.

"No. Not really."

"No?"

"You're blushing, too, Miss Bonnie."

"I'm just so happy for you."

I wanted to buy Monica chocolates. I asked Miss Bonnie if Monica preferred dark or milk chocolate.

She laughed. "Why don't you ask her?"

"That's crazy," I said. "And how do I make sure she knows they're from me?"

"You gotta talk to her."

"That's crazy."

At the grocery store in Sibley was a special aisle full of cards and stuffed animals and chocolates. At the end was a bucket of rose bouquets.

We met at checkout. I wasn't holding chocolates, but roses.

"Changed your mind, then?"

"I guess so."

I left them on the kitchen table for her. Hours later they were gone. I think she brought them to her room.

In Macy's, the biggest shirt I can find for less than ten dollars is an XXXL with the words "Just Big Boned" printed on the front. It almost reaches my knees. The clerk, reeking of the lemon zest sample perfume from the station beside her, looks at me like I'm wearing a bathrobe and cowboy hat. I buy the shirt, tip the brim of my hat toward her, and leave the store.

In the bathroom, I strip down to my underwear, put the gigantic shirt on. I leave the rest of my garments, cowboy hat included, in the waste bin. Then I walk to the Target on the other side of the mall and find a pair of khaki shorts long enough to hide my bandages but short enough for the shirt to cover them. After sliding them on in a secluded nook in the men's department, I return to Macy's to exchange the shirt for one that fits.

"What's wrong with it?" asks the teen at the returns desk. He has a mullet-mop of black hair, pupils so dilated his irises appear black.

"It's too big," I say.

"Didn't you try it on before you bought it?"

"I really should've, huh? Next time."

"Whatever. We can give you store credit."

"Fair enough."

My new shirt is plain grey. I go back one more time to Target for fresh socks and a pair of sneakers, which I wear as I walk out the front door unimpeded. After a swig of water at the fountain, I find the nearest exit and step into the sunlight again.

Immediately I'm pitting out, sun-sapped. I head back toward the four-lane highway that runs north back to Sibley and south to Saint Cloud and Minneapolis. Revenge or escape?

Wait, how the fuck did I get to the hospital in the first place? Dorian. Dory. Dorian the Mute. Bunkie. He's the one who gave the doctors my name, too.

After a brief pause at its apex, the rickety wooden roller coaster descended, and my stomach rushed into my skull and Monica's hair stuck straight up. She opened her mouth to scream but didn't or maybe I just couldn't hear her over the ride. She'd come to the Crow Wing County Fair because The Concrete Nipples were performing at the talent show. She watched my solo from the crowd of two dozen. I was real afraid of putting my fingers on the wrong frets or missing a string entirely like a moron, so I couldn't look at her. After, she tried talking to me but I was acting shy. I couldn't speak loud enough for her to hear me, even as she inched her ear closer to my mouth, the motion almost disastrous since I'd devoured two deep-fried pickles just an hour before.

"Let's go," she said.

"Where?"

"The roller coaster, duh!"

It made sense later on, how confidently she took my hand and on the way to the ride talked to me about my "awesome" show and the "fun stuff" she was doing at the fair and "stupid" Mr. Trevino, who confiscated her cell phone during Algebra after he caught her texting. Later on, Miss Bonnie admitted to delivering those roses to the Spencers' address on Valentine's Day, with an attached note ("To: Monica, From: Heath"), to running into Monica at the Fourth of July parade earlier that summer and mentioning that I liked her.

I can't blame Miss Bonnie for having no idea what she was getting me into, can't blame her for something that brought me closer to Monica. That brought me Thursday morning second-period bakery runs, "Ditch for Donuts Days," and Sunday afternoon cuddles on the school's high jump landing mat, our spearmint tongues warm and spongy and frantic. We'd sneak out to meander around Sibley, through the Koetter Farm where fields of baby's breath sort of snoozed, looking like pilling cotton, and we gawked at distant thunderstorms and the stars blinking like they were arguing with one another, and we talked about horoscopes and space travel and Islam and Sitting Bull and carbon emissions.

The night I learned Monica was pregnant, I called her and told her to meet me in front of the school. "Don't bother to grab your things, either." More out of curiosity than logistics, she asked what I planned to do for money. "We'll figure it out, baby." And how we'd slip town. "In Miss Bonnie's car." She doubted that Miss Bonnie would forgive me for stealing it, that Miss Bonnie would sacrifice anything to see me happy. It was futile. Still, I said Miss Bonnie would understand when we came back to Sibley one day with her grandchild.

"They'll come after us, Heath."

"Let them," I said. I was gonna drive fast. Everything would be better once we crossed state lines. I'd never been more sure about anything. These schemes of mine.

Maybe they haven't put it together yet and so there's still time. I gotta get to her. Gotta try one last time. Maybe she'll look at me differently now that I almost died.

"You ready, baby? Let's go," I'll say.

"My God, Heath, I thought you were ..."

"There's no time to talk. This is our only chance. I'm leaving today with or without you."

"That's crazy."

"Don't call me crazy. Please. I don't like that word. You know that."

"Heath—"

"It's true, Monica. Let me rescue you."

"Okay," she'll say, so relieved.

"I love you."

"I love you, Heath."

"Honey."

"Heath."

"Monica."

But whose car will I take? Miss Bonnie's is still at Franklin's Auto and there's a bill for almost a grand magnetted to the fridge (a sweetheart deal on a new transmission). She might've saved her own life by paying it. And she had the cash, in an envelope in a kitchen drawer. I might've gone for a drive that night instead of pacing around the block thinking about what Delia told me.

After the anthill burial I went to the Spencers'. My argument with Delia is what did it. What changed everything. It wasn't Monica's fault, what she did. Not really.

Monica stripped me down and put me inside her and broke herself aching and trembling around me so that I didn't last three seconds. Then I tried to play it off like I never came at all, but she could tell. I believed myself when I told her not to worry. "It won't happen." It couldn't. I'd have worn a condom if Monica and me had one at the time and the implications of having a baby with her didn't occur to me until at least a week after she told me she was pregnant. When it hit me, really hit me, I was delirious. I was gonna be a dad with a no-explanation-needed-ever-again family and I'd never be alone. The next day I pawned my electric guitar for two hundred dollars, bought a gold wedding band, and went to Monica's house to ask Travis for her hand. I expected a no. But he and Delia had to accept me at some point, after the child was born or after Monica finished college or after she left her first husband, how I figured things. I presented the ring as a symbol of my commitment, which is what it is anyway.

Delia answered the door and wouldn't let me any farther than the stoop. She dug her ocher-painted fingernails into her palms, ivory from lack of blood. One of her knuckles cracked when she retrieved the wedding ring from the three-by-five-inch envelope I handed her—somehow I misplaced the box—and she held the ring between her pointer and thumb and dropped it onto the lawn like it was a strand of hair or piece of lint plucked from the dustpan. She snapped and was somehow more terrifying for her quiet-voice that kept Travis and Jeremy from overhearing. I couldn't look into her eyes, couldn't talk. Not that anything I might've said would've stopped her. She'd gone so far out of her mind that if I'd interrupted her just by saying her name she'd have shaken her head and shouted, "That's not me, you lying little fuck!"

South or north. Escape or vengeance. Scavenging until I bleed out or seeing Monica and bleeding out, seeing Monica and killing as many as I can, seeing Monica, Monica, Monica, Monica.

I reach the stoplights and start north along the four-lane, holding my thumb up and doing my best to attract the attention of passing trucks, especially rusty shitcans since they're most likely heading to Sibley and, if not, another nearby junkyard of a town. When one arm weakens, I hold up the other.

Monica was the first person I called. I told her to come to Miss Bonnie's place, met her on the stoop. I had a plan. In the morning I'd pay for the transmission. Cash in an envelope in a kitchen drawer. Then we'd hit the road.

I kept saying, "We gotta go. We gotta go."

And she, "You killed her? You killed her? You killed her?"

And me, "Stop crying, Monica, baby. Stop crying. Stop crying."

And she, "This is insane, Heath. Don't touch me. Don't touch me."

There are no vehicles anymore, just the here-and-there blur of red and blue and black metal. And searing pain. My arms are limp. Blood-juice trickles down both legs. At some point I stopped walking. There I stand. Goods news, though, up on the shoulder of the road is a true beater. An old grey truck, the bed crammed with lawnmowers and weed-whackers, a bunch of rakes and hoes and shovels strapped to the railing with bungee cords, the four-way flashers on. The tires look brand new, probably cost more than the truck itself.

I wanna sprint to it, jump in or tie myself to the hitch, but I only take a few haggard steps. Then the truck creaks and starts backing up. It parks alongside me, and the driver reaches across the front seat to open the door. Taking the grab-handle with both hands, I pull myself up onto the passenger's seat. I drag my legs inside and shut the door. My eyes water from the stench of the cab, sauerkraut and cigarettes and vodka. Vodka, what luck. As he puts the vehicle in gear and accelerates, his wooly hands crawl over the steering wheel, two tarantulas. He's got full-sail jowls. His beard melds with the collar of his short-sleeve forest green checkered flannel and climbs clear to his ruddy eye bags. His plump and flaky cheeks are breaded chicken breasts prepped for a pot of oil. His windburned brow is tawny and wrinkled as a rotting apple. He wears that shit-eating sneer folks put on to defend themselves against things society won't.

His voice is a yowl whistling from his beard-shrouded mouth. "You're the oddest sight I've seen in years. Can I take you to your parents? Maybe a pharmacy or something?"

"Pharmacy? No, I need to get back up to Sibley."

"Don't you need ..."

"Just Sibley, please."

"It's okay, kid. You see, the wife ran out on me twenty years ago, so I raised Mary alone. That's my daughter. Hadn't a clue what to do about it when it happened the first time. I just handed her a roll of toilet paper and called the neighbor lady. Sweet woman. She came right over. You got what you need?"

"Just my legs bleeding."

"Oh, I see—"

"I'm a dude, dude."

"Shit, you are, aren't you? Sorry about that ... Um, my name's Crosby."

"Nice to meet you. I'm Spunk. Spunk McDougle."

"Spunk, eh? The hell happened to you?"

"You got an aspirin and I'll tell you."

"In the glovebox. I'm not going as far as Sibley necessarily but I'll drop you off there."

The way his underbiting bottom row of teeth nervously chomps at his mustache compresses his expression to the top half of his face. A real sight, this Crosby character. I like him a bunch. The aspirin bottle is on a stack of wadded up invoices. When I struggle to open it, he takes the bottle, twists the cover off, and hands me three pills. I pop two in my mouth, accidentally drop the third on the floor mat. While looking for it I try to make enough spit to slide the pills down my gullet. Eventually I resort to munching them into pieces and tilting my head back and swallowing until my throat stops burning.

He lights a cigarette and sips vodka from a disposable coffee cup. I breathe through my mouth, exhale through my nose. This way I mask the scent.

"Well, bucko?"

"Yep."

"What you gotta get back to Sibley so bad for?"

I give him a sure-why-not-best-come-clean sigh. "It's all about my little sister. That's how it started. Can I get one of those smokes?"

"Sure."

I take one from the pack, light up, push the seat back, put my hands behind my head, suck down as much sweet and earthy tobacco as my lungs can hold, and exhale. I hold the cigarette right below my nose, huff it good. "Mom raised us right. Curfews, homework, extracurricular, straight As. Dad ran off with his fishing buddy, that's a long story, but Mom was an angel. Worked two jobs, one at the grocery store, another at the hardware store. Always putting food on the table. Always listening to our gripes. Always tucking us in and doing prayers with us. Always in church on Sunday. It's important that you know what a woman she was, because of what happened to her and why you found me this way, all gashed up."

"You bet, Spunk."

He's hooked now. It's a nice distraction, having Crosby here. I think about telling him everything because what difference would it make, really? And Monica's in my ear. "Why? Why? Why? Why?"

Then I get a whiff of vodka breath.

"Mind you, Sis, she isn't fifteen years old even ... She mentions this older boy who's my age. He's been following her around after school, watching her during choir class and asking her out to dances, shit like that. He's one of those rough types. An orphan. Running around and getting into fights with other kids in detention. Playing loud music on his electric guitar, acting out in class. You know what I'm talking about. He's calling the house all the time. Obsessed with her. I suppose he thought it was a cute little love story. She was a way out of town for him, maybe. He gets to thinking about college and a family and a good job, maybe. For the first time in his life, he'd be part of a respectable family with a respectable name. Sis was his ticket. That's the nicest explanation I got for why he tricked her into having sex with him. Got her high on some of his dankest bud and schemed his way into the house when Mom and I were out running errands. Sis didn't see it this way. By then she'd started saying how she's in love with him."

"Young love," he says, all wistful.

"Right. Give me a goddamn break. I know what he was thinking, too. He figured that a baby would tie them together forever. You can imagine where Mom's head was at when she found out what her fifteen-year-old daughter had growing inside of her and who was responsible for putting it there. Can I have another?"

This time I pull two cigarettes from the pack and smoke them both at once, one in each hand. Every time he sips his vodka, he peers over the lid at me. If I quit talking, even pause for anything but another drag, I'll pass out.

"Sis did always require some prodding. Had one foot on one path, the other on a different one. Mom would pour her a glass of milk and a glass of orange juice at every meal, that's how hard decisions were for her. My baby sis was so afraid of missing out on one, she couldn't choose between them. Then she'd throw fits, of course. It was easier just to appease her. Eventually Mom changed her approach, quit buying orange juice altogether. A sad day for me, I remember it well. So, there she was, Sis, researching pregnancy, maternity clothes, onesies, diapers, car seats, carriers, strollers, formula, breast feeding. Had an entire folder on the desktop devoted to her fetus. No sooner did she have her next appointment marked on the family calendar on the fridge than I learned that she was gonna have an abortion instead."

"Oh, my."

"Mom had to have spoken to her. There's just no way around it, because Sis wasn't picking that route on her own. Not a chance. And I don't know what Mom said to coax her one way over the other. The more important question is *why* Mom told her whatever it is she told her. To be honest, she'd always treated Sis's boyfriend fairly. She was a tad cold toward him at times, sure, but not rude. Never rude. Even when they came home late from the movies that time and he escorted her to the door, and he needed to use the bathroom and so he did but then he slammed the toilet seat real loud. Damn near shattered it.

He was a slam-the-toilet-seat-hard-as-you-can type of fellow. I doubt Mom quite hated him, even if she was determined to not let him hold Sis back from the future she wanted. Sis' future, that is. For Mom, it was about her daughter's opportunities. But see, the biggest question and the one that just won't quit bugging me is, what'd Sis's boyfriend think? Did he murder my mother out of—"

"*Murder* her?" he asks, sounding almost sober.

"Yes, murdered, strangled her with some type of rope he brought over. You know how these pro-lifers can be. Maybe that was it, huh. He was foaming-at-the-mouth pissed about her sin and only knew one method of making it right."

"My God, sonny—"

"Or maybe in his mind Mom was always the thing standing between him and my sis, just he was looking for a reason to do it. Maybe he had it planned out long before, knew where and how he'd do it."

"What was her name? I might've read about it in the papers."

"Gwen Bonnie. I'm sure you did."

"Doesn't ring a bell."

"But you would've read about a suicide, not a murder, because my idiot sister helped cover for him. I can imagine how those conversations went. He manipulated her, threatened her, pleaded with her. He did everything possible to get his way. She was distraught, obviously, but she didn't wanna lose both her mother *and* the love of her life. Told the police she's the one who found Mom hanging in the kitchen, cut her down herself, all this. The bozos didn't investigate any further than that."

"Gee-zus, that's some tale."

"That's how it happened." I press my forehead against the side window, my eyes burning again, my tears, with each blink, a soothing lubricant.

"Then, what?" he asks, miffed.

"Huh?"

"What's with your legs?"

"I'll tell you what's with my legs, Crosby. That dipshit convinced my sister that it wasn't enough to murder our mother. There was still someone else keeping them from their everlasting love. And could he talk to me like a man? Could he fight me face to face? Nope. My sister texted me last week, said she needed help. I came home right away, stepped inside the door, and there's her boyfriend slashing at me with a knife. If she hadn't intervened, I'd have bled to death. She called an ambulance and the two of them took off in my car. God knows where they went. I just got discharged from the hospital so now I'm heading back to gather what clues I can. If I track them down … Well, if I find them … I don't know quite what I'll do."

"Call me drunk, bucko, but you don't look so good. You sure they told you you're free to go?"

"I'll be fine. All's I need is a little nap."

I start tapping my head against the window, gently at first, then a bit harder, until I gotta roll it down so I'm not tempted to try to break it with my forehead. "You don't understand," I tell him, "just how important Mom was to me. She did everything she could so that Sis and I were never without meals, never without a bed, never without a ride to and from school or sports or dances. We were fortunate to have her. I know plenty of kids who'd give anything to be so lucky."

"I'm sure sorry for your loss, Spunk."

"Poor Spunk."

When he turns off the highway to drive me into Sibley, I ask him to drop me off in the parking lot behind the school, between the tennis courts and the football field.

He does. Like I'd hoped, it's deserted. I'm about a mile from home. He parks his truck and trailer at a slight jackknife and shakes my hand with his scruffy mitt.

"You take care of yourself. Get some rest," he tells me.

Off he goes, driving slowly, eyeing me skeptically in his rear-view mirror, like we share the same premonition of me taking one last walk through this ratty town before I save it from its own misery. Like he can hear me counting shotgun shells in my head. Two in the tube, one in the chamber. Pocket the rest.

***

I take a step and my right leg gives out like I've been sitting on it for days and I list to the right, barreling into the chain-link fence that surrounds the tennis courts. My face smooshes against the metal, my leg hanging limp, my fingers barely holding me up. Grass has grown through cracks in the courts. My fingers begin to cramp. I try to pull myself up but can't, so I rap my knuckles on my head, grab a clump of my hair, and yank my head side to the side. Then I'm walking again. Strands of hair are sweat-shellacked to my hands and for a while I struggle to slide the hairs free and flick them into the breeze.

I make my way out of the lot toward the long gravel road that leads to Bongo's street. Bongo is probably getting bronzed at the beach with his guitar and Sonya, waiting for rain or the heat index to clear the sand so they can fondle each other. But Bongo Light, Bongo's little brother who, unlike his older brother, doesn't tan so well, will probably in the inflatable pool on the patio behind Mrs. Bongo's, blazing up beneath that rollout canopy she bought to keep him from sunburning. Bongo is good people. He had my back last spring when those bungholes jumped us after Battle of the Bands and one of them tried to snap the neck of my guitar by leaning it up on the curb and stomping on it with his boot. Bongo tackled him just in time.

That was just before prom. For months Monica kept saying she wanted to lose it with me and didn't wanna lose it with me and wanted to lose it with me right away and wanted to wait until prom to lose it with me and wanted to go to prom with me wearing a hot-pink corsage and strapless turquoise dress and glitter-lotion on her collarbone and wanted to go to prom with Samuel Dunch wearing a turquoise corsage and strapless honey-brown dress and glitter-lotion on her collarbone. She went with him, and I stayed home and cranked my amp up and Miss Bonnie came into the room and stroked my head while I whimpered because it seemed Monica had been leading me on. Then two nights later she came by, glitter still on her, tears cutting through her prom rouge and cleansing again and again the same thin cheek-to-chin streaks, and talked about how she still burned from the condom and how she didn't feel about him the way she felt about me and I teared up because it seemed now she hadn't been leading me on but was just like me, confused and childish at times, which is fine.

"It won't happen," I told her.

"How do you know?"

"Does it hurt? Is it still sore?"

"It feels different."

"We don't have to."

Aching and trembling around me so that I didn't last three seconds. I tried to play it off. She could tell I came. I passed Dunch in the hallway, and he smirked at me the way he must've at her after he pulled out and thought to himself, That's all I needed from you. A sad thing, that smirk is the closest he'll ever get to being a man.

From up on Miss Bonnie's roof I could shoot up a whole four blocks, one in each direction, before anyone got a clear line of sight to snipe me, and I wouldn't be a sitting duck with the eave there and those chunky cops parked half a mile away, pretending they didn't hear the call go out. No turning back now unless Monica says she's coming with me. If she says yes, I'll save the bullets for the road.

If Dorian shows up, he'll die with the rest of them. He couldn't even bother to say my name. I disgust him just like I did back when he came to Miss Bonnie's and somehow just knew what had happened to me. Maybe I gave it away somehow. Maybe there was some tell. No, his brother must've told him. Murphy. Murphy. Always slamming Miss Bonnie's toilet seats.

I turn left onto Spruce Avenue. Mrs. Hankerson is jogging toward me in black tights, a grey sports bra, and a canary yellow headband. I stop. Forty feet out, she sees me. As she approaches, she keeps glancing at me warily like I'm wearing a ski mask.

"Excuse me, ma'am. Excuse me," I say not because I have anything to ask her for but so she'll veer wide and ignore me, which she does. I keep walking, pass Julie Ann's place. I've never shared one solitary word with her, then one time she spotted me in Target, walked right up to me, snorted, and spat a loogie that hit me in the chest only because it didn't have the trajectory to hit my face like she aimed to. Standing in the window with a baby on her hip is Julie Ann's stepmom, maybe thirty. She cocks her head forward and scowls at me. I keep going. Bongo's isn't far.

Monica must've called me a killer a hundred times that night. After she saw the body on the kitchen floor, I offered her a hit to calm her down. It only made her more paranoid and somber. She sat on the stoop. I sat beside her. She wore jean shorts and a long-sleeve V-neck shirt. She said an awful lot. Said she wouldn't visit me in jail, wanted no connection with me whatsoever anymore. Then she stared at her phone forever. It was agonizing. Some moments last so long they can't ever really pass.

"Go ahead," I said. "Call your dad, tell him what I did." I meant it. I'd given up. For the first time in forever, I couldn't see a way out.

She didn't lift her head. For a long while we were silent. There was no sound but my swallows and her mucusy inhales, noises that crept up on me as she scooted closer and closer even though she insisted I don't put my arm around her.

"But why, Heath?"

I hushed her.

"Why?"

"I killed her."

"But why?"

"I killed her."

"Why? Why? Why? Why? Why?"

She put her phone atop her knee and slid her thumbs into the waistband of her jeans and stared at the steps.

"What are you doing?" I asked when she suddenly stood.

She didn't reply. She walked into the house, and I followed her into the kitchen and she knelt next to Miss Bonnie. Eyes closed, she put her hands on Miss Bonnie's face and neck, traced her fingers through the blood, which was still leaking quite a lot. She stained her jeans and the gut of her shirt with blood, then called Travis. "Daddy," she said, "I did something terrible."

I went outside, I couldn't listen to it. She came out and said her dad was on the way. She asked which drawer the money was in. It was the closest thing to salvation I've ever felt, how sure I was that she'd run off with me, if not that night, soon.

"Don't touch me!" she said. "Don't!" She retrieved the cash. "And don't do anything stupid with this, either. It's for the funeral."

There never was a funeral. I still don't know what happened to that money.

Bongo Light is on the other side of the picket fence that separates his mom's back yard from the dirt alley. Like I figured, he's lounging in the inflatable pool. He's got headphones on, a baseball cap pulled down over his eyes, curly brown locks furling out from beneath it.

"Light," I say. He doesn't flinch. I toss pebbles at him one by one. After I plop a few in the water, he finally looks out from under the brim of his hat, his small and slightly divergent brown eyes doped up good.

I wave at him. "Light. Light."

He takes off his headphones, climbs out of the pool in his Hawaiian trunks, saunters to the fence, presses his face between two pickets, and looks me over, frowning.

"Heath?"

"What's up?"

"My brother's not home."

"That's okay. I came to talk to you."

"He's pissed at you. Everyone's been saying you capped yourself."

"You got a blunt, Light?"

"My mom found my stash. She said she flushed it but I think she sold it to her friend Caroline. They let you leave the hospital like that?"

"I didn't go to the hospital."

"What happened to you, then?"

"Just sick. Can I use your phone?"

"Let me call my brother first."

"Don't do that. Don't tell anyone we talked. Not Bongo. Nobody."

He grimaces. Just how he is. He takes as an insult anything that makes him think.

"You'll understand later, Light. We didn't talk. I don't wanna ruin your summer."

"Who you calling?"

"Don't worry about it. Whatever you don't know you won't have to lie about later."

"Lie about what?"

"Just trust me, dumbass."

He mutters something as he gets his phone from the patio. He holds it out between the pickets. When I grab it, he doesn't let go right away. "You're creeping me out with all this. I was on a good buzz."

"Thought you said you were out of bud."

"I am now."

I jerk the phone out of his hand.

"Got any gum, Light?"

"In the house, maybe."

He slips through the back screen door and into the house. I call Monica's cell twice. She doesn't answer, so I call the Spencers' house. Jeremy picks up, of course.

I talk like a muttering old man. "Monica there?"

"Who's this?"

"Luther."

"Luther who?"

"Luther Jones. She won a contest and I'm calling to notify her of her reward."

He pauses. "Heath?"

"Huh?"

"That you?"

"This is Luther. Is Monica avail—"

"You know I've got people accusing me of murder because of your crazy ass? My cousin—"

"No idea what you're talking about, young man. Is Monica there?"

"I'm gonna end you."

"Good."

"I'm serious. If I don't my dad will."

"I'm serious too. I'm calling from the hospital. Come and get me."

I end the call. Before I can try the house again, Monica's number pops up on the screen.

"Heath?! I thought you were ... What'd you do to yourself?"

"Nothing. It's all a misunderstanding. I'll explain everything later."

"I had to, Heath."

"I know."

"I had to tell them about Jeremy, except he's here at the house and people are out looking for you. I think they figured it out."

"Don't worry. Everything's gonna be fine."

She breathes into the phone. "I've been crying nonstop."

"You have?"

"Of course, Jesus, I thought you'd—"

"I never wanted you to be sad," I tell her.

"Fuckin A, how'd you think I'd feel?"

"I didn't know you still loved me."

"I never stopped. I'm still pissed at you. So pissed. But that doesn't mean I—"

"You still love me?"

"No shit," she says.

"Monica, I'm so sorry. I couldn't have messed things up worse. Is your mom there?"

"Yeah, why?"

"I've got a little money. We'll put Miss Bonnie's plates on your mom's car. We'll be in South Dakota before they have any clue we're gone."

She doesn't answer. I checked to see if she's ended the call.

"Monica."

"No."

"I'll find us a car, then."

"I'm not skipping town with you, Heath."

"Goddamn transmission."

"This isn't about the transmission. You never think things through! You don't even have a plan for living. It's just a plan to not be here anymore."

"The hotel—"

"That'll cover, what, one night?"

"You said you love me."

"I do."

"I don't believe you."

"Heath ..."

"I don't. And another thing, what happens when they start asking questions about what happened to her? What if the wrong people start wondering about who was where and when, and what people had to say after the ... crime took place?"

As she speaks, her voice grows nasally, cracks. "I don't know what they'll do to me, jail or who knows. If I go down with you, at least I'll have a clear conscience, which is something you could use. Sometimes I think you obsess about me and leaving town and all that just because it keeps your mind off of what you did."

"Don't say that. You don't know how I feel. Just come meet me at Miss Bonnie's."

"No."

"Please, please, Monica."

"No."

The screen door smacks against the door frame. Light comes toward me holding a glass of water and a lit fatty.

I plead with her. "I'll be there in fifteen minutes or so. Please just ... I need to see you. If I can see you, maybe I can hang on a while longer. And I'll tell you what all happened to me, too. Be there."

"We'll see."

"That's all I needed to hear. I love you, baby."

"Love you too."

I hand the phone back to Light, drink the entire glass in two gulps.

"Sorry, bro," he says. "I rolled you one to make up for lying about not having none."

I belch, hand him the empty glass, take the blunt, and draw a deep hit. "It's all good. And no matter what happens after this, it wasn't your fault, Light. There was nothing you could do to change it. Got it?"

"Not really."

"Just remember what I said."

"You're creeping me out. Don't do nothing stupid. I'll send Bongo over to check on you later."

I look him hard in the eyes, one then the other, which isn't easy the way his eyes are. "Don't send anyone over. No one. Keep them far away from that house, okay? And one more thing. You. Didn't. See me."

I leave in the direction of Miss Bonnie's.

"You're a good kid, Light!" I yell. "Always been kind to me! Kinder than I deserve! Don't forget sunscreen!"

I roast the blunt down to my fingertips and flick the stub onto the gravel. It whirls twice before it stops, its smoke-plume one tall ray piercing the wet, still air.

She's coming. She has to. She'll be waiting for me, parked in front of the house, tapping her thumbs on Delia's leather steering wheel. There's a secluded rest area south of Brainerd where I can pull over to hold her and wipe her tears on the shoulder of my shirt and kiss her lips, thin and supple and plum pink. On the highway, she can say everything she must, and I can say everything I must.

If she doesn't come, she'll tell everyone where I am. They'll show. I'll be ready for them.

As soon as I step onto my street, that stray mutt Herbert is on my heels. A menace, he's had his fangs on me before, once on the calf, once on the hip, so I keep my eyes on the alley and move as quick as can be while he's back there huffing and grumbling.

Monica isn't there yet. On the block are four vehicles. Mr. Schlitz's Ford is always locked. The keys are probably just inside the door or in his bedroom. I could smash his bedroom window with a shovel, a rock. Corey Dinkelmann's parents leave their car keys on a hook just inside the front door but they installed double bolt locks on the front and back doors after Corey denied pawning his mom's jewelry enough to convince them they were victims of vandals. The other two are maybes. Anyway, she'll take her mom's car because she's not walking and she's not asking anybody for a ride. She'll be here.

That night, before the murder, I walked to the Spencers' place. Delia answered the door, this time to confront me about the "procedure" I'd "forced on" her daughter. She'd convinced herself I did it on purpose, to punish her for scoffing at my proposal to Monica.

I couldn't get much in, words-wise.

"The abortion—"

"Procedure," she corrected me.

"Abortion."

"Procedure."

"It wasn't *my* idea. I wanted her to keep it."

She went off about how somebody had to have wanted something other than what happened, "otherwise why does anything we don't want to happen happen?"

"She didn't wanna do it, so why did she?"

"Do what, have an *abortion*?"

"Procedure," she said. You know, because the word was the real tragedy, not the act itself.

"Call it what it is."

"Why'd she do it if you didn't want her to?" she asked.

I crouch on the sidewalk in front of Miss Bonnie's. Herbert nuzzles his face into my hands, and I scratch behind his ears. He closes his eyes, twists his neck so he can face the sun, and grins with his tongue hanging out lazy and slick. My shadow's all stretched out, misshapen. A car turns onto the street from the east. The sun bakes the back of my neck as the car cruises past, some geezer driving. Could hardly see over the wheel.

"What'd you kill all those people for, baby?" Monica will ask.

"For you."

"Everyone was so sad at my brother's funeral, but not me."

"He shouldn't have come by that day. I warned him not to but he had to stick his nose where it didn't belong one last time."

"What about those other people? They didn't do anything to you."

"Never did anything for me, either."

"Heath."

"I had to."

"You didn't."

"I had to. I did, Monica."

And that night Delia going, "What do you suppose she had to say about you, Heath? What'd she say to my daughter? I've wondered..." Because in her mind it must've been Miss Bonnie who told Monica something, something jarring enough to make the choice easier for her. "What'd she say, Heath, what'd she say to Monica?" Delia's words were so precise, so measured, so premeditated, so spiteful. I had to look down at her bare feet to comprehend them. "What do you suppose Miss Bonnie said? That you were broken, you were sick in the head, you weren't to be trusted, you couldn't be a father any more than a husband any more than a boyfriend because you're a twisted little twerp, those wires in your head like a rat's nest all kinked up, what do you think...?"

How was I supposed to explain this to Monica?

"I killed her."

"But why?"

"I killed her."

"Why? Why? Why? Why? Why?"

195

How was I supposed to explain this to her when everything Miss Bonnie said about me was true. Everything. No, I couldn't explain this to Monica. I can't. I never will. Because Monica's the last person I want believing these things.

Everything moves slowly now. The dead air blisters my skin. I let it. A feisty cat named Maxine wobbles toward me, gunk-eyed and grubby and looking punch-drunk. She hisses at Herbert, and they fight. I watch them for a bit. If Herbert wins, Monica will show up any minute because she loves me, and if Maxine wins, Monica's isn't leaving with me because I'm exactly what Miss Bonnie took me for in her heart of hearts. In the distance is the long peal of the firetruck horn. I don't want Maxine and Herbert getting clipped by a ricochet but I don't have time to corral them inside, either. I hustle in, slam the door behind me, and scream until I'm lightheaded and queasy.

What Miss Bonnie took me for. Didn't she, deep down? I should've died yesterday. The house stinks of mothballs and compost, of the salty remains of sweat-stains, of death. I look for the shotgun.

I walked home from Monica's after talking to Delia for the last time. Miss Bonnie was standing in the kitchen, humming to herself, sniffing her upper lip merrily. Like nothing on Earth could ever alter her tidy Christ-loving existence. Nothing. I rushed up to her.

"Hello, my handsome boy."

"Why'd you tell her those things about me?"

"Who?"

"You told Monica I wasn't good enough for her, that I was broken and couldn't be fixed."

"Heath—"

Until that instant, I never had the guts to really smack someone. It felt like every swing I hadn't taken I'd been saving up for her all along. The room was dark after that. Dark for a long while. I wasn't sleepwalking and I wasn't really awake. When I came to. When I came to. When I came to. There she was. There she wasn't.

There's the horn again, closer and cruder now. And with it a siren. The police.

The shotgun's in the utility closet. I can hardly lift it. I put it down. The shells are downstairs. Fuck, what if I actually survive? What could be worse? I have a better idea. I sling the shotgun over my shoulder, head up to the front-facing bedroom. It's gloomy, dust motes like tiny devils calling me home.

I call Monica again.

"The police are on the way," she says the instant she answers. "Please, please, please just do what they say."

"I have to ask you something before … I have to ask you."

"Heath, what's going on? What are you gonna do?"

"Hush, baby. Don't worry. I'm not gonna hurt anyone else. I wanna tell you why I did it."

"Did what?"

"Your mom said you and Miss Bonnie talked about whether or not you'd keep the baby. She said Miss Bonnie told you a lot of things about me. That I wasn't any good for you, that I was fucked up in the head."

"You moron, I wanted to do it. I didn't want my mom to be mad at me, so I told her Miss Bonnie talked me into it. If my mom told you that, it's because she hates you so much."

I start to whimper.

"Heath?"

"I'm here."

"Don't do anything dumb. Promise me, Heath."

"I'm so sorry to have put you through ..." I trail off.

"Heath, are you there?"

"I'm here. You're right not to come with me. Stay home, baby. I have to go now."

I end the call. She calls right back, and I don't answer.

Unsteadily, I climb through the window, onto the awning, and up to the roof. The sun is in the west, grim and apricot-colored, the closest to healthy it's looked in weeks. The neighborhood stretches out before me in every direction. Emergency vehicles come from the east. Trailing them are two trucks. I stare down at the street me and Murphy used to shovel together. He meant well. He did. He was only trying to toughen me up, trying to keep me from getting raped in the future. My weakness disgusted him. Him and Dorian both. That's all he knew of compassion. He and Dorian came here, their shit in garbage bags like they might run away at any moment. Once upon a time, they loved me, one then the other, each for a short while. Two brothers who in another life may have let me be the third.

My legs give out and I slide down the roof on my ass. Braking with my elbows against the shingles and jamming my feet into the gutter, I manage to keep myself from flying down onto the lawn. As the vehicles park on the street and Doleman and Travis and all their goons swarm below, I crab-walk back up the roof, kneel, and take aim at Travis.

Suddenly my knee explodes, and I topple onto my back, bullets whistling overhead. The shotgun slides down the roof and disappears. I wriggle for a long time, shrieking loud, my leg burning, blood like an overturned can of crimson paint. If just one of them would finish me off, I'm ready. Been ready.

"Heath," a man calls out from further up on the roof.

I kink my head back to look but there's only the glare of the sun. He comes closer and when his crouching frame blocks the sunlight, I see him.

"These guys are gonna kill you," Dorian says.

"How'd you get up here?"

"You hear me?"

"Let them."

"You have any other weapons on you?"

"Why?"

"Do you?"

"I dropped my shotgun, that's all I had."

"Come on, then."

"I told you already, let them take me out."

Too weak to fend him off, I let him drag me up the slope toward the back side of the roof. He lifts me onto his shoulders, carries me to the front of the house and down onto the awning, then feeds me in through the bedroom window and dumps me down on the cot before crawling in after me.

He steps in front of me, turns to face the door, squats down on his haunches. "Climb on."

"They'll shoot you, too, you know."

He reaches back for my arms, pulls them over his shoulders like two seatbelt straps, and carries me sort of piggyback out of the room and down the stairs. He sets me down and I crumble onto the living room carpet.

"We'll go out there together," he says, crouching in front of me again.

I don't respond.

"Heath."

"You know what I did, don't you?"

"I'll carry you the rest of the way. We'll go straight to the police car. They won't shoot us both."

"I killed her, Dorian."

He looks at me for several seconds. He has no expression, like some sliver of him knew her fate before I did, before anyone. "You ready?" he says.

I get on his back again and he lugs me out onto the sidewalk and down the walkway. At least three officers have guns pointed at us. Judd has a rifle. Travis is holding Miss Bonnie's shotgun.

"Release him!" an officer directs Dorian. "Step away from the suspect!"

"Don't shoot! Don't shoot!" Dorian replies.

"Step away from him!"

Dorian takes me all the way to a police car parked sideways in the street. He sets me down and I put my hands on the vehicle, standing with all my weight on my good leg. "Stay put," he whispers.

"Step away from him!" the officer barks.

"Okay! Okay! I'm stepping away!" Dorian says.

He steps to the side and stands beside me and puts his hands on the trunk next to mine.

"Do everything they say, Heath," he tells me. His voice is gentle, like he's waking me from a nightmare.

I look down at my gory knee. I close my eyes.

Then comes the shame.

We All Fall Down

Dorian
Seven years later ...

Early one morning in late October, I sit on Juliette's single bed and nudge her awake. She groans but doesn't open her eyes. There's a gold tiara with jewels next to her pillow. She's wearing her Halloween costume, a blue gown with white shoulder poofs, having changed out of her pajamas after I kissed her goodnight the night before. I grin. To her this is mischief.

"The queen is asleep," my girl mumbles.

"We gotta get going."

"It's already time for school?"

"You're not going to school today."

Her eyes spring open and she sits upright, grinning my grin. She has Kelly's happy auburn eyes, ash-blonde hair, slender nose, and ears, the left sticking out a tad farther than the right.

"It's a surprise," I say. "But you have to change into normal clothes."

The Saint Cloud Zoo is two hours away.

Tigers pace side to side. Wolves nap in the shade. Monkeys fly between branches. There are fish, snakes, lizards, bugs, bears, giraffes, and gorillas. For lunch we eat burgers, then I buy her cotton candy and chocolate ice cream. It's unseasonably warm but I don't take off my sweatshirt. Over the years, she's often asked why I wear long sleeves all the time. I shrug, like it's just a personal preference of mine. In a way, it is.

After a long day of surprises, excitement, treats, and giggling, she naps on the drive home. It's almost her bedtime when we get back to Walker. We have fish sticks for dinner. After, she puts her gown back on, climbs onto her "throne" (bed) in her "castle" (bedroom), and talks to her "handmaidens" (Janie and Millie and Po, the dolls on her dresser).

"Juliette, did you brush your teeth?" I ask from the hallway.

"Duh!"

"You're in your jammies?"

"Yep!"

"And in bed?"

"Yep, yep!"

I open the door and she rushes across the room to hide under the covers. She closes her eyes, pretends to be asleep. I sit by her feet. "Juliette."

"Juliette is asleep," she tells me.

I poke her belly until she laughs and opens her eyes.

Now it's time. This is the plan.

I scratch my beard.

"I'm sorry, Daddy, I'll go brush my teeth now."

"It's not that ..." I rub her leg over the covers. "Remember how I used to be gone some nights visiting my friend? And remember that time you and I drove out to that big house a long ways away? There were a bunch of men living there and we talked to one of them?"

"He seemed wacky."

"It's just that he'd been locked away for a while."

"Where?"

"In a jail."

"What for?"

"He did a very bad thing a long time ago."

"Steal somebody's car?" she asks.

"No, not that."

"Break into a house?"

"Someday I'll tell you, but that's not what I wanna talk about—"

"He did something real bad, then," she tells me, her mind busy now.

"Do you remember what I told you about him?"

"No."

"Yes, you do."

"Okay," she says. "You two knew each other when you were boys."

"That's right. His name's Heath."

"Like the candy bar?"

"Yep. And I care about him a lot. He's a little brother to me. I got it okayed through the right people so that tomorrow when you're in school I'll pick him up from his house."

"Uh-huh ...?" She's putting it together.

"Then ... I'll bring him home with me. He'll be here when you get home. He's gonna work for me and stay with us. Just for a bit."

I wait for her to speak. She's still processing, like she knows it's bad news but isn't sure why yet.

"You know how there are tornadoes and floods on the news sometimes?" I ask. "And they interview the people who lost everything they have? He's like one of those people. We're gonna be very nice to him, honey."

I wait again. Wait for mystification to become anger.

"Where's he gonna sleep?" she asks.

"That's the thing."

"I'm not sharing my room with him. No way."

"Of course not. He's—"

She snaps upright. "No, he can't. That's not fair, Daddy. That's her room. You promised, you promised, you promised!"

"I know I did, Juliette. But this is different. I'm sorry, there's no way around it."

"What about her stuff?"

"Some of it can go in the garage."

"And the rest ...?" she asks.

"We're gonna get rid of it. Sell what we can. We don't have room—"

She yells and kicks and sobs for a bit. I hug her and when she stops yelling, she repeats, "You promised, you promised," again and again, weeping.

Eventually I give up trying to get her to brush her teeth and put on her pajamas. While she cries, I say alone the nightly prayer we usually say together, kiss her on the forehead, shut the light off, and leave the room. I have work to do.

The house is a quarter-mile from the nearest neighbor and two miles from downtown Walker. It's small. There are two bedrooms on the main level, each on the backside of the house. Juliette's is on the right, mine is on the left. There is also a kitchenette and a small living area. The TV rests on an entertainment center. The large avocado green rug I bought at a garage sale covers the scratched-up hardwood floor. Between the bedrooms is a short hallway that leads to the basement stairs. There's a spare room in the basement.

It's really the only place Heath could experience some privacy and quiet in this house, two things he hasn't had much of in the past ten years. His parole officer thought he'd benefit from a change of environment. Given his record of compliance during and after incarceration, and his struggles to find long-term employment in the Twin Cities, she agreed to transfer his case to Crow Wing County so he can live with and work for me.

I head down to the unfinished basement. Grey concrete floors and walls. A washer-dryer set next to a sink with exposed pipes. A bedroom little bigger than a king-size bed. I've been in this house longer than Juliette's been alive, yet I've never bothered to carpet the floor in the room, paint or wallpaper the walls, haven't even mudded over the nails in the drywall. When I first moved here, I was swamped with roofing projects and needed money for Kelly's hospital bills, the nursery, diapers, baby clothes, formula, and countless other necessities. After Kelly left, I had to pay for daycare on top of everything else. By the time I saved enough to feel financially stable I moved the things Kelly left behind into this room. Since, I've had no desire to go downstairs. It isn't pleasant, the thought of sorting through her belongings, even if it means I can discard some of them afterward. It reminds me of an old bitterness I don't identify with anymore.

Juliette is coming down from her tantrum. She's gotten better at this the past couple years, at calming herself down. I used to have to hold her, and we'd talk until she was too sleepy to be wild, to sob and throw limbs at me. She's always been dramatic, and I'd say she didn't get it from me but there's no one around to tell me what I was like when I was eight. Might be my fault, anyway. This room and the owner of its contents are things I haven't discussed with Juliette all that much, leaving her imagination to fill in the details. Her imagination is good for that. Vibrant and reckless.

Years ago, when she first asked about her mother, I was ready. Or thought I was. I didn't hesitate to tell the truth, at least as much as I felt she needed to hear. "She left." "You were eighteen-months old." "I don't think she's coming back." It's not that I thought what I had to tell her would head off her follow-up questions. Just, I figured the spigot of questions would turn off quicker than it did. I kept thinking, You're a baby. My baby girl. You don't need to know all that shit.

It never does me much good to think about Kelly. She's another bitter memory, and something hope does is start you thinking you're done making those, bitter memories. That's how I feel these days, which is good. I can't much fight them anymore, either. I'm too tired most of the time. Then again, I don't mind a little tussle here and there. My memories are plenty worn out by now too.

I open the door, turn on the light, step into the cool bedroom, and look over Kelly's abandoned possessions. A chaise lounge chair, a dresser, a record player, and boxes full of clothes, books, receipts, records, bank statements, and coupon books. Juliette has pushed everything to the sides, clearing an area in the middle for her trainset. I move the train and wooden tracks upstairs and begin hauling things into the basement living area.

I suppose someday it might be appropriate to tell her how Kelly's postpartum Percocet addiction got so bad I considered giving her an ultimatum, get clean or leave. In the weeks before running off, she slept all day, was up all night. She reclined on this chaise lounge chair, which she stole from the Holiday Inn, smoking Camels, drinking rum, watching *Friends* reruns, crying in a way I couldn't stop. I tried. She had a job at the dollar store downtown but only worked ten hours a week. Outside of a few dresses for Juliette, the paychecks went toward drugs and liquor and smokes. Communication was something we just couldn't ever pull off. I knew it, she knew it. The topics I wanted to get into, her addiction, her coldness toward Juliette, the household budget, were things she didn't want to hear about. And the topics most important to her, feuds with her mom, Melissa, and constant complaints about body aches, aggravated me because she and Melissa were always feuding about one thing or another and Kelly might've been a hypochondriac in addition to a recovery addict. Out of revenge, she started sleeping with a drifter who hooked her up with prescriptions. She even arranged for a girlfriend to give me the details. She was disappointed when the news didn't faze me all that much. I was focused on my baby girl. What she needed for food, clothes, toys. What I'd do if Kelly wasn't around. What I'd do if she tried to take Juliette from me. I thought about an ultimatum but I didn't have the guts to follow through on the threat. So I did what any bright guy would do when he finds out the mother of his child is sleeping with a drifter who gets her Perc. I proposed.

She laughed awfully hard, harder than *Friends* ever made her. I'd never heard her laugh like that before. Of course, there wasn't a lot of laughter in the NA meetings we met each other in, and our relationship was built on talking about substance issues and the hardships of her childhood, her emotionally abusive father. The way she carried on almost made the proposal seem feasible, even though there was mockery and resentment in it. Even though it seemed she was laughing at me. I got home from work a few days later and she was gone. I picked Juliette up at Melissa's. Melissa told me Kelly was going to Colorado to be with her dad and wouldn't be coming back to Walker for a while.

That was seven years ago. Seven years of hearing that laugh of Kelly's. Each time the mockery and resentment sounded less like they were directed at me and more like they were directed inward. Like she was laughing at herself. This sound is among the many things in my life I don't care to remember. Because what use are they to me, to Juliette when she's old enough to hear more than, "She left." "You were eighteen-months old." "I don't think she's coming back."

My baby girl's right. I did promise to keep Kelly's things in the room. But whether Heath moves in or not, this stuff can't be here forever.

I'd been optimistic about the plan, splurging on a day at the zoo before breaking the news to Juliette, but only because it was Emma's idea.

She'll be eager to hear how it went, and now that the tantrum's over, I call her.

"How'd it go?" Emma answers.

"Real good. I was gonna do it on the drive home but didn't have the chance. She had a fit a bit ago."

"Oh, no."

"I expected it. I think she's asleep now."

"Have you talked to Melissa yet?"

"Tomorrow. Plus, I need to ask her what she wants of the things her daughter left. I'm not worried about the other part. It's still better I tell her than she finds out on her own."

"I know, people can be so cruel. Don't forget that you're doing a good thing."

"We'll see how it goes," I say, aiming to clip this part of the conversation. "How was your day?"

"Just got the kids to sleep a while ago. Wine, a little work to do tonight. Are you anxious?" she asks, pulling us right back to Heath.

"Not really."

"I guess if you're not worried about the change, what's the problem? It's a very good thing you're doing."

"I should get going, Emma. I have a lot of work to do to get his room ready. I'm tired."

"Okay," she replies, sounding somewhat reluctant to end the call so quickly.

"I didn't know the zoo would be such a to-do."

"It's always a nightmare."

"I've never been there before."

"The zoo in Saint Cloud?"

"Any zoo. Next time, the five of us can go."

"Can't wait."

"I love you."

"Love you too," she says.

I end the call and start lugging Kelly's stuff out of the basement, some to the garage attic, some to the burn pit next to the shed in the back yard. I move quickly, carrying larger loads than I would if I were in a better mood. It's true, I do have a lot to get done. And I am tired. But we both know I'm not too tired to talk, not to her anyway.

Thing is, even if she's never outright says it, sometimes I get the sense she'd rather I didn't bring Heath in like this. Whether in Walker or at her place in Brainerd, where most of her book-keeping contracts are, we and the kids will be happy together someday. We're both committed to it, we're both people who get what we're committed to getting. Derek and Marybeth like me, and Juliette adores Emma. Heath is a hitch in the plan and though Emma would never admit it she'd feel different about what I'm doing if he were flesh and blood. I heard it again just now on the phone, in her insistence that what I'm doing is "a good thing." Like it'd sure be generous to offer your home to a sibling in need, but to do it for a stranger, well, that's really special.

Maybe I'm being too sensitive. I probably am and she's just bummed that our dreams are on hold.

Maybe it's all in my head and she truly understands and isn't bummed at all. I really am tired.

Tomorrow, I think, his life starts over. A fresh start here with me. Give him time, he'll blossom in Walker. It'll be a long road.

Second-degree manslaughter. Seven years in prison, where he grew four inches but on account of stress never had much of an appetite. He weighs the same today as he did at seventeen. Over the years, his hairline receded, the limp that resulted from his gunshot wound became more noticeable, tension in his shoulders gave him a slight hunch and chronic neck pain, and his eyes, bulging from his emaciated face, took on an almost neon hue. His rare and brief attempts at smiling make him seem cynical. Even a little nuts.

The last three years he's lived in a halfway house in Minneapolis. Understandably, he didn't make many friends there. He spent his idle time reading fantasy books in the tidy room he shared with a convicted murderer. When I visited, we'd go to a nearby Starbucks and do the same things we used to do in the visitors area of the correctional facility north of Minneapolis, play cards and chat about Southern classic rock. ZZ Top, The Allman Brothers, The Marshall Tucker Band, Lynyrd Skynyrd. And books. I'm a slow reader but have worked my way through both *The Lord of the Rings* trilogy and the series *A Song of Ice and Fire*.

I used to ask about his plans for life after parole. He never had much to say about the future, so I quit asking. It hurts to see him all out-of-it, kind of sedated, and I still can't tell if he's this way because of shame or the side-effect of his anti-anxiety medication or the anxiety itself or some combination of these factors. I think back on the first time we lived together, before either of us met Miss Bonnie, before the sexual abuse. I think back on the enthusiastic and trusting and innocent child who seemed to look up to me for no other reason than I showed no signs of minding being called Bunkie. The idea that he's permanently numb, as a consequence of his own crime or not, does something to my soul that I don't like.

I'll say, though, he has a sense of humor. It's dry and quiet and gives me hope.

After dusting the cobwebs from the corners of the ceiling and hanging the framed map of Minnesota that Kelly left behind, I carry a couch from upstairs down to Heath's room, put fresh sheets and a blanket on the couch.

Before falling asleep I decide I have been too sensitive about Emma and Heath's move to Walker. I chide myself for conjuring up sentiments and views she hasn't put into words herself and likely doesn't actually own. I tell myself it'll be good for Juliette to have Heath around.

And I'm reminded that Kelly is an only child, so Juliette, who's never asked many questions about Murphy, will finally meet one of her uncles.

Juliette

The morning school bus ride is cold. Paul takes all the bumpiest roads he can find and so we fall onto each other's laps. Then during guard-the-pin in gym class, Marlon Torpler smacks me good right on the thigh with the ball and my leg stings and it's red. Later Mrs. Grindle gives us all popcorn and Torpler rips one real loud and blames it on me. My face is hot, and I almost start crying and I yell at him until Mrs. Grindle puts us in the timeout corner. Then on the bus ride home one of the Carson twins pukes and since my window won't open, the bus stinks the whole ride.

I know who's to blame for this cruddy day. When I get home Daddy's friend is sitting at the kitchen table like he's just part of the family now. Swapped in for Mom. Daddy said his friend is younger than him. He doesn't look younger. He looks like an old, creepy, bony, giant spider. A spider so old he can't grow hair anymore where he's supposed to and that's the only reason he even looks sort of like a human. His eyes are the worst part because they stick out far, and they are the color of pickle juice.

Daddy says, "Juliette, this is Heath."

"Spider, come with me quick," I tell Daddy's friend.

He looks at Daddy, then back at me. He frowns and points at his chest.

"Yes, *you*, Spider."

"Juliette, be nice," Daddy says.

"I'm sorry, Daddy. *Mr.* Spider, come on, please and thank you, I wanna show you something."

I lead Spider down the hallway and stand just outside my room. "This room is my realm. Everything in here is under my domination. My people all respect their queen and listen to my rules. You can't go into my realm. Don't even look at it. You're doing that now. Stop it!"

With a little sleepy grin, he throws his hands up and steps back and looks back down the hallway at Daddy. I shut the door.

Halfway through dinner Daddy sends me to bed early for calling Spider by the name I gave him. I don't mind. Spider was bugging me by being there.

But that's just how Spider is.

And he turns more spidery every day. No matter what's for dinner he always takes a slice of white bread and wipes his plate clean and folds his bread in two and scarfs it. Spaghetti or macaroni or split pea soup from the can. And he's always reading books that are big as shoeboxes with dragons and swords on the cover and his voice is way too soft and he won't say much unless I ask him two hundred questions all in a row. Or else sometimes, he'll just sit there with his eyes glossed over and his lips moving but nothing coming out of his mouth.

"What are you mumbling about?"

"Nothing. Sorry, Juliette," he says.

"It wasn't nothing, Spider."

"Nothing important."

"Why don't you talk?"

"Shy, I guess," he mumbles.

"What for?"

He shrugs.

I whisper, "Are you a moron? There's this kid in my class named Torpler. He farts and blames it on me. Are you like him?"

"I'm not sure. Maybe Torpler and I would get along good."

I can't tell if he's joking or not.

Me and Spider sit in the cab of Daddy's truck whenever the three of us drive around town together. It's just big enough for me but it's way too small for him. He's all folded up with his knees almost to his chin. He holds his book between his legs by reaching his arms underneath them. Never seen such a thing.

"What are you reading?" I ask him on the way to the grocery store. "Is it Dandy Log Legs books?"

"No."

"How come you don't go to church with us?"

"Maybe someday I will," he says. He goes right back to reading.

"How come ...?"

"How come *what?*"

"How come you don't go with us?"

"To church?" he asks.

"Duh! Gosh!"

"I don't know."

"You're the wackiest, Spider."

"No, he's not," Daddy says. "Be nice. And please use his real name."

"It's okay," Spider tells him.

"*Juliette,*" Daddy says.

"Sorry, Daddy," I say. "Sorry, Spider," I mutter to him.

I know I'm supposed to like him. I just can't and there's nothing to do about it but give him the meanest scowls and put rocks in his work boots and sit real close to him on the couch when he's already stuffed himself into the end of it. And when he's talking to himself, I sneak up behind him and get on top of a stool and flick his ears. Sometimes he doesn't even move his head the tiniest little inch even when I get him good.

Soon he's my slave. All he does is work for Daddy and read books and do what I say. If I'm thirsty, he gets me a glass of water. If I'm hungry for a snack, he makes nachos by putting chips and shredded cheese in the microwave. And he never changes the channel on the TV if I'm already watching something.

Sometimes he looks all mopey and droopy and heavy like an ugly flower that doesn't have much color. The reason is that Daddy's the only one in town who doesn't think Spider's the worst. Grandma thinks he's the worst. I even overhear her whispering about Spider to her friends on the phone. "Scum," she says.

That's why Thanksgiving is so weird and sad. I usually go to her house for turkey. Except since Daddy won't go unless Spider goes and since she doesn't want Spider to go, I eat at home. Daddy can't cook a turkey and Spider probably doesn't even know what Thanksgiving is, so I have turkey sandwiches with meat from the deli at the grocery store instead. It's the saddest thing ever that I can't be with Grandma because I know she's home alone watching football and she can't eat a whole turkey herself, can she?

That night there's a knock on the door. I'm standing in the kitchen.

Spider creeps downstairs to hide in his room. Daddy opens the door. It's Grandma holding leftovers and pie.

"Dorian, honey, we have to talk," she says.

"Go to your room, please," Daddy tells me. But I don't wanna leave the kitchen.

She tells him she's held her tongue long enough, and now I really don't wanna leave.

"Go to your room," he says again. I don't move.

"Dorian," she says, "I've heard some bad things. My heart is breaking thinking that something might happen to my grand-baby. Something you and I would regret for the rest of our lives."

"Melissa—"

"Not like he was a drug addict or something. What he did—"

"Let's not talk about it now. Juliette, room!"

"That's just it, it's so bad that we can't talk about it in front of Juliette. Tell me you think he's right in the head. I don't trust him one bit."

"Juliette!" he shouts. His voice breaks like I've never heard it do before.

I run to my room and slam the door. They're talking out there but I can't really make out the words.

When she's gone, I come out. Spider stays downstairs all night. Daddy brings him down a slice of pie on a saucer. He comes right back upstairs with it. At bedtime I set all the people in my kingdom up on the dresser and put on my gown and warn them that the kingdom must be on alert for any evil forces that might try to invade it.

"Your queen has learned that Lord Spider's armies are on the move. They're mean and ugly and wicked. We must be on guard like never before. Any deserters or traitors will be punished with death. Your choices are scorpion bath or beheading."

"Juliette, you ready for bed?" Daddy asks.

"Just about!"

"Don't be afraid," I tell them. "Your queen will protect you from any invasion. Our enemies will wish they never came here."

I stroke their heads to calm them. I brush Millie's hair until Daddy comes into the room.

"Where are your jammies?" he asks.

"The king has them in his chambers."

"Put them on, please," he says.

"Okay. Is something wrong, Daddy?"

"Would you just get ready for bed like I asked you to?"

Dang, he's mad about something. Probably something Spider did. I brush my teeth fast as ever and change out of my gown and into the jammies that have planets on them, and I crawl into bed. Daddy comes in and sits by my feet. It looks like something awful has happened to him and he's about to tell me all about it. He doesn't know how to cry. Never learned, maybe.

He says, "Remember when I talked to you about the tornadoes and floods, all the people who lost everything they have?"

"Nope."

"Think hard. What'd I say about them?"

"You said Spider doesn't have other people to help him, but maybe it's because—"

"Don't listen to Grandma," he says. "She's not right all the time."

"Did Spider hurt somebody and that's why he went to the slammer?"

"Slammer? Where'd you hear that word?" he asks.

"Grandma."

"He hurt one person. He was young and wasn't thinking right. He's different now than he was back then. Anyway, Jesus forgave him."

"He did?"

"Jesus always forgives us no matter what we do wrong," he says, "as long as we ask Him to."

"And Spider asked for it?"

"Yes."

"At our church, he did?"

"No, on his own."

"So, he's not gonna hurt anybody else?" I ask.

"Don't think about what Grandma said. She doesn't know Heath at all."

"You'd never let anything happen to me, though?"

"What do you think? That's enough questions for tonight. I don't wanna get you all wound up before you go to sleep."

"One more?"

He sighs. "One more."

"What ... No, um, who'd Spider hurt?"

"I'll tell you some day."

"That's not fair," I say. "You said I had one more question."

"Pick another one."

"That's the one I want, though."

"Sorry about your luck," he tells me.

Daddy prays but I don't say anything the whole time because I'm thinking. After he leaves, I can't sleep. There's too much to think about since I've figured out what Spider did. Duh, he killed a little girl like me. That must be it and that's why Daddy wouldn't tell the truth and why he wouldn't let Grandma talk about it in front of me. So I think and think and think and I can't sleep at all. I can see Spider sneaking into my room and stealing me and driving off in Daddy's truck. Soon I'll be a fly in Spider's web he's made in a big tree somewhere.

What helps me fall asleep is Daddy on his cellphone outside my room. He's talking to his friend. Emma is my friend, too, even though she's old like Daddy. She brings Derek and Marybeth and we go sledding or ice skating or swimming and it's fun. From his voice I can tell he's smiling on the phone. He says my name and Spider's. He even laughs. I wish he'd laugh more. Maybe he would if Spider wasn't moping around all the time. Daddy always laughs when he's with Emma. She has a pretty laugh, too. Sometimes there are tears in her eyes from giggling.

Maybe I won't get kidnapped after all. Except I have an idea then that would fix so many problems.

I sleep well, thinking about what I'll do in school tomorrow.

***

The other kids have been asking about Spider and why he's there at our house and how long is he staying and is he a creepo or what. All this time I said I didn't know anything about it. But today during pizza slices and fruit cocktail at lunch, I say, "You don't wanna know. You'll never sleep again."

They all stare at me. Nobody's eating their food.

"He kidnapped kids. A whole bunch, at least twenty. He ripped their toenails out and ate them. Then he drowned them in the Mississippi."

The girls are super grossed out. They groan and put their feet up on their stools. But another girl named Patricia is sitting at the table over and she just laughs at me.

"I don't believe you," she says. "You also said that you knew an astronaut and that turned out to be a juicy lie."

"That was just a misunderstatement, Patricia. I'm telling you the truth about Spider. Ask your grandma. She'll lie and say she doesn't know anything about it. That's how you know it's true. I snuck into Spider's room once. Under his bed there was a jar. Guess what I found in the jar."

"No! Icky!" Marie yells.

"Yep. Toenails! I sleep with ten pairs of socks on now. Just in case."

Patricia stands up and says, "You're so full of crap, Juliette!"

"Maybe *you* like eating toenails."

"No, I don't, Juliette!"

The thing about Patricia is that she lives with her grandma. I know this because we used to be friends before I went to stay the night at her house one night and her grandma was weird and gave me the willies from being old. So I never went to Patricia's after that.

Later on, in gym class, I sling a kickball right at her legs and she falls down. "Oops!" I say.

That night I'm playing cards with Daddy and Spider comes creeping out of his lair and into the living room. I even kind of feel bad for him sometimes because he's so slow and creeping it doesn't seem like he could actually hurt somebody. For sure he couldn't pull out someone's toenails. I tried pulling on mine on the bus ride home. They're stuck on there pretty good.

The three of us play cards until Daddy's cellphone buzzes and he goes into the kitchen. He's on the phone for a while.

"I'm sorry you don't like me," Spider says. "It must stink having me here. Maybe I'll be out of your hair soon."

"You're actually probably not the worst, Spider."

He looks up from his cards and smiles all tired-like.

Daddy comes back to the game with his face full of red blotches. Just the way he looks when he's been roofing all day and it's real muggy and hot out.

"Juliette, come with me," he says.

I tell Spider not to look at my cards, then follow Daddy into his bedroom. He shuts the door, and we stand face to face. He's mad.

"I just got off the phone with Mrs. Portis," he says.

"Who's that?" I ask, playing dumb.

"Patricia's grandmother."

"She's a liar. Everyone knows that."

"Patricia told her you bullied her today."

"Not even."

"Juliette ..."

"I didn't. The ball slipped out of my hand."

"First of all, Juliette, it's not okay to bully. But Mrs. Portis also said that you told some girls a story."

"What story?"

"You tell me, Juliette."

"I was only joking."

"Go on ..."

"It was about Spider. I told them that he was in jail for eating toenails."

"What else?" Daddy says.

"That's it."

"Before you go on, think very carefully about how long you wanna be grounded."

"Then ... Then I just said that he drowned them all afterward," I whisper.

"Speak up."

I do. "I said he drowned them. The girls whose toenails he took. But I only said that to scare my friends."

"You think it's okay to make up lies about him?"

"No."

"Why'd you do it, then?"

"I don't know," I say.

"All those girls are gonna tell their parents he's dangerous, then their parents are gonna tell their friends and it's gonna be even harder for him to feel welcomed here."

"I was just pranking him," I explain.

"It's not funny."

"Sorry I'm not funny, I guess."

"What should we do, Juliette? Maybe we don't get to play softball this year. Maybe we're grounded until spring."

"Till spring?! That's like the rest of my life!"

"That should give you enough time to think about what you've done."

"I already said I'm sorry."

He takes a deep breath. He sighs. My eyes start to burn, and I know I'm gonna cry but I don't wanna.

"Can I go to my room?" I ask.

"Yes. And don't come out until I get you."

On the way to my kingdom, I look for Spider. He isn't in the living room. His cards are overturned on the couch. My bedroom seems darker than normal. My bed doesn't feel anything like a throne. Janie and Millie and Po are up on the dresser, and I turn them so they face the wall and aren't looking at me anymore.

At first, I think this is all Daddy's fault because he's the one that's grounding me, Patricia's fault too because she's whiny. Then I think it's actually Spider's fault. Everyone would be happier if he wasn't creeping around all the time. But, see, that's just the problem I was trying to fix. I don't know what to do.

Daddy calls me out for dinner. He made me two fried eggs and I ask him if I can have French toast but he says no. While I eat he just looks down at his hands. It seems like he could fall asleep right there in his chair. I can tell he's got something to say and he's waiting for me to finish eating, so I eat slow. But even after I'm done, he doesn't say anything. He's grumpy.

"You wanna play cards with me, Daddy?"

"No."

"Can I have ice cream?"

He shakes his head no.

"Can we make brownies?"

"Juliette ..."

"What?"

"You're not getting dessert."

"Okay, that's all you had to say, geez."

He sighs long and loud. "Do you know what happened to Patricia's parents?"

"No."

"They died in a car accident. That's why she lives with Mrs. Portis. She told her grandma she didn't mind you bullying her. She said she can stick up for herself. But her grandma had told her that Heath not only didn't have parents, he didn't even have a grandma."

"Uh-huh."

"So, when you lied about him, Patricia got mad. Do you understand that?"

I do. I nod.

"I thought you and Patricia were buddies," he says. "What happened?"

"I don't know." I really can't remember.

He sighs. Then he tells me all the things I have to do. Apologize to Patricia and tell the class I was lying about Heath and apologize to Heath for lying about him.

"Do you know why I'm so upset?" he asks.

"Because I shouldn't lie."

"And ...?"

"And I shouldn't bully."

"Why not?"

"Because it's mean," I say.

"Why is it mean?"

"It hurts people."

He says, "Because people only bully those who are already hurting a bunch."

"Daddy, if I do everything you told me to, am I still grounded?"

"Definitely."

"I was thinking that if I'm gonna be grounded anyway can I at least have some ice cream tonight?"

He shakes his head no. Dang.

"How long am I grounded for?"

"I'm not sure yet."

"A week?"

"Probably longer."

"A month?"

"I'll let you know," he says. "You don't understand how lucky you are. Maybe I've tried too hard to ... To keep you from seeing that some people never feel love like you do every day. I don't know what I'm supposed to do. I love you, Juliette."

"I love you, too. That's why ... See, because of Emma. I thought you'd be happy if she was around more, and I thought you could see her more if Spider was out of your hair."

"Heath. Uncle Heath."

"It's weird that he's here, Daddy. Don't you see that?"

"I don't care if it is. I don't care what others think about it. I don't care what you think about it. He's part of our family. He needs us. Emma knows that, Juliette. She understands. She cares about him, too. There's so much you don't understand."

"But—"

"You don't ever have to worry about me being happy. You're what makes me happy every day."

"Okay, Daddy."

I brush my teeth and put my jammies on and when I'm in bed I get the sniffles thinking about how Daddy once said he wasn't treated too good when he was a boy my age and about how he had bad luck just like Spider. If only I knew Daddy back then, I think. If only, I'd have treated him the best. I'd have said "I love you, Daddy" every night. Duh.

***

In the morning, before school, me and Daddy go down to Spider's lair. It's kind of like that hotel room we stayed in one time when we went to see the Twins play. There's the couch and the dresser and Spider's duffel bag and that's it.

I feel really bad for a whole bunch of reasons and not all the reasons are the things I did to him and Patricia. But some of the reasons are the things I did to him and Patricia. I feel really bad.

He's sitting on the bed. Daddy stands behind me.

"Sorry, Spider," I say.

"How come?"

"Whoops, I forgot you don't know. I told a lie about you."

"Oh, that's okay."

"It was a bad lie."

"Don't worry about it," he says.

"I'm gonna fix it, though. Unless ... Have you ever eaten a toenail?"

"Juliette," Daddy says.

"Never mind, Spider. See you later on."

At school I say sorry to Patricia for being mean and I tell my friends I was only fibbing about Spider.

Daddy grounds me for four weeks and I say okay. Then I remember that four weeks is a month and I'm mad again. There's no going to the movies. No sleepovers. No zoos or baseball games. All I can do is go to school and play cards and blow raspberries and watch whatever Spider and Daddy are watching on TV. It's usually shows about houses being built. Those shows are by far the worst crap anyone's ever been forced to watch.

The only fun thing I do is around Christmas time when Emma and Derek and Marybeth come over to open presents. It's different because there's usually five of us. Now there's six. While me and the other kids make snow angels and snowmen and have snowball fights and all that, Daddy and Emma and Spider drink cocoa by the fire. Emma is talking to Spider and they're smiling and laughing like she doesn't know he's not funny or fun and like she doesn't know he's even a spider at all.

After that I'm done being grounded. Then something strange happens to Spider that gets me wondering what he and Emma were talking about when they were by the fire, or if there was something in their cocoa. A magic potion, say. Because he changes. He's still skinny and going bald and still looks older than he's supposed to. But he's not as creepy and mopey and he doesn't mutter all the time and he smiles more. It's really just a smirk but that's pretty good for a spider. Plus, when Daddy steps out of the room Spider turns on cartoons for me until Daddy comes back.

"No, you're not the worst, Spider," I tell him one day.

"Thanks for saying that. I appreciate it."

"You're welcome."

Then Spider buys a janky old grocery-getter car and now he doesn't have to ride all scrunched up in the back of Daddy's truck. I can tell he's got something brewing behind his pickle eyes, I just don't know what it is.

"What are you gonna do with your new car?" I ask.

"What do you mean, Juliette?"

"You're scheming."

"How can you tell?"

"Because, duh. What are you up to, then?"

"Nothing."

I scoff.

"Fine, I'll tell you," he says. "It might not look it but that car is for racing."

"Racing?"

"Right, like you see on TV. I just need to tinker for a few weeks, then I'll be ready to make some real money, get some sponsors. By the time I'm done with her she'll top-out around three hundred and twenty miles-per-hour, I bet. Faster than anything on NASCAR."

I don't know if he's goofing with me or not. Then he starts to smirk, and I know he's goofing.

"I got you," he says.

"No, you didn't," I tell him. "I knew all along that your car's a piece of junk."

"It is."

Spider thinks he's funny.

One day after church, Daddy says it's the day we'll go to the beach. We wear coats and boots and hats because it's way too cold to swim and the path out to the beach is icy so Daddy carries me. It's sort of a holiday like Easter since we did it last year and the year before that. Except we're not there long and Daddy promises me ice cream afterward and as far as I know, no one celebrates this holiday but me and Daddy. Spider stays in the truck even though Daddy invites him along to be nice. Anyway, we're not out there a few minutes when here comes Spider walking out to the beach. He stands next to Daddy.

Daddy talks to the sand all covered in snow. "We sure miss you. We're doing well." Things like that. I've asked about it a hundred times since I don't know who he's talking to. I can't see her, and I can't hear her. He says he'll tell me all about it when I'm older and that's fine since there's ice cream afterward. Then there's Spider. At first, I think he's cold and his eyes are red for some reason. Then I wonder if maybe he's crying, a thing I guess a spider can do.

After we get home Spider skips lunch to hide out in the basement. He comes up with his duffel bag. It's fat with all his things stuffed inside.

"I'll see you at work. Thank you all so much for your hospitality."

"Of course," Daddy says.

Daddy gives him a hug but Spider doesn't quite hug him back and so it looks like Daddy's squeezing the life out of him. If Daddy grabs him just a bit harder, a tear might drip out.

Spider waves goodbye to me and walks out of the house. His bag makes his shoulder slump low. He drives off in his car.

I ask Daddy why he didn't tell me Spider was leaving.

"I didn't know," Daddy says.

"He was up to something. I knew it. But why is he leaving?"

"We'll have to ask him later."

"Is it because I was mean to him?"

"No."

"How do you know, if he didn't tell you why?"

"Juliette, wash your hands for lunch, please."

"Where's he going? You think he'll be okay?"

"You seem awfully worried about him," Daddy says.

"I'm not worried. He's just the wackiest, is all."

All afternoon I throw a rubber softball against the wall above the entrance to my kingdom. Po and the rest are just as confused and grumpy about Spider.

At dinner Daddy tells me Spider moved into the apartments above Grover's Bar downtown.

"How come?"

"That's where he wants to be now."

"No, how come did he leave? Was it me?"

"Why do you keep thinking that?" he asks.

"I don't know."

"He's dealt with much meaner people in his life, if that's what you're worried about. It sounds like you miss him ..."

"Not even a little bit. I will never ever miss him."

"In case you do ever start to, we can go visit him. Or else he can come over for dinner again sometime. What do you think of that?"

"Whatever," I say.

The thing is, something is bugging me. It bugs me and I just can't make it stop.

So I come up with another tricky idea.

I wait until Daddy is sleeping and that's when I crawl out of bed. The house is dark like the deep woods and there are lots of things to bump into. I gotta walk super careful to find the front door. I put on my hat and mittens and Vikings coat. My snow-pants and boots. I unlock the door and step out into the night. It's cold and spooky and windy and it smells like hard snow. I start toward downtown.

The walk takes forever. I worry I went the wrong way and even think about turning back. But I keep going. Thank God, Grover's Bar is where I thought it was. And it's still open. I go inside and it's stinky and there's stinky people all over the place drinking stinky beer. They stare at me like they've never seen a little girl before. The bartender guy is named Floyd. I know him from church. He has a backward baseball cap and hair so twisty it looks like it was done with a thousand little curlers. The bar stools are too high to climb on top of without maybe falling off. Instead, I just stand between two of them and wait for him to see me.

"You and your dad need a table tonight?" he asks, peeking over the edge of the bar.

"Nope. Daddy's parking the car. We're just looking for Spider."

"Spider?"

"Sorry. The man who lives here now. He's real tall and skinny."

"Reynolds? I haven't seen him. He might be up in his apartment. Want me to call him down?"

"I'll go see if he's home."

"It's the first door on the right," Floyd says.

He points to a door at the end of the bar. I go through the door and climb the stairs and head down the hallway at the top of the landing. I can't remember which room Floyd said Spider's in. There are two doors. I pick one and knock and knock and knock. Nobody answers. Then the other door opens and out steps Spider. He's wearing pajama bottoms and a plain shirt and no socks or shoes.

"Juliette?! Is everything okay?"

"I came to ask you about something."

"Where's your dad?"

"He doesn't know I'm here. I was sneaky."

"I bet he's worried about you." He pulls his phone out of his pocket.

"Wait. Before you call him, can I ask my question?"

"How about you and I wait for him together downstairs?"

"Okay, Spider."

He calls Daddy to explain what happened and we go downstairs. Spider stays barefoot. He helps me onto the stool and Floyd pours two lemonades from the soda gun behind the bar. We suck our straws while we talk.

"Why'd you leave?" I ask him.

"I needed to give you and your dad some space. He wouldn't take any money for the house bills, either."

"How come?"

"Proud, I guess. Is that your question?"

"No ... So, Spider, um ... So, what'd you do to have to go to prison ...? Because you hurt somebody, right?"

He nods.

"Who was it?"

"My foster mom."

"You were adopted?"

"A foster mom is different. But kind of, yeah," he says.

"Was she bad to you?"

"Not at all. But I was angry and not too good at controlling my anger."

"Why were you angry at her?"

He frowns. It's funny. See, his eyes are still big but not as big as they used to be because he has more face now to hide them. And the pickle color isn't so pickly anymore. It's more of an olive color that is actually kind of nice. Years and years and years ago when he was a boy, maybe he wasn't the grossest spider around. Maybe.

He says, "At the time, I thought I had a reason. But I didn't. I was just angry in general. Had been for a long time."

"But ... And why were you so angry?"

"I thought everyone hated me and that they were right to."

"That's sad."

"It is."

"I was trying to make people hate you, too," I tell him. "That was dumb of me. Spider, I have another question."

"Okay?"

"Did Jesus forgive you?"

"Not yet."

"That's not what Daddy says."

"I know, Juliette."

"When do you think Jesus will stop being mad at you?"

"Not sure."

"Okay."

"Is that all your questions?" he asks.

"Yeah ... But ..."

Spider turns around and I look too. Daddy's in the bar window. He's got on his winter coat and stocking cap. His hands are in the pockets of his pajama bottoms. He's confused but sort of grinning at the same time.

"You ready to go home?" Spider asks.

"But my other question is about, um, when you were my age. Did you have to sleep outside at night?"

"Sometimes."

"Were you hungry and didn't get food?"

"Here and there, yeah."

"How come? And how come that stuff doesn't happen to me?"

He scrunches his face up, frowning again. It isn't just olive now. In his eyes are all every type of green you could think of. And flecks of orange and red and yellow. He's alive, except he wasn't always. He's alive.

"I don't know, Juliette."

"That was my main question. I was hoping you could tell me that." I slurp the rest of my lemonade and now I have to pee.

"I'm sorry I can't help you more."

"It's okay, Spider."

Daddy walks up behind me and puts his hands on my shoulders.

"Am I in trouble?" I ask him.

He nods.

"Dang," I whisper.

I hop down off the stool and Daddy hugs me. Then Spider says, "Juliette, why'd you ask me all this?"

"Because did you know there are floods and tornados?"

He squints at me like I told him the start of a joke and haven't finished it yet. He stands and takes out his wallet and puts five dollars on the bar for the lemonades. Then he walks off toward the door to his apartment.

Me and Daddy go out into the cold and head down the sidewalk toward Daddy's truck and I ask him how long I'll be grounded for.

"I'll probably add on another week."

"But do you think …? I was wondering something."

"Yeah?"

"Do you think Spider, um, Uncle Heath, will wanna come back to our house some day? I think I should keep an eye on him."

He doesn't answer. He puts his arm around my shoulder and pulls me close. With his warm, hard hand on my cold, soft cheek, he hugs me tight.

He takes me home.

Heath

My apartment's hardwood floors are mottled with mold. The walls are mint green and bare. No mirrors, no photos. There's spider silk strung from the still ceiling fan to the Styrofoam tiles above, those stained too, the threads remnants of autumn which I don't dare dust away because Juliette will get a kick out of them. In the middle of the fan is a shadeless lightbulb. Due to the short ceiling, my shadow stretches partway up the wall behind me, my own wraith. It tails me into the kitchen, where I make tea, then back into the living room, where I sit on the floor beneath the ceiling fan and open my notebook to journal. I write for some time though it's difficult to get started. Today is Miss Bonnie's birthday.

Prison can be quiet, even tranquil. Yet at any moment chaos, violence of some order or another, might destroy your peace, raid whatever sanctum your conscience has permitted you to invoke. Tranquility contingent on the whims of madmen is not true tranquility, go figure. It'll be years yet before I come down from the bracing to which prison conditioned me, the readiness to defend myself physically and emotionally, to have my reflections interrupted, to not accept these interruptions as merely another manifestation of deserved torture.

Today, Miss Bonnie's birthday, I decide to try something I haven't done in a decade. Hum. Hum one of the hundred songs

I've had stuck in my head since I was a boy. I don't sing. I'm not ready for that, neither my voice nor my spirit prepared. So Alanis sings for me. I hum along.

"I'm broke, but I'm happy. I'm poor, but I'm kind. I'm short, but I'm healthy, yeah."

The frigid path to the Sibley Beach was narrow, icy, clogged with dense snow and wind-toppled trees and brush, like the beach itself aspired to forbid our passage, or her ghost had whiled the winter away erecting barriers, snowfall, fallen trees, thickets. Dorian supposes it's there that under different circumstances we'd have deposited her ashes. It must've occurred to him that she had no plan for her ashes because she, Christian and deeply so, preferred burial. Then again who's to say what her preference was? Murphy, it turns out, was closer to her than any of us were and on this point even he isn't certain. I know because I asked him.

Five years ago, he visited me in prison for the first time. I had a fever at the time so when he appeared from out of the hallway and sat on a stool across from me in the glass-partitioned cubicle, dressed in a police officer's uniform, clean-shaven, hulking, glints of deviance and malice in his eyes—they were dark grey though I'd remembered them black, as though they'd faded over the years like fabric does, the tone faded, deviance and malice as well—I looked over at the guard and nearly asked to return to the infirmary. Obviously, I was hallucinating. It would've helped if he'd picked up the phone right away. He just stared at me, sizing me up, I felt. You'd have thought I was the one who played dead out west all those years, how astonished he looked. When he finally reached for the phone, I picked up mine. All he said was, "Reynolds."

I don't remember much from those early visits, irregular, once every six or seven weeks or so, except for the joke he told about how no one ever asks Barabbas, the man Pontius Pilate allowed the people of Jerusalem to pardon over Jesus, to "take the wheel," even though he almost certainly would've been a better driver than Jesus. "It's true," he said, "I've spent a lot of time with criminals. Great reflexes, real tuned in to their environments." He thinks Miss Bonnie coopted the joke. "The real one is that if you're gonna pray for someone to take the wheel, shouldn't it be Dale Earnhardt Jr or someone like that?"

I may've cracked a smile.

"The comedian tells it better, I guess," he said.

There was never a fitting moment to ask why he'd come. Anyway, I got the sense he didn't have an answer or wouldn't have told the truth if he did. Suppose he wanted to know why I did what I did, whether I was remorseful, anything of the variety, he didn't ask. At times, how else to put it, it seemed I was chatting up a new cellmate, that mutual confinement established our kinship, that the reasons for this confinement were less important than the patent truth that we were and would remain in each other's company for a period of time determined by those with more power than either of us possessed. The obvious caveat ought to have been that Murphy had a choice as to where he spent his time, only it seemed to him no choice at all, somehow his notion of freedom akin to mine. It was all so startlingly familiar, his jaw muscles at work as he ground his teeth, his hands two balls of knuckles, his shoulders tense. His uniform notwithstanding, the guards must've wondered which side of the glass he was supposed to be on. Subjecting himself to my chains for a time, deliberately assuming the psychology of captivity, was in my eyes a tremendous act of compassion.

Here and there I could even mistake him for Dorian, myself for a brother to each of them. Then again and perhaps more likely, Murphy's body betrayed him, as though for him existence implied only incarceration and efforts to evade it.

"Her janky nose," he said. According to him, she hadn't broken it in some snowmobiling disaster involving a seesaw. It wasn't the result of a freak waterskiing accident, shark attack, faulty bungee cord, or cage fight, these just a few of the explanations she'd thrown around over the years.

"She told *you* the truth?"

"She did."

"How do you know?"

"I know."

I believe him. It happened when she was eleven or so. Her stepfather caught her kissing the neighbor boy in front of the hardware store. A couple pecks on the cheek. She lied to her mom because she was ashamed to admit it. She lied to the rest of us for the same reason.

"Did you know she was married once?"

Of course I didn't.

All in all, she'd told Murphy, Puck Bonnie was good to her, called her beautiful years before she realized he meant it, though by then he was gone.

They were twenty when they got married. They put their wedding money toward an RV, planned to honeymoon at the Grand Canyon. It was meant to be a lengthy, cheap adventure during which they'd have all the "loving" (her term) they missed out on while living in sin with his parents. They spent their first night as a married couple at a campground twenty-five minutes from his parent's place in Sibley. The next night, the transmission blew just across the border into Iowa and they hitchhiked home.

The first three miscarriages drove Puck toward the bottle and an unsettling infatuation with agates. He collected them, polished them, sold them to other collectors, "each fellow stranger than the last," she told Murphy. She mused about whether it would've worked out between her and Puck had they quit trying to have kids then. Because the fourth miscarriage pushed him over the edge.

One night in spring he strapped on his headlamp and told her he was going to scour for stones in Bristow's gravel pit, about fifteen miles north of town. By morning he still hadn't returned. She didn't go to the police because she noticed that his toiletries and some of his clothes were missing. Weeks later she received a letter. It was addressed to "Gwen," said nothing about why he'd left but mentioned he was in West Virginia with his cousin Moses, leaving Miss Bonnie to assume Appalachia was rife with all sorts of glorious gems. The letter contained logistics: how to install the AC window units stowed in the attic, how to ignite the pilot light on the water heater, how they ought to divide the assets. She kept the house, he took the savings and vehicle.

She'd developed the rosacea during her pregnancies. So aside of grocery store runs and Sunday church, she rarely left the house, and so in her mind the prospect of remarrying was fanciful. But she still wanted like hell to be around children, and she needed money.

All these things he told me, mimicking her voice and expressions at times, the way she pressed her upper lip into her nostrils. Somehow imitation—no less, from a man whose deceit was legendary artistry—reinforced the notion that I really, truly, ought to trust him. I did. I couldn't imagine a motive in bullshitting me. And I felt the stakes were low.

About the stakes I was wrong. Following these conversations, I often returned to my cell confused and ashamed. Confused because Murphy, whom I took for a mere brute all those years ago, had been the one to come by this information, ashamed because I wasn't the one to ask her these questions myself, as she certainly would've shared her past with me if I'd been persistent enough in my asking. Rather, all throughout my youth my mind was this splendorous labyrinth of inane logic puzzles and despairing theological concepts, a maze from which I couldn't escape. Nor wished to. The real escape, it seemed, was mastery. Such is youth. I'd obsess over the strangest images (say, rapid-elapse footage of a rose bloom), sensations (my fingertips touching the frets of the guitar just right), fears (the absurd and the reasonable inundating me in equal measure).

"Heath," she'd tell me, "you have that look about you ... What are you thinking about? How can I help ...? That look about you ... Face all twisted up, it looks like you had a glass of orange juice right when you just woke up." As if it truly didn't matter how many times I read a road sign before passing it, or what position I fell asleep in.

The closest I ever came to reciprocating even a portion of the care she showed me was when she'd tell me she prayed I'd stop punishing myself with tricks of the mind and I asked her not to lose sleep over my insanity. Oh, she assured me, she didn't lose more sleep than any typical mother would over her child. I'd hug her goodnight, then lay in bed wondering what proof she had that life's enigmas aren't God's profoundest and most sincere expressions of adoration, that I wasn't speaking to God when I learned a new language in the span of a dream, that I wasn't seized by God's essence whenever I went numb from the tip of my head to my toes and the only sound was a portentous baritone hum, the only smell and taste iron, the only image a spot on the ceiling from which materialized a swirling aurora? How can anyone tell you what does or doesn't, should or shouldn't matter when it all seems to so damn much?

Eventually, I gave up these self-imposed torments. Or they quit me. Maybe it was the lack of nutrition in prison. Maybe it was a biological factor, a natural dip in testosterone levels. Maybe it was the shame, which for many years nullified all other psychic activity. I prefer to believe it was God's grace. Whatever that means, grace. Still, I bet a good number of atheists would accept that there are miracles whose mysteries are their own verification.

I regretted not hearing first-hand how much we children frightened her because she worried she could never do enough for us, how much she feared she frightened us. The little ones, with her perpetually flushed complexion, her crooked nose, her imposing figure. The older ones, with her warmth, her embraces and patience, by showing us the part of her we harmed each time we harmed ourselves. But I was too narcissistic to concern myself with others in this way, at least instinctively. For me, it needed to be premeditated, almost rehearsed, before it became second nature. This was the gift of Murphy's visits. Dorian's too, to a lesser extent, how guarded and loath to imposition he is.

One time Murphy mentioned his son. Accidentally, it seemed.

"I sorta understand what she meant," he said. "Carter is the only person who ever scared me."

"Carter?" I asked.

He blushed.

Carter is thirteen. He lives with his mother, Courtney, Murphy's ex-wife, in Montana. When he was eighteen months old, he tried to swallow an acorn whole. "I'd never known anything like that, pulling a damn acorn out of your boy's mouth. If that isn't bullying, what a child will do to you, shit…"

After that apparent slip of the tongue, something happened between us. I asked things and he answered, though he often came off abashed, too quick to laughter. Imagine that, Murphy cowed. He had an awful lot to tell me. Say, how all these years later he still wasn't sure why he had Courtney, his fiancée at the time, call up Miss Bonnie and tell her he'd died. She went along with it because he spun some yarn about owing an old lady cash. To this day Courtney has no idea who Miss Bonnie was. Initially, he thought it was a good prank, no different than how he tricked everyone into thinking he was in Afghanistan. Then he figured that by the time he stopped getting a laugh out it, it might well be the truth. "Or I suppose I just didn't want her fretting about me anymore."

He'd "saved up some coin" in Santa Fe, working as a bellhop at a swanky, old-fashioned hotel. About the time he and Courtney were set to be married he got fired for stealing from the guests. They postponed the wedding and moved to Illinois, a compromise—she was pissed about the postponement, so he agreed to their living in her parent's guestroom in Champaign for a while. Unfortunately, as their new wedding date approached, he got the urge to track his father down in Montana.

"I'm sure you're sensing the pattern here," he said. "It wasn't her, I'll tell you that much. Wasn't her."

Last Murphy had seen his old man, Mr. Murphy was managing a grocery store in some trailer park community just outside of Billings, and though only a boy at the time, Murphy could still recall the smell of his father's trailer, Swisher Sweets cigarillos and dank sawdust, as despite the rain they'd taken up repairs on the porch. He remembered drinking Coca Cola through a Twizzlers straw.

Some locals pointed him in the right direction. "An impressive accomplishment, really," he said of Mr. Murphy, who in only a few years had gone from disgruntled grocery store manager to disgruntled cashier to trailer-park-shut-in to bum-in-front-of-grocery-store to bum-behind-trailer-park. Murphy found him sitting by a creek, his pants rolled up and his feet in the water, drunk to the point of delirium, salty about "some bitch," who might've been Murphy and Dorian's mother, whereabouts yet unknown. The man had soiled himself.

"He didn't even notice me. Me and him, two ships passing in the night." At one point Mr. Murphy tapped himself on the cheek, a little slap. Murphy supposed he did this to keep his head from quivering so much. "Something I'd done from time to time when I needed a drink. Seeing that made me wanna cut my hand off."

Something about the image—some all-too-typical "I'll show you, pops" impulse, maybe—pushed him back home to Courtney, with whom he eloped when he returned to Illinois, having charmed her into forgiving his procrastination. They had a son and for several years "a normal, middle-class go at it." The Champaign Police Department issued him a badge and a gun he claimed to have never fired, never drawn, never even wanted to. Regardless of his priors, he didn't abuse his power. He got off in other ways, aggravating the chief by intentionally misfiling paperwork, driving his partners insane. With one, he spat tobacco in his coffee. With another, he constantly sang "The Battle Hymn of the Republic." "Always hated cops," he told me.

The career outstripped the marriage. Courtney, he said, ate more than anyone he'd ever met, yet never seemed to gain weight. She was too anxious, he reasoned, anxious about Carter, anxious about her husband's moodiness, evasiveness, secrecy, compulsive fibbing, "the list goes on." Her eyes were light blue, "the most beautiful shade, like aqua, when she teared up." They were paradoxically magnetic, drew him closer the wetter they were, all the wetter on account of his genius for estrangement.

Ever sense, he's been a yo-yo, with ever a reason to make himself scarce. "There's a year or two here and there. I'm out making a lot of women smile and a lot of men jealous." Not that Courtney hasn't had her share of flings herself. It seems neither takes the other's trysts too seriously. Then he and Courtney make up and he's the father Carter needs, "the boy's hero."

"He's a good kid. Gets good grades, says please and thank you, eats his veggies, doesn't curse, no temper, all that. She raised him well."

By his own admission his problem is his need to embark on adventures to demonstrate to himself he's worthy of them. Only after coming back from them does he realize he's failed. Hence the yo-yoing.

"Is that what I am to you," I asked. "An adventure?"

"Sure."

I'm not sure what made me do it. I only wanted to help. Maybe I should've waited a little longer to mention Dorian, or been more tactful about it. Maybe he was bound to run from me eventually, just as he had from Miss Bonnie, from Dorian, from Courtney and Carter, and all the others too numerous to recount.

"You still have one in the chamber," I said.

"What do you mean?" he asked though in an instant that old deviance, that old malice, emerged in his glare, as poignant and stark and hostile as ever, and he seemed to coil up as if suddenly aware that the manacles binding him to that prison, to me, were illusory.

There seemed no point in playing coy. "Dorian," I said.

"What about him?"

"I haven't told him about you."

"You'd better not."

"But he'd sure wish to see you again. And Juliette—"

"That's enough, kid."

He said some hurtful things after that, things I remember only because they have merit and maybe even needed to be said. It *wasn't* my place. I *am*, in my worst moments, *pathetic* and *wicked*. So I didn't protest.

After he left, I returned to my cell and feigned sleep so my cellmate couldn't see the tears draining from my eyes, spreading down my face, slow as cracks in a windshield. Had I known this would be the last time we'd speak—for the time being, at least— could I slow time, reverse it, say the things I ought to have said, I might confess to merely emulating his tactics, engaging in the very emotional jujitsu he employed against the universe. I myself was pushing him away, keeping the spotlight on his life because in recent visits he'd steered me toward considerations I wasn't ready to entertain—in essence, that Christ has "already washed away" my sins, that the rest of my life needn't be lived so near the gravitational pull of my crimes, that that pull would weaken if only I began to forgive myself.

Springtime next year, my parole ends. I could leave Minnesota. Lately I've had the thought often. It may just be the winter, which always gets me dreaming, antsy for flight. Suppose

I stayed. Suppose I bought a guitar, acoustic, used, good for picking. Suppose I let my fingers bleed until callouses formed. Suppose I sang. So few who said only God can judge them meant it. If ever I said it, I sure didn't mean it. Judgment is an early lesson, as inborn and vital as breath. It hones the soul, only you hope not so sharply that another can never touch it.

Some morning, I have to imagine—for the sake of my soul, I must—I'll get ready for work and head down to my car and the wind will feel different on my hands, my neck, my face. Someday these pines lording over my drive to the site will be greener and prouder, the dawn nobler, and I'll work a full day without remembering my sins. Dorian will invite me to dinner and Murphy will be there. Emma and her children, too. He'll meet his niece. He'll hug his brother. We'll reminisce. We'll laugh. And missing them on the way home after, I'll crack the window to feel the air, hear once more that uncanny exhale of wind whispering, "Hush, my son."

Acknowledgements

I'm forever indebted:

To my wife, Ashley, my biggest fan, the love of my life.

To my baby girls, Clare and Nora, who inspire me every day.

To my parents, who encouraged me to chase my aspirations as a novelist and whose decision to shelter foster kids during my childhood in northern Minnesota made my siblings and me more compassionate and curious people.

To the foster kids with whom I shared a home as a child, imparting to me many lessons, not the least of which was the importance of community.

To the extraordinary team at Vine Leaves Press: Jessica Bell, publisher; Amie McCracken, publishing director; and Melanie Faith, my developmental editor.

To my readers: Aaron Sinner, Robin Soukup, Cord Jennings, Scott Richardson, Joe Dammel, Rachel Haase, Angela Sinner, Emily Schuster, Mikael Carlson, and Karol Lagodzki.

To Mona Power and The Loft Literary Center.

Vine Leaves Press

Enjoyed this book?
Go to *vineleavespress.com* to find more.
Subscribe to our newsletter:

Vine Leaves Press

Milton Keynes UK
Ingram Content Group UK Ltd.
UKHW040700030424
440478UK00005B/51

9 783988 320551